Barry Norman, son of film producer and director Leslie Norman, was show business editor of the *Daily Mail* until 1971 when he was made redundant. He describes this as 'the best thing that ever happened to me', since it has enabled him to turn his hand to a wide variety of activities. He has been a television critic and show business interviewer for *The Times*, occasional leader writer and Wednesday columnist for the *Guardian*, sports writer for the *Observer* and scriptwriter for 'Flook' in the *Daily Mail*. He has also presented *Today* for BBC Radio 4 and is well known for his many television presentations including *Film 81*, *The Hollywood Greats* and *The British Greats*. He is currently presenter of the BBC arts programme, *Omnibus*.

He has written seven other books, several of which – *The Hollywood Greats*, *The Movie Greats* and his last novel, *A Series of Defeats* – are available in Arrow.

HAVE A
NICE DAY

Barry Norman

ARROW BOOKS

Arrow Books Limited

17–21 Conway Street, London W1P 6JD

An imprint of the Hutchinson Publishing Group

London Melbourne Sydney Auckland Johannesburg
and agencies throughout the world

First published by Quartet Books 1981
Arrow edition 1982
© Barry Norman 1981

Set in Linoterm Times by
Book Economy Services
Burgess Hill, Sussex

Made and printed in Great Britain
by The Anchor Press Ltd
Tiptree, Essex

ISBN 0 09 929130 4

This book is dedicated affectionately to all those who worked with me on 'The Hollywood Greats' and 'The British Greats'. They will not, I can say with complete confidence, recognize anyone herein, for any resemblance between anyone in this book and any person, living or dead, is not only coincidental but quite astonishing. But I hope it will remind them of Hollywood and one or two of the bizarre things that happened to us out there.

1

Mark Payne leant against the parapet wall at the end of a parking lot on Sunset Boulevard and prepared to address himself to an Eclair. Behind him the small, untidy one-storey houses staggered down the hillside to Santa Monica Boulevard and beyond them, way over in the distance, downtown Los Angeles coughed and wheezed beneath its crown of smog.

On Sunset, halfway up the Hollywood Hills, the air was comparatively clear and the sun shone. It was spring in California and not yet particularly warm but the conventions of television insisted that no matter what the season or the weather anyone addressing the nation on film from Hollywood must appear to be baking gently in a constant, golden heat. In Hollywood it is always high summer. The movies issued this dictum many years ago and television has never seen any reason to challenge it. Hollywood, as everyone knows, is a magic place, a fairyland inhabited by beautiful people of immeasurable wealth living in homes of unimaginable grandeur and eternally clad in lightweight clothes by Gucci and Pucci and Yves St Laurent.

Thus the cameraman had placed his Eclair so as to disguise the fact that what actually lay between Mark Payne and the black skyscrapers of downtown Los Angeles was simply urban sprawl, a mass of wide streets and narrow gardens, of tourist shops and fast-food joints, of small factories and massive freeways; an

unplanned, unscheduled disaster of a town, designed –
insofar as it could be said to have been designed at all
– for cars and not for people.

And Mark himself, unquestioningly believing that
what the people wanted was glamour and only glamour,
wore the traditional uniform of the T.V. presenter
reporting from Hollywood – blue check shirt with
epaulettes and button-down pockets, dark-blue slacks
and Gucci shoes that had been made for him in twenty-
four hours by an elderly Chinese in a backstreet shop in
Kowloon. His lips moved silently as he rehearsed the
message he was about to deliver and behind his black-
framed glasses his eyes shone with great sincerity.

'When you're ready, Mark,' said Geoff Warbottle,
the producer. He was propped up against the hired
production car and was finding it difficult to stay awake.
A combination of jet-lag and several lunch-time tumblers
of what passed for Chablis in California had managed,
not surprisingly, to dull the keen edge of his interest in
what was going on around him.

'Do you mind?' said Mark. 'I'm trying to memorize a
piece to camera. Of course I'll go when I'm ready.' Idiot,
he thought, scowling at the dozing Warbottle. Incipient
wino. How could the old fool expect a performer – he
would go so far as to say an artist – like himself to give of
his best when he was plagued with these burbling inter-
ruptions? He didn't need a producer fuddled with plonk
to tell him when to go. He would go when he was good
and ready and not a moment before.

'I'm ready,' he said.

'Okay,' said the cameraman. He made a last-minute
adjustment to the focus. 'Camera running.'

'Sound running,' said the soundman, squatting on a
wooden box and crouched over his tape-recorder. The
assistant cameraman moved in with his clapperboard,
said his piece, brought the arm of the board down with a
firm smack and eased quietly out of shot.

'When you like, Mark,' said the cameraman.

Mark Payne took a deep breath, stroked his chin pensively with his left hand and gazed over to his right for a moment with the deep sincerity of one who was trying to collect his thoughts. Then, with even greater sincerity, he turned his head and looked the camera squarely in the eye.

'Willard Kaines,' he said, 'can truly be described as one of the great men of our time. He is not only a great movie star – anyone, given the right breaks can be a movie star. Willard Kaines is – or was, because we haven't seen him on our screens for twenty years now – also a great actor, an actor bowed down with honours. From the time he won his first Oscar fifty years ago in *The Life and Loves of Pontius Pilate* his has been one of the names to conjure with in any examination of the cinema. But that's not the whole story. Because, apart from being a great star and a great actor, Willard Kaines is a great Englishman, a great ambassador for his country. And above all he is a great . . . a great . . . Shit!'

Geoff Warbottle, some T.V. producer's sixth sense alerting him to possible danger even in his wine-induced reverie, heaved himself away from the comforting support of the production car. 'I don't think you can call him a great shit, Mark,' he said. 'See what you're trying to do, of course – lull them with all that flannel and then bring 'em up sharp. But. . .' He shook his head. 'Shit's a bit strong. Family programme, after all. Going out at peak hour. They won't let us get away with calling him a shit.'

'I wasn't calling him a shit!' Mark said. 'Bloody hell.' There was an empty Coca-Cola tin at his feet, carefully placed there by the cameraman to mark his position, and he kicked it viciously away. It hit the top of a Rolls-Royce, bounced from there onto the bonnet of a Mercedes and finished up in the driving seat of an open

Porsche. 'I said "Shit!" because I'd fluffed, that's all.'

'Oh yeah?' said the soundman, addressing his tape-machine. 'Fluffed, did you? Well, well, I am surprised.'

'What was that?' said Mark.

'Nothing,' said the soundman. 'Talking to meself, that's all.'

'A performer's entitled to fluff occasionally,' Mark said. 'It's all right for you sitting there with nothing else to do but fiddle with your little box of tricks. My job's not easy, you know. I might make it look easy but that's the whole art of it. I'm at the sharp end of this operation and don't you forget it. It's my reputation that. . .'

'Yes, we understand that, Mark,' Geoff Warbottle said soothingly. He put his arm round Mark's shoulder and breathed wine into his face.

'Well I mean to say,' Mark said, pouting sincerely.

'Of course you do,' Warbottle said. 'Of course you mean to say. You. . .' It suddenly occurred to him that he had no idea how to finish that sentence if indeed it was a sentence for which any conclusion was possible. He tried a different approach. 'What I mean to say and I expect what you meant to say is what you said, that anybody can fluff. I know. We all do. It's perfec'ly un'erstan'able.' This was the longest speech he had made since lunch-time and during the course of it his tongue appeared to have grown lethargic with disuse. 'I understand. We all understand.' He hit the d's firmly this time and retired with the lurch of a man who had the situation perfectly under control to his previous position against the production car. 'Soon as you're ready, Mark,' he said, 'Soon as you're ready.'

'All right,' said Mark. 'We'll try it again. We. . .' He stopped, looking sharply across at Warbottle. 'What did you mean by "flannel"?'

'Did I say "flannel", Mark? Sorry, old man, sorry. Slip of the tongue. Didn't mean to say "flannel".'

The cameraman sighed. 'Aren't we ready yet? I mean,

I don't want to rush anybody but the light's not getting any better, you know.'

'I'm ready,' Mark said. 'If we could have done without the snide remarks I'd have been ready ages ago.'

The cameraman readjusted his focus and the sound-man put on his headphones.

'Camera running.'

'Sound running.'

The assistant cameraman held up his clapperboard in front of Mark's face. 'Great Men of Our Time,' he said. 'Willard Kaines documentary. Shot one, take nine . . .'

Mark Payne stroked his chin and gazed briefly over to his right, once again apparently plucking random though fluently constructed thoughts out of the air, and then turned his sincere gaze to the camera. 'Willard Kaines,' he said, 'can truly be described as one of the great men of our time. He is not only . . .'

William Pendleton had deliberately taken no part in the foregoing exchanges. As the researcher he was aware that he was the junior member of the outfit – not only by virtue of age but also by virtue of status – and that any interjection by him would have been an invitation to the others to round jointly on him and berate him soundly. He was twenty-nine years old and, with his blue eyes and curly blond hair, looked even younger. But between leaving university and joining National-Metropolitan T.V. three months ago he had worked in Fleet Street and if he had learned nothing else in that Rabelaisian atmosphere he had at least learned enough not to put his head above the trench when there were snipers about.

So when, just under an hour ago, Mark had first embarked upon what now appeared to be the marathon performance of delivering a fifty-seven-second piece to camera, William had wisely tucked himself away, not out of sight but certainly out of eyeline, behind the very

Porsche on whose driving seat the Coca-Cola tin had landed.

In any event he couldn't really understand what they were all doing in this parking lot at this particular stage in the documentary they were making. Mark Payne, old Warbottle and his assistant, the camera team and the soundman had only arrived in Hollywood the previous night and William himself had been there barely a week. Indeed, just over a week ago they were all getting ready to go to Burnley to film a lengthy interview with an aged and retired bishop who had won the V.C. in the First World War. Around that interview they would have constructed a biography of the bishop which, along with other similar biographies, National-Metropolitan would have distributed to the commercial T.V. network under the generic title 'Great Men of Our Time'.

Mark had not been at all keen to do the bishop's biography because it was highly unfashionable in T.V. circles even to believe in God, let alone to give apparent support to organized religion. Mark's public image, he always felt, was the image of the professional iconoclast, not a cynic exactly but certainly a sceptic, one who listened with sardonic sincerity to the arguments of the Establishment and then, with devastating accuracy, pounced on the flaw in their logic. (There was, of course, another and more critical body of opinion which said he merely talked long enough and persuasively enough to convince the watching public that he had pounced on the flaw in their logic, but Mark did not subscribe to this.)

Buttering up bishops, he had said to Nat-Met's head of production over lunch at Wheelers, was not exactly his line. He was the voice of the liberal conscience (small 'l', naturally), the challenger of accepted conventions. His public wouldn't expect to find him kissing bishops' backsides.

'Ah, but that's the point, Mark,' the head of production had said, 'that's exactly the point. You're a star,

Mark, no doubt about that – you're an S-T-A-R. But don't you think you're in danger of becoming just a little bit too predictable?' He softened the effect of the wounding remark by ordering another dozen oysters each. 'You see, there's nobody on T.V. who can put forward the liberal (with a small "l", naturally), trendy viewpoint in half an hour, minus time for commercials, of course, as brilliantly as you can. And, what's more, without offending anybody. And you know and I know, Mark, that a commercial T.V. company can't afford to offend anybody. I mean, you're in a class of your own, Mark. But . . . and you might give a bit of thought to this, Mark – people are beginning to know what to expect. I mean, they know you're an agnostic. All right, all right, not the kind of agnostic that's going to upset anybody. You're not – how can I put it? – you're not going to piss icewater over the Archbishop of Canterbury. But, by God, I remember – well, we all remember – the way you ripped into that African evangelist. Know the one I mean? That big, black woman – could hardly speak English, right? Well, I mean, you ripped her up for loo paper. Marvellous demolition job. But the point I'm making is this: while that is still fresh in the public mind, I reckon it would really make everybody sit up if you suddenly appeared on the network with this clinical, but sympathetic and above all sincere, biography of Bishop what's-his-bloody-name. See what I mean? Suddenly, unexpectedly, you'd be coming out of a different trap, Mark. It could only do your image good.'

'Clinical,' Mark said. 'Sincere. Yes.' Was he really becoming predictable? Good God. Terrifying thought.

'And sympathetic,' said the head of production. 'Sincere obviously because sincerity's your hallmark, Mark. But it's got to be sympathetic, too. I mean, the whole purpose of this series is to honour these old bastards, not put the boot in. I tell you, it can only do you good, Mark. It'll show people you're not only liberal and trendy but catholic (with a small "c", naturally) as well.'

Predictable, Mark thought and swallowed his last oyster with a shudder. 'Okay, Charles,' he said, 'I'll do it. But only because it's you who are asking. I wouldn't do it for anybody else.' A bloody bishop, he thought. Jesus. And then, to underline the fact that his acquiescence was only to be secured at a price, he said, 'I think I'll have the fresh salmon next. And another bottle of Montrachet, perhaps?'

So it was decided and at once William, the newest recruit to the research staff and the only one with journalistic experience, was instructed to look deeply into the blameless and, on one notable afternoon on the Somme, heroic life of the bishop. Geoff Warbottle, senior producer in the Religious Affairs Department, a practically moribund branch of Nat-Met which, by and large, produced five minutes of religious television a week that went out at 11.55p.m. on the Sabbath under the title of 'Your Sunday Prayer', was appointed as producer and director.

William, accustomed to meeting deadlines, did his work swiftly and well; various friends and colleagues of the bishop were interviewed by Mark on film and announced, in their various ways, that he was a truly saintly man who had never had an uncharitable thought in his life and the programme was beginning to take on a cogent, if somewhat boring, shape when, on the eve of the team's departure to interview the man himself in Burnley, the bishop was inconsiderate enough to have a heart attack and die.

'What shall we do?' said Mark. 'Carry on anyway?'

'Carry on?' said the head of production. 'Like hell. It's bad enough making programmes about old buggers but I'm buggered if I'm making any about dead buggers. No, scrub it. We'll have to find something else.'

William interrupted deferentially. 'There is a slight problem. The bishop's widow is still expecting us

14

tomorrow. She called up to tell us he was dead and said she'd like to do the interview herself.'

'Do the interview herself?' said the head of production. 'With the bishop hardly cold? Bit bloody callous, isn't it?'

'I don't think she saw it that way,' said William. 'She thought it would be a sort of tribute. You know – it would be nice for him, she said.'

'Yes, well,' said the head of production, 'what would be nice for him hardly matters any more, does it? I mean, he's stiff, isn't he? No, no, tell her we can't possibly do that. Bloody hell, who wants an interview with a bishop's widow anyway – unless she's about twenty-five with big knockers?'

'No, she's eighty-three actually,' said William.

'Well, that settles it then. Get rid of her. Who can we do instead?'

And so there ensued a high-level conference to decide, urgently, upon a replacement for the bishop in the series 'Great Men of Our Time' and eventually, and in some desperation, it was agreed that the team should turn its attentions to Willard Kaines.

Willard Kaines had been born Alfred Hornchurch in Penge, Kent, towards the end of the last century. Nobody seemed to know anything about his early life but in the 1920s he had turned up in Hollywood and, being tall, lean and dark with a good profile, had become a star of silent western movies. By the time talkies were introduced he had, fortunately for him, acquired a passable Californian accent and since, even more fortunately for him, he had never received any stage training and therefore knew nothing about projecting his voice and hitting the back of the stalls, he had moved without any noticeable difficulty into the sound era.

In the early thirties he had received the Academy Award for best supporting actor for his role as King Herod in *The Life and Loves of Pontius Pilate* and ten years later had been given another for his part as Napoleon's father in the comedy *Boney and I*. It was rumoured at the time that he had only won the second Oscar because the film, though appalling, had been extremely expensive and the opinion in Hollywood was that if it didn't win something to boost the box-office the studio itself might go bust. Willard Kaines, being the least appalling ingredient in the picture, was thus boosted by the power and wealth of the studio publicity department towards nomination and eventual victory more or less *faute de mieux*.

Thereafter, his own career revived by this second award, he carried on acting in films and T.V., playing older and more dignified roles for another decade or so before retiring, having made an enviable fortune out of real-estate deals. Nothing had been heard of him since; no biography had ever been written of him and there hadn't even, as William discovered when he began his hurried research, been a book of 'The Films of Willard Kaines', which was odd since there seemed to exist a book of the films of almost every other Hollywood star up to and including Lassie.

His inclusion, therefore, as a Great Man of Our Time was hard to justify except on three counts – he had made more than 100 pictures, he had retained his British nationality despite living for more than half a century in Hollywood and, most important of all, there was talk of awarding him a special Oscar the following year in recognition of his considerable feat of having lived a very long time. The members of the American Academy of Motion Picture Arts and Sciences, being on the whole pretty aged themselves, have a deep reverence for their very old colleagues and are always anxious to heap honorary awards upon them; unless, of course, they happen to be not only very old but also very poor, in which case they are best forgotten.

To achieve longevity with wealth is the ultimate sign

of success in Hollywood but longevity accompanied by poverty is obscene and anti-social and a slur on the entire cinema industry.

Willard Kaines, being both very old and very rich, was thus an obvious candidate for honours, even though he had hardly appeared in public for the best part of twenty years and even the most passionate movie buff would be hard-pressed to remember the names of more than three of four of his films. So he was promoted by Nat-Met to the status of a Great Man and William was dispatched to Hollywood to begin research into his life.

The job had to be done fast because the transmission date of the Great Men series had been unexpectedly brought forward by the network and the programme had to be completed in weeks rather than months. Nat-Met had naturally complained, saying that such a rush job would damage its artistic integrity but this was merely a token protest. Nat-Met had very little interest in its own artistic integrity at the best of times and none at all when it threatened to get in the way of the profits. Although it ranked among Britain's Big Six independent T.V. companies, it did so only by virtue of being one of the three that were based in London. It was, in fact, a small outfit compared with the others and employed only the minimum staff permitted by the trade unions. Thus, armed with a few reference books and a small pile of photocopies of faded newspaper and magazine articles, William had been sent out alone to investigate what Nat-Met confidently expected to be the fascinating life of Willard Kaines.

He had continued with that work this morning while the others, being but newly arrived, occupied themselves with the far more essential task of visiting Ralph's supermarket on Sunset Boulevard in order to stock the refrigerators in their motel rooms with such necessities of life as beer, wine, taco chips and dry-roasted peanuts.

For them this was supposed to be a rest day to help

them recuperate from their flight and so William had been a little surprised, when he returned to the motel at lunch-time, to learn that Mark had insisted upon recording a piece to camera in the afternoon.

'What exactly are you going to say, Mark?' Geoff Warbottle had asked, washing down his bacon, lettuce and tomato sandwich with yet another tumbler of wine.

'I thought I'd do my summing-up piece,' Mark had replied, sniffing. He was the only man on T.V. who could even sniff sincerely. His nostrils dilated and the corners of his mouth turned down.

'Bit early for that, isn't it?' William had said. 'I mean, you haven't interviewed anybody yet.'

'I have your notes, William. They tell me all I need to know to sum the man up. I have a clear vision of him – up here.' He tapped the side of his head as if to indicate that his clear vision of the man lay somewhere behind his left ear. 'Too much information can be an embarrassment sometimes, it clouds the issue.'

'Facts get in the way, you mean,' William had said, nodding. His experience in Fleet Street had taught him that this was a view widely held by a number of quite famous journalists.

'I don't mean that at all,' Mark had said, sharply. 'My view of the man has nothing to do with facts. It's a personal impression, an emotional but thoughtful analysis, if you like. It's the sort of thing I do particularly well. I have an instinct for it.' He had then returned to his room to write the piece to camera which he was now attempting to deliver, for the ninth time, to the Eclair in the parking lot on Sunset Boulevard.

This was the part of any television programme that Mark liked best: the time when the camera, moving in from medium close-up to close-up, was concentrating on him alone and when his opinions, delivered in that slightly suburban but infinitely sincere voice, would insinuate themselves into millions of homes. Television,

18

he believed, had been invented for just such moments.

'. . . apart from being a great star and a great actor,' he was saying, 'Willard Kaines is a great Englishman, a great ambassador for his country. And above all he is a great . . . a great . . .'

'Shit?' said the soundman helpfully.

2

Mark Payne poured a generous measure of Mountain Chablis into a plastic tumbler and pushed it across the coffee table to William. Then he sank back onto the imitation leather settee in the living-room of his tiny motel suite. 'Cheers,' he said.

Apart from the settee and the table the room contained a couple of armchairs, a lamp or two, a television set and, in the corner, a bar complete with sink and small refrigerator. Behind the partition wall that reached up three-quarters of the way to the ceiling were his bedroom and the bathroom. Outside the sitting-room window was an open corridor looking down on the motel swimming pool and around it the small expanse of plastic grass that was Hoovered daily by the Mexican cleaner. And in the distance, on the far side of Sunset Boulevard, were the lights of Century City.

'Went pretty well today, I thought,' Mark said. He had completed his piece to camera on the twelfth take. 'I always feel better when we've got something in the can.' He yawned and stretched. 'God, I'm tired though. You've never done any work in front of camera have you, William?'

William sipped his Mountain Chablis. It was too sweet for his taste, but then all Californian wines were. 'No,' he said.

'Amazing how it takes it out of you. All that adrenalin, you know. The tension. Of course, one doesn't show it.

The art that conceals art, I suppose. One takes no credit for it, naturally. Either one is good on T.V. or one isn't.' He smiled with sincere modesty.

'I suppose so,' said William, missing his cue entirely.

'Of course, that's something of an over-simplification,' Mark said with less modesty and more sharpness in his tone.

'Mmm,' said William, absentmindedly letting another cue go by. He was leafing through his notes preparatory to giving Mark his schedule for the following day. Mark took a handful of dry-roasted peanuts. As a sign of his displeasure he did not push the jar across to William who, unperturbed, leaned over and helped himself.

'About tomorrow,' he mumbled through the nuts.

'Later,' said Mark. 'Switch the telly on, there's a good fellow. I want to see the news. A man in my position has to keep abreast of what's going on, no matter where he is.'

William switched on the T.V. The picture showed two men with green faces talking in a chemist's shop.

'Same old stuff,' William said. 'It's all about hae-morrhoids again.' It was always the same on American T.V.; whenever he tuned in there were these two men, one complaining of piles and the other, elderly and avuncular, prescribing a miraculously healing ointment. They were usually followed by an equally green-faced woman suffering from pre-menstrual tension and then by a senior citizen, no less green, who claimed that every known brand of chewing-gum, save one, clamped his false teeth inextricably together. After a few days of this William had come to the firm conclusion that the news in America was invariably about haemorrhoids and other embarrassing ailments and had therefore abandoned television entirely.

The men in the chemist's shop were followed, as William had known they would be, by the woman with the pre-menstrual trouble and the old man with the false teeth.

21

'Why are they all green?' said Mark.

'I don't know. Everybody on American T.V. is green. I think they're raising a special breed of green-faced people . . .'

'It's just not tuned properly, that's all,' said Mark. 'Twiddle the knobs a bit.' William did as he was told and a woman appeared on screen, puce, as if she'd been fed from infancy on fine old port. 'The penalty for premature withdrawal . . .' she was saying sternly from behind an executive-style desk.

'The penalty for what?' said Mark, startled.

'Premature withdrawal,' William said. 'It's a commercial.'

'Of course it's a bloody commercial. But what the hell is she advertising?'

'. . . will be a loss of interest,' the woman said. The puceness of her complexion made her appear, despite the wide red-toothed smile, to be in a state of extreme bad temper verging on apoplexy.

'It's a commercial for a bank,' William said. 'Something to do with a special offer on savings accounts. I keep hoping she'll say that the penalty for premature withdrawal will be a loss of your deposit but she never does.'

Mark studied the screen for a moment. 'Turn them back to green,' he said. 'They don't look so angry that way.'

William touched the control knob and a middle-aged man appeared, reassuringly green, to discuss his acid indigestion. Mark leaned forward, watching with deep interest. This was his first visit to the U.S.A. and so his first experience of the doubtful pleasures of American T.V. 'Is it all commercials?' he said.

'Pretty well,' said William. 'They break them up with bits of programme occasionally but not very often. What they do here, you see, is they find the lowest common denominator and then aim about five miles underneath it. Well, that means that they're making T.V. shows for people who can't watch more than thirty seconds of anything remotely serious without suffering severe brain-ache so . . .'

'Shut up,' said Mark. The commercials had finally ended and the newscaster was on screen. She was a Eurasian girl in her late twenties who, despite being quite as green as everybody else, was undeniably beautiful. The name caption flashed across her apparently green bosom said 'Tina Ling'.

'Tina Ling!' said Mark. 'Bloody hell. I was reading about her in the paper this morning. Do you know how much she earns? You won't believe it – 400,000 dollars a year! Can you believe that? Two hundred thousand quid a year and for what? Just for being able to read! That's all she does – she reads the autocue. My God! Do you know how much I earn?'

'No, Mark,' said William, although he had an idea that, by British standards, it was rather a lot.

'Well, never mind. But let me tell you that it wouldn't keep that girl in . . . in . . . in knickers.'

'I expect you could buy an awful lot of knickers on your salary, Mark.'

'Not for her. With her money she probably wears them made of mink.' Mark was silent for a moment, possibly brooding resentfully over his mental picture of Tina Ling reading the news in mink knickers.

'The police,' said Tina Ling, 'affirmed that the rapist was pro'lly . . .'

'Did you hear that?' yelled Mark. 'Did you hear what she just said? She said "pro'lly". Dear God, she can't even speak bloody English and she gets 400,000 dollars a year!'

'I know,' said William. 'There you are – she just said it again. I think she's cute. Do you notice the way her lips move when she says words like "pro'lly"? It's very sexy. I think I could fall in love with her.'

'I could fall in love with her money,' said Mark. 'I wonder how hard it is for an Englishman to get on T.V. over here? I mean, after all, if what she does is worth 400 grand what I do must be worth at least a million.'

'. . . coming right up after these messages,' said Tina Ling. She gave them a green smile and vanished, to be replaced by a young matron who was enquiring earnestly, 'What does it mean when the baby's diaper has an ammonia smell?'

'It means the baby's struck again, twit!' said Mark and switched the television off. 'I shall need a woman tonight, William.'

'What?' said William, looking up from his notes.

'I shall need a woman. I always need a woman before I start the real work on a programme. Weren't you aware of that? I'm rather famous for it. I'm surprised nobody told you.'

'Good heavens,' said William, 'do you mean you're always randy before you go off to do an interview? It must be very uncomfortable for you.'

'I don't like that word, William. Randy. It's nothing to do with being randy. It's simply a matter of excess energy. You may have noticed how often I snap my fingers.' He snapped them a couple of times to prove the point. Snap, snap. 'Well, that's another sign of excess energy. You'll find a good number of intellectuals suffer from it. That's why we need sex more often than the average man.'

William shrugged. 'Well, good luck then. Got anybody in mind?'

'No. I thought you might have some ideas.'

'Me?' William said, startled. 'It's no good looking at me. I don't know any women in this town. Besides, I have enough trouble finding girls for myself without pandering for you.'

Mark nodded. 'You haven't been with us very long, have you, William? You have quite a lot to learn, I fancy.'

24

'Come off it,' said William. He was beginning to feel decidedly uneasy. 'I'm having a hard enough time trying to find people for you to interview without chatting up crumpet on your behalf. My contract says I'm a researcher, not a procurer.'

Mark stood up and looked at himself in the mirror beside the bar, frowning sincerely – black hair, flecked with grey at the temples, the vague beginnings of a paunch disguised by his well-cut sports jacket. He noticed the paunch reflected in the glass and drew it in slightly. 'Let me put it this way, William,' he said, 'I'm not asking you, good heavens I wouldn't dream of asking you, to pander for me. What I would say, however, is that if I don't have a woman tonight, I shall be very disappointed indeed.'

'Yes, well, I can understand that, Mark. If I don't have one I'll be disappointed, too. I've been disappointed every night this week.'

'Ah yes, but not as disappointed as I shall be, William. And if you want to know how disappointed I can be, I suggest you ask Geoff Warbottle.'

William found Geoff Warbottle in his room on the next floor up, getting at the bourbon and watching T.V. He looked old, though in fact he was only just into his fifties. His hair and moustache were both grey and limp and his nose and cheeks were faintly mottled by broken capillaries. Unlike Mark he allowed his paunch to swing free and a small expanse of pale, hairy stomach peeped out between two straining shirt buttons.

'Have a drink, William,' he said, waving towards the bourbon bottle. 'It helps with the jet-lag.'

'I haven't got jet-lag any more,' William said. 'But I'll have a drink anyway.' He poured bourbon into a plastic glass and helped himself to ice from the refrigerator in the corner. 'Geoff, there's something . . .'

'There's no hope for this country, you know,' Warbottle said sadly. 'No hope at all. It's doomed.'

'Well, I expect we're all doomed. We certainly are if you listen to the economists. Geoff . . .'

'No.' Warbottle shook his head. 'America is more doomed than anybody. There is no hope, no hope at all, for a country that can put up with television as bad as this. I've just been watching a quiz show in which there was a man dressed up as a banana. Ordinary member of the public, dressed up as a banana. There was a woman there, too, dressed as a toilet roll. Another ordinary member of the public. She won a refrigerator for knowing the capital of France, or something equally obscure. There's nothing to be said, William, for a country in which people dressed as toilet rolls can win refrigerators for knowing the capital of France.' He poured more bourbon into his glass and drank deeply. He looked very unhappy.

'Ah,' said William. 'This, of course, is your first visit, isn't it? I always used to think like that too, but what I've learned is, you've got to forget the television. The television is just a sort of small area of collective American madness. What you've got to do is, you've got to get out into the streets and look at the bookshops. You should see the bookshops in New York, Geoff. London's got nothing to compare with them. There must be hope for a country that can support as many bookshops as America does.'

'I haven't seen any bookshops,' Warbottle said. 'I walked up and down this street for half an hour and I didn't see any bookshops. I saw a lot of liquor stores, thank God, but not a single bookshop.'

'Yes, well, this is Hollywood, Geoff. You can't judge America by Hollywood. Nobody in Hollywood can read anything longer than a two-page synopsis. They employ people on the East Coast to do their reading for them. Geoff, there's something I want . . .'

Warbottle topped up his bourbon again. 'William, I have been in this town for twenty-four hours and I've seen the worst television in the world and more liquor shops to the square mile than anyone could possibly imagine but I have not seen any sign of God. You know what they're doing here, William? They're drugging the people's minds with pap and their bodies with booze. But where in this frightful place is God?'

'He's about somewhere,' William said uneasily. He had just remembered that Warbottle was attached to National-Metropolitan's religious department and for the first time it occurred to him that the man worked there from choice and not, as it had seemed only natural to assume, because he was no good at anything else. 'He must be about. They've got more than a thousand religions in this country.'

'Ah. A thousand religions – but no God,' Warbottle said, nodding wisely. 'You've put your finger on it, William.'

'Listen,' William said. He hitched his chair closer to Warbottle's and stared earnestly into the producer's sad and faintly red-rimmed eyes. 'Can we discuss all this later? I mean, I'd like to talk to you about it but there's something rather more urgent that I want your advice on. I think . . . I think Mark Payne expects me to pander for him.'

'Are you going to do it?' Warbottle asked.

'You're not surprised? That he asked, I mean.'

'No. He always does, apparently, on location. Well, for the last few months anyway. All to do with his image, I gather. You know, powerful telly personality with menials running around keeping him happy.'

'Really? He told me it had to do with his intellectual nervous energy.'

'That too, I suppose,' Warbottle said, shrugging. 'Are you going to do it?'

'Am I hell.'

Warbottle gazed thoughtfully into his glass. 'He'll be mad if you don't try. I mean, I don't think it's necessary to succeed. As a matter of fact I'm not sure that anybody has actually succeeded yet but he likes to think you're trying. The power thing, you see.'

'The hell with him,' said William. He finished his drink and stood up. 'Are you eating tonight?'

'I expect so. Where?'

'There's a place down the road that's not bad, if you stick to American food.'

'What's American food?' asked Warbottle.

'Steaks, baked potatoes, hamburgers, chips, salads, that sort of stuff. But take my advice and steer well clear of anything that purports to be French or Italian. It'll be smothered in sweet tomato sauce.'

'All right. Serve wine at this place, do they?'

'Oh yes.'

'I'm on then. Will you round up the others?'

'Yes,' said William. 'Meet in the foyer in half an hour?'

'Good,' said Warbottle. 'That just gives me time for an aperitif.' He reached for the bourbon bottle again.

3

'You're Australian, aren't you?' said the waitress, giving them the benefit of all her teeth in a huge, friendly smile. They were splendid teeth, flawlessly white and there seemed to be an awful lot of them. 'I can tell.'

'That's clever of you,' said William, 'How did you know?'

'From the accents,' said the waitress. 'I'm a student of accents. What part of Australia you from?'

'London,' said Geoff Warbottle.

'Oh really? London, Australia? Is that near Sydney?'

'Not very near,' said William.

'Oh,' said the waitress. She was a tall, well-built girl who looked as if she had been specifically designed by nature to grace the centrefold of Playboy one day. Preferably one day soon, William thought, looking at her carefully, or she would be too old for the job. She must be pushing twenty already. Her hair was long and blonde and her eyes were large and blue; her nose was small and slightly retroussé and her mouth was wide and eager. Her gingham waitress's dress was cut low to reveal the top of her breasts and high to reveal her shapely, powerful thighs.

'I should like,' said Warbottle, when the food had been ordered, 'some wine. Some red wine.'

'Okay,' said the waitress. 'How's about a bottle of Hearty Burgundy?'

'Yes, well,' said Warbottle, 'its mood is immaterial to

29

me. Hearty or jovial or even ever so slightly down in the dumps, it's all the same to me so long as the stuff is red and there's plenty of it.'

'Okay,' said the waitress. 'Right.' The smile was as wide as ever but there was a nervous uncertainty about it now. It looked as if someone had lowered the wattage.

'She's very pretty, isn't she?' asked Alice Flitton wistfully as she watched the strong bronzed thighs disappearing towards the kitchen. Alice Flitton was not pretty. She was thirty years old and rather plump and for the last three years she had been working as Warbottle's assistant. Warbottle said she was the best assistant he had ever had because she was the only one who never tried to interfere with his drinking. She was also, he would add – though this was clearly but a secondary consideration – the most efficient assistant he had ever had. Alice Flitton did her work neatly and without fuss and even Warbottle knew hardly anything about her private life, though it was rumoured that she had once been married.

'She'd do quite nicely for Mark,' said Warbottle, his eyes too following the progress of the waitress's legs.

'I'll tell him then,' said William. 'He can come and chat her up.'

'No, think about it, lad. It would give you a leg up with him if you helped him to get his leg over her. Shouldn't be too difficult. She's bound to want to be in show business, girl like that. Why don't you give Mark the build-up – big telly star, powerful contacts, able to put in a word for her with the right people. That sort of stuff.'

'It isn't even true,' said William. 'He doesn't know anybody over here.'

'She doesn't know that. And it wouldn't do you any harm to have Mark as your friend.'

Alice Flitton looked at William with disdain. 'You're not procuring for Mark Payne?'

'No, he isn't,' said Warbottle. 'That's just the problem.

Mark wants him to but he won't do it. All I'm saying is that he should at least give the appearance of trying because a friendly report from Mark will stand him in good stead back at the factory. Conversely, an unfriendly report . . .'

'You're disgusting,' said Alice Flitton, 'both of you. And you,' she added, turning fiercely on Warbottle, 'a religious producer, too.'

'Where does it say "Thou shalt not pimp"?' said Warbottle. 'Anyway this could turn out to be a very religious affair. That's probably quite a devout girl.'

'And that's another thing,' said Alice. 'Why pick on that poor girl? She's far too good for Mark Payne. I think she's terribly nice.'

'On what evidence,' said Warbottle, 'do you base that assumption? All she's done so far is take our order, recommend us a wine purely on the grounds that it appears to have a happy disposition and mistake us for a bunch of bloody Australians. If you ask me she's thick.'

At this point Mark Payne and the waitress arrived simultaneously, she bearing hamburgers and Hearty Burgundy and he wearing the look of brisk sincerity that he always donned for public appearances whether or not there was much likelihood of anyone recognizing him.

Mark's gaze did a slow pan from the legs to the breasts and eventually to the nuclear-powered smile. He moved in to medium close-up and gave her his most sincerely amorous look. 'Hello there,' he said. As an opening gambit it was not particularly original but it seemed to satisfy the girl.

'Hi,' she said, finding even more teeth to reveal. 'I'm Larraine. I guess you must be another Australian, huh?'

'Australian?' said Mark, deeply and properly offended. 'Good heavens, no. What on earth gave you that bizarre idea?' His accent which, on television, sometimes had the faintest of transatlantic twangs to suggest to his viewers that here was a man who was at home in all parts of the English-speaking world, was now wholly and traditionally B.B.C.

'Gee, I'm sorry,' said the girl, looking faintly puzzled. 'But your friends said you were Australians . . .'

'Not really,' said Warbottle, helping himself to the red wine. 'We simply said we came from London, which was not very near Sydney. This may have led to some understandable confusion on your part, of course.'

'Oh,' said the girl.

'You mustn't tease her,' said Alice Flitton and was rewarded with a smile of pure gratitude.

Mark grasped the waitress's hand and squeezed it gently. 'I wouldn't tease you,' he said. 'These other uncouth fellows might but not I. You're far too beautiful.'

'Why, thank you,' said the waitress. She took his order and said, 'I love your accent. I'm a student of accents, you know. I guess you must have come from Scotland.' She turned the smile on him again and headed for the kitchen.

'Scotland?' said Mark. 'Bloody Scotland?'

'How can anybody smile as much as that girl does?' said Warbottle. 'She must have cheek muscles of coiled steel.'

'They all smile like that in California,' said William. 'They're given smiling lessons almost from birth. I believe they even have annual competitions to find the quickest smile in the west. And they always say "Have a nice day". They never mean it. They don't give a damn whether you have a nice day or not but they say it all the same.'

'I would say,' said Mark, judicially, 'that that girl is probably slightly thicker than pigshit but she likes me.'

'Of course she does,' said Warbottle. 'William's been giving you the build-up.'

'What?' said William.

Mark patted him on the arm. 'Thank you, William. I knew you'd come through.'

With Mark's arrival the dinner-party was complete. The camera crew and the soundman, old Hollywood hands all, were staying at another, cheaper motel further along Sunset Boulevard, partly in order to save as much as possible of their daily allowance by spending as little as possible on accommodation, and partly because, as technicians, they had no desire to fraternize socially with the production team. William, who had been charged with booking accommodation for the entire party, had found this demand for segregation rather puzzling at first but Geoff Warbottle had explained that it was, in fact, quite normal. Just as people like Mark Payne, he said, were the stars of the production team, so the cameramen were the stars of the technical unit. Cameramen were indeed even bigger prima donnas than most presenters and their assistants were apprentice prima donnas. Since no television unit was big enough for both presenter and cameraman to hold court simultaneously they quite frequently chose to set up separate courts on location. This was particularly so, said Warbottle, when Mark Payne was the presenter.

William had, nevertheless, phoned the cameraman to ask whether he and his acolytes wished to join the production team for dinner but had been met with a courteous refusal. The impression he had received was that while the technicians found him, William, perfectly agreeable, liked rather than disliked Alice Flitton and even had an amused affection for Geoff Warbottle, whose ability to consume alcohol they sneakingly admired, they had no wish to spend any more time than was strictly necessary in the company of Mark Payne.

'Has he got you pimping for him yet?' asked the cameraman.

'Well, he's tried,' said William. 'But I don't reckon I'm going to do it.'

'Good for you,' said the cameraman. 'Oh, hold on. Ernie's just come in.' Ernie was his assistant, a tall, good-looking young Cockney with the swaggering self-confidence that went with being a karate expert. There was a brief pause and then the cameraman returned to the phone. 'Must go,' he said. 'Ernie's found a place down the road where you can get a steak dinner for $4.95 and a supermarket where they sell red wine for two dollars a gallon. Guaranteed lead-free, he says. See you, and good luck with Mark.'

William returned from the reverie induced by recollecting this conversation to hear Mark complaining about his meal. 'You wouldn't believe this,' he was saying, 'but this spaghetti's sweet.'

'They always make spaghetti sweet in America,' William said.

'Well you might have warned me when I ordered the stuff.'

'You didn't ask.'

'So you're all in T.V., huh?' the waitress was saying to Alice Flitton. 'Gee, that's exciting. I'm an actress too, you know. Larraine Laroux. Well, you wouldn't have heard of me, I guess. I haven't done much yet. But one day . . . See, I just wait table because it gives me time to go to auditions and like that. I've been in Hollywood for six months. From Oregon? That's my home. Oregon. I had a walk-on once in a comedy show on T.V. I was the dumb blonde? You know? But, gee, I don't know what happened. I guess they overran and they cut me out. I was so disappointed.' She glanced with a certain respect at Mark. 'And he's your star, huh? Is he famous in England?'

'I suppose so,' said Alice Flitton, grudgingly. 'Quite famous.'

'Gee, and he seems so ordinary. You know? I mean, mixing with everybody and all. You wouldn't find an American T.V. star eating in a place like this.'

'Well, he is ordinary,' said Alice. 'He's very ordinary.'

'What's that?' said Mark, suspiciously, aware that he

was being discussed.

'Alice was just telling me you're a big T.V. star in England,' said the waitress.

Mark turned down the corners of his mouth with sincere modesty. 'True,' he said.

'Gee, I'd like to talk to you all about that some time. Like, I'm an actress too, you know. Larraine Laroux? Well, you wouldn't have heard of me. But I'd sure like to talk to you.'

'Why not tonight?' said Mark. 'I'm at the motel just across the street. What time do you finish here?'

'Well, not till midnight. Isn't that kinda late?'

'Certainly not. I need very little sleep. I don't know whether you find this too, as an actress, but I think the small hours of the morning are often the best for us creative people. It's a question of nervous energy.' Mark snapped his fingers once or twice to hint at the pent-up nervous energy within him. 'I find the small hours are the best time for formulating and exchanging ideas. Don't you agree?'

'Er, yeah,' said the waitress, uncertainly. 'Are you all staying at the motel?'

'Yes,' said Alice Flitton.

'Okay. Right. Well, sure, I'll come over when I'm finished here if you're sure that's all right. You wanna give me your names?' They gave her their names and paid their bills.

'Okay, you guys,' said the waitress. 'I'll be over later then, huh? Bye now. Bye. Bye, honey,' she said to Alice Flitton.

'I think I'm going to score tonight,' said Mark, when they were all outside. 'I rather fancy I impressed her. Did you notice how she kept looking at me?'

'Got William to thank for that,' said Warbottle. His voice was a little thick, as it had a right to be since he had consumed most of the two bottles of Hearty Burgundy that he had summoned.

'Of course,' said Mark. 'You did the groundwork, William, and I shan't forget that although in the end I flatter myself that she would have gravitated towards me anyway.'

'Look,' said William, conscious of Alice Flitton's ironic stare, 'I didn't do anything . . .'

'You did enough, William,' Mark said. 'Obviously you did. I believe, immodestly perhaps, that the result would have been the same, whatever you did. But nevertheless, credit where it's due.' He seemed somewhat light-headed, a combination, William thought sourly, of a couple of large glasses of wine and the anticipation of his forthcoming sexual conquest. 'What's her name – Larraine, is it? – anyway, just the sort of girl I'd have chosen for tonight. Lush but dim. There are times, William, when people like myself need, positively need, a sort of intellectual roll in the gutter and this is one of those times. Well, I'll . . . er . . . I'll say goodnight, then.'

'Me, too,' said Warbottle. 'Quick nightcap and crash out.'

'It's been a long day,' said Alice Flitton, 'I think I'll turn in too.' She gave William an oddly enigmatic smile. 'Good night, pimp,' she said softly.

William found himself alone outside the motel. It was barely eleven o'clock and he didn't feel in the least tired. He did, however, feel a certain amount of self-contempt, which was very unfair because there was no reason why he should. He had done nothing whatsoever to procure that girl for Mark Payne and yet everyone was behaving as though he had. Consequently he almost believed himself that he had done so. He had handled the whole thing very badly. He should have told Mark clearly that he had not even attempted to procure for him; that he had no intention, ever of procuring for him.

'The hell with it,' he said and, moved by a sudden desire for a stiff drink, he got his hired Datsun from the car park and set off along Sunset Boulevard in the direction of Beverley Hills. About a mile up the road was what purported to be an English pub, the King and Queen by name, that looked dark and cosy and not at all like an English pub.

In the room behind the bar a rock group was thumping out some heavy music and in the bar itself men in leather trousers were whispering softly to other men in tight jeans and frilly shirts, while girls with boyish haircuts were sitting close to other girls in flouncy dresses.

'You cruising?' asked the barman. He stared at William with cold, disdainful eyes.

'Pardon?'

'You sure came to the right place,' said the barman, gesturing towards the clientèle at large. William looked carefully around him.

'Is this a gay bar?' he said.

'It is tonight, buddy,' said the barman. His hostile gaze went contemptuously from one whispering couple to another. 'Like I said, you sure found the right place.'

'No, no,' said William, 'you misunderstand me. I'm . . . er . . . I'm straight. I didn't realize this was a gay bar.'

'One night a week. One night too many, you ask me.'

William sipped his bourbon on the rocks. 'I thought they had their own places.'

'Right, they do. But that ain't good enough for 'em. Goddamn faggots. They wanna come into our places, too. We don't let 'em in, they call it discrimination. So, one night a week, the boss lets 'em have the joint. Discrimination. Jesus, I'll discriminate the bastards. Don't talk to me about goddamn Gay Lib.' William, who wasn't about to do so in any case, remained silent.

The barman said, 'Jesus, I mean, Gay Lib. You know what's gonna happen? One day they're gonna make it compulsory, know what I mean? One day there's gonna be a federal edict – one night a week everybody's gotta

be gay, just so there's no discrimination. You may laugh
. . .' William didn't laugh. 'But you mark my words, it'll
happen. Want another of those?'

William had another of those. He was feeling
increasingly depressed.

'You want a girl?' asked the barman, sympathetically.

'Yes,' said William, 'I want a nice, warm, kind-hearted
girl that I could cuddle and tell my troubles to.'

'Jesus,' said the barman. 'I don't know where you'd
find one of those. You just wanna get laid, there's no
problem. This is the easiest town in the world to get laid.
The whole place is lousy with hustlers. But you want
companionship, you came to the wrong town. You can't
even buy that here.'

'It's a rare commodity anywhere,' said William.

'Right,' said the barman. 'Right.'

It was half-past twelve when William returned to the
motel. He stood for a moment on the plastic grass surrounding the swimming pool and listened to the noise of
the traffic and the occasional scream of the police sirens
on Sunset Boulevard.

'Psst,' said a voice above his head.

He glanced up to find Mark Payne in a Chinese silk
dressing-gown glaring down at him from the first-floor
balcony overlooking the pool area. The door to Mark's
room was open behind him. 'Where's that bloody girl?'
Mark said.

'What?'

'That girl, that big, stupid waitress. Where is she?'

'I don't know,' said William. 'She was your date, not
mine.'

'But you were supposed to arrange it!'

'Correction,' said William. 'You thought I'd arranged
it but I didn't. I didn't even try.'

'You what?' Mark leaned dangerously over the

balcony, emanating a sincere rage. 'Listen, go across the road and find her. Tell her she's supposed to be here – now! Tell her . . .'

'Hello, boys,' said Alice Flitton. She was looking over the balcony on the floor above Mark's and she was wearing a short pink nightdress.

'What the hell do you want?' said Mark.

'Just thought I'd ask you to keep your voices down. I think there are people around here who are trying to sleep.'

'Don't you tell me to keep my voice down!' said Mark, turning his wrath on Alice. 'How dare . . .'

Yet another voice said, 'Come back to bed, honey,' and Larraine, the waitress, clad only in a shirt appeared beside Alice. 'Oh, hi, William,' she said. 'Hi, Mark.' She put her arm around Alice's shoulders. 'Why don't you get some sleep, fellers? 'Night.' And led Alice firmly back into the bedroom.

'You idiot!' Mark said. 'You were supposed to pull her for me, not for that . . . that . . .'

'I didn't pull her for anybody,' William said. 'I keep trying to tell you. I . . .' But with a furious rustle of silk Mark had returned to his room, slamming the door behind him.

For a moment William stared thoughtfully into the swimming pool and then, slowly, he began to smile. By the time he had finished he had created a smile that would have been the envy of Larraine, the waitress.

4

It was three o'clock in the morning when the burglar came into William's room and at first he didn't even realize it was a burglar. His first impression, as he emerged slowly from a heavy sleep, was that a white suit was somehow propelling itself slowly across the carpet towards his wardrobe but as his eyes grew accustomed to the darkness he realized that inside the suit was a black man, a very large and powerful-looking black man.

Immediately he was seized by fear. He lay naked and trembling beneath the sheet and watched through half-closed eyes as the suit made its slow, cautious way across the room. What to do, what to do?

Inside the wardrobe were, of course, William's suits and in one of those suits was his wallet containing travellers' cheques, credit cards and several hundred dollars. He couldn't afford to lose them but, on the other hand, could he afford to challenge an American burglar? Challenging American burglars, he knew from all he had read, was a most hazardous enterprise since they were, without exception, psychopathic drug-addicts armed to the teeth, and even the merest tyro was likely to have at least a machine-gun concealed about his person. Furthermore, although it was hard to tell in the dark, this particular burglar didn't look at all like a tyro and William hardly dared to imagine what kind of artillery he might have in his possession.

While he lay brooding thus and consoling himself with

the thought that a live coward could at least get his credit cards and travellers' cheques replaced while a dead hero couldn't even report their loss, the white suit had almost reached its destination. And then, unexpectedly, William's fear was swept aside by honest British indignation.

Chap comes into a chap's bedroom to steal his wallet. Well, chap can't have that. Mean to say – bloody cheek, after all. Impulsively he sat up and switched on the bedside light. There was a brief flurry of movement across the room, and the burglar vanished behind the wardrobe.

'Look here,' said William firmly, while part of his mind still marvelled at the foolhardiness of his action. 'I haven't seen you and if you leave now I shall never have seen you. Okay?'

There ensued a long pause during which William's surprising courage ebbed even more swiftly than it had flowed and the burglar presumably weighed the pros and cons of the argument that had been put to him. William wondered what would happen if he began to scream. Nothing probably, except that Mark Payne would bang on the partition wall and tell him to shut up. And the burglar would no doubt come out of his place of concealment with guns blazing.

Suddenly the burglar came out of his place of concealment and advanced towards the bed. He was smiling. My God, William thought, in California even the burglars smile at you. He sank back against the pillows and prepared for the murderous assault that was bound to be launched upon him.

But no such thing happened. The burglar walked briskly to the bedside and there he stopped. He had about him the air of a man who had been absurdly misunderstood but was nevertheless prepared to take the reasonable view.

'Hey, man,' he said, 'like maybe I owe you an explanation. See, what it was, I was looking for a hooker. You got any hookers in here, man?'

'Certainly not,' said William, indignation returning. 'You can see for yourself I'm perfectly alone.'

'Right,' said the burglar, giving the room a close scrutiny which indeed revealed a noticeable absence of hookers. 'Right. Only, see, there used to be a hooker in this room, man, and I was looking for her.'

'In the wardrobe?'

'Well, it was kinda dark. I couldn't see too good. Anyways I didn't wanna disturb you. Or her. Or her john. Or whatever. Mind if I sit down?' He sat down without waiting for a reply on the side of the bed. It sank markedly under his huge bulk. William had no previous experience of burglars but it occurred to him that, by any standards, this must be a very large burglar indeed.

'You got a cigarette?' asked the burglar.

'No, I'm sorry. I don't smoke.'

'How's about a joint then?'

'No. I don't use them either.'

'Shit,' said the burglar. 'This sure ain't my night.' He sat brooding for a moment with his chin in his hand. 'You ever have any truck with hookers in this town, man?' he asked.

'No,' said William. 'I've only been here for a few days.'

'Well, that's good, man, because, see, the hookers in this town are bad people. They real bad people, man. You keep away from them hookers, you hear me?'

'Yes, of course,' said William. 'Anything you say.'

'Right.' The burglar sat there, nodding thoughtfully to himself. 'You sure you got no joint, man? Little speed maybe?'

'No, nothing I assure you. Um . . . I hope you don't mind my asking but what exactly did you want with this hooker you thought might be in my room?'

'What?'

42

'This hooker . . .'

'What hooker? You mean you do got a hooker in here, man?' The burglar gave the room another swift examination and then stooped to peer under the bed.

'No, no, it's all right,' William said. 'My mistake. I just thought you said you were looking for a hooker?'

'So what if I did?' The burglar looked at him with dark hostility. 'You wanna make something of it?'

'No, no, not at all. None of my business.'

'You are wrong, man.' The burglar gave a deep sigh and sat in silence for a moment. Then he looked at his watch and rose to his feet in the purposeful manner of one who really had far better things to do with his time than sit around discussing hookers all night.

'Guess I'd better be getting along,' he said. 'Mind if I use the door this time?'

'Be my guest,' said William.

'Appreciate it,' said the burglar. He turned the smile on again and proffered his hand which William took and meekly shook.

'Anything else I can be doing for you?' asked the burglar.

'No nothing,' William said. 'Thank you very much all the same.'

'You're welcome,' said the burglar. 'Any time, man.' And he went to the door and let himself out.

William waited for a second or two then leapt from his bed, locked the door and went to the wardrobe to check that his wallet was still in his suit. It was. He carried it back to his bed and had just stuffed it under his pillow when there was a knock on the door and from without the burglar said, 'Hey man, you awake in there?'

William froze. There was a pause and then another tap on the door and the burglar said, more irritably this time, 'You hear me, man? Wake up, huh.'

William went to the door. 'What do you want now?' he asked.

'This is kind of embarrassing, man. Could you let me have ten dollars for cab fare?'

'What?'

'Jesus, man, what language you think I'm talking? All I want is a lousy ten dollars for cab fare. I'm asking you for a loan, man, like between friends.'

'If I let you have ten dollars,' said William, 'will you promise to go away and let me sleep?'

'Sure I'll go away. You think I wanna hang around this dump all night?'

'Hold on, then.' William returned to the bed, took a ten-dollar bill from his wallet and then, unlocking the door but keeping the safety chain on, he slipped the note into the waiting hand outside.

'Thanks, man,' said the burglar. 'I'll remember this. Sleep tight and don't let the bedbugs bite.'

William shut the door and locked it again. But he didn't return to bed until, through the window, he had seen a large, dark shape in a white suit cross the plastic grass and walk purposefully away from the foyer to the cab rank outside.

The next morning Mark Payne was to interview an elderly but extremely famous actress who had co-starred in three films with Willard Kaines. William's preliminary interview with her had made it clear that she had hardly known the man at all and that her contribution to the finished profile of him would be more or less negligible. But against that she was a Good Name and the makers of television programmes would always prefer to feature a Good Name spouting banalities than an anonymous face talking sound sense.

William was not accompanying the rest of the unit on this enterprise. Having arranged the rendezvous and provided Mark with background information and a list of suggested questions he was going, alone, to interview a much better prospect, an aged actor – another Good Name – who had frequently played the heavy to Willard Kaine's hero during the fifteen years of the Great Man's greatest success – a period that began some years after he had won his first Academy Award and lasted until the mid-1950s. William had met this actor, Rex Angell, briefly, three days earlier. Now he was to see him once more to extract the information that Mark would extract from him again during the interview on camera that afternoon.

'You're all clear about this morning, then, Mark?' William asked when they met for breakfast in the motel coffee-shop.

'Of course I'm all clear,' Mark said. His manner was, and had been since his first appearance, decidedly cold.

'Good. Then this afternoon, three o'clock, we all meet at Rex Angell's place. I've given Alice the address.'

'Don't talk to me about that fat dyke,' said Mark. 'And don't mention anything about last night. Not to anybody. Do you understand me. Because if you do . . .'

'Don't threaten me, Mark.'

'This is not a threat, William. It's a promise. I could ruin your career – just like that.' He snapped his fingers to show how swiftly he could ruin William's career and then, as an afterthought, snapped them twice again – snap, snap – as a reminder of his nervous energy.

William sighed. 'Mark, I spent a long time in Fleet Street. I've lost count of the number of people who were going to ruin my career.'

'Ah, yes,' Mark said. 'But the difference is, I could do it. I could have you out of Nat-Met in seconds and then where would you go, with your lack of experience? You'd be lucky if you got a job at the B.B.C. at half the pay.' In British television working for the B.B.C. was the financial pits and, as William had discovered in his brief period at Nat-Met, the prospect of somehow being drummed out of the independent network and obliged to go cap in hand to the Beeb, with its legendary starvation wages, had kept many an incipient rebel in line.

William said, 'You don't have to waste your breath on threats. I wasn't going to talk about it anyway.'

'That's good. Because you'd better not. And I might tell you, William, that I shall not lightly forget your part in last night's events. You tried to make a fool of me . . .'

'No, I didn't. You made a fool of your . . .'

'. . . and that's not the kind of thing I forgive.'

He broke off as the waitress brought William's breakfast – two eggs over and easy, crispy bacon, hash browns and, on the same plate, a large slice of orange.

'Good God,' said Mark. 'Fancy putting a lump of orange on the same plate as bacon and eggs.'

'That's nothing,' William said. 'They do it all the time here. You get the impression that they like to promote oranges rather urgently in this State. And besides I saw a man the other day, sitting right where you are as a matter of fact, who had all this *and* two great heaped spoonfuls of strawberry jam. All on the same plate. What do you think of that?' He shovelled a mound of egg, bacon and potato into his mouth and champed upon it with vast enjoyment.

'Do you mind?' said Mark. 'I'm not at my best this morning.' He nibbled morosely at a piece of rye toast.

'I had a burglar last night,' William said. 'In my room. I woke up and found him there. Big black chap.'

'Really? Pinch anything?'

'No.'

'Oh,' Mark said. He seemed disappointed. 'That's all right then, isn't it?'

'What do you mean – that's all right then?' William said indignantly. 'He was in my room and I challenged him. I was extremely brave. Let me tell you what . . .' But before he could do so Alice Flitton arrived. She looked pink and contented and somehow softer than she had done the previous day.

'Good morning,' she said. Indeed she very nearly sang it. 'What a lovely day. Did you sleep well? I did. I slept beautifully.' Mark got up, glowering at her.

'If you'll excuse me,' he said icily, 'I have some work to do.'

Alice watched him as he marched with sincere dignity out of the coffee-shop. 'Poor Mark,' she said, a trifle smugly, 'I expect he hates me, doesn't he? Well, come to that, I expect he hates you too.'

'Yes, he seems to,' William said, polishing off his bacon and eggs.

'Serves you right. You shouldn't have agreed to pander for him.'

'I didn't pander for him,' William said, gritting his teeth – not an easy thing to do with a mouthful of crispy bacon. 'And I told him so. It seemed to make matters worse, if anything.'

Alice yawned and stretched. 'God, that's a marvellous girl. Didn't you think so?'

'I didn't have a lot of opportunity to find out, did I? As far as I could tell she had big tits and a five-watt brain.'

'Male chauvinist pig,' said Alice Flitton.

'Dyke,' said William. They grinned at each other. 'I had a burglar in my room last night,' said William. 'He . . .'

'Good morning,' said Geoff Warbottle. It was merely a token greeting. He didn't sound as if he thought it was a good morning, nor did he look as if he thought it was. 'Christ, what have you been eating?'

'Eggs,' said William, 'bacon, hash browns . . .'

'All right, all right. I didn't really want to know. The sight of all that congealed yuk on your plate makes me feel sick.' The smell of fresh bourbon lingered on Warbottle's breath. He had clearly broken his fast on the stuff before coming to the coffee-shop. 'Seen Mark today?' He lowered himself, grunting, into a chair and signalled to the waitress for coffee.

'Yes,' said Alice Flitton.

'Did he lay that girl last night?'

Alice looked at William with the same enigmatic smile he had seen last night. 'No,' she said.

'Damn,' said Warbottle. 'That'll mean he'll be in a terrible mood all day.'

'He is already,' said William. 'He seems to hold me responsible.'

'Told you he would,' said Warbottle. The waitress poured his coffee and he lifted the cup carefully with both hands. 'They tell me you can have as much of this stuff as you like in this country.'

'That's right,' said William. 'They keep coming round and filling your cup.'

'First civilized thing I've heard about America,' said Warbottle.

'Mind you, it's lousy coffee.'

'You ought to take it intravenously,' said Alice Flitton, watching her producer's shaking hands without any indication of sympathy.

'I had a burglar in my room last night,' said William. 'It was about three o'clock . . .'

'Do you mind?' said Warbottle. 'I'll listen to your memoirs later.' He passed a hand over his pale, damp forehead. 'Oh God, I feel terrible.'

Rex Angell lived in a penthouse apartment in one of the black skyscraper blocks in Century City. Century City had once been the back lot of 20th Century Fox Studios but that was in the days before Fox, like all the other major studios, fell on hard times and had to unload its real estate. Now great office and apartment blocks, hotels, shopping centres and entertainment complexes had sprung up where once the stars of 20th Century Fox had played cowboys and Indians and re-enacted the Second World War. The studio itself still stood, rather insignificantly, on the fringe of what had once been its own land. With its entrance dominated by the turn-of-the-century New York street scene which had been built, years before, for the film of *Hello, Dolly* and which for some reason had never been struck, it looked like an eccentric factory.

Just before 10 a.m. William turned left off Santa Monica Boulevard, parallel with the Avenue of the Stars, and a few minutes later drew up in the parking lot outside Rex Angell's apartment block. A large door-man, very possibly armed, William thought, stopped him, questioned him, checked his credentials, phoned through to the Angell penthouse to make sure he was indeed expected and only then, grudgingly, let him pass. In apartment blocks such as this the residents paid heavily for privacy and, most of all, for security.

A silent, middle-aged Mexican maid let William into the penthouse. He trudged through thick, dark nylon carpet to a sitting-room furnished incongruously, bearing in mind its situation, like a western ranch-house. From a room down the corridor his host issued a summons, 'In here, pal.' The voice was loud, authoritative and still bore traces of New York's lower East Side whence its owner had sprung. William followed it to its source – a bedroom, or rather a boudoir, furnished and carpeted in dark blue with satin drapes and matching bedspread. In the bed itself, a vast king-sized affair, lay Rex Angell, small, plump and eighty-five years old.

His head, once famous for its black, sleek hair, was now quite bald, save for a few white wisps above the ears and at the back of the neck, but the startling blue eyes were still as blue and as startling and his skin was very pale and remarkably unlined. Propped against his blue satin pillows he looked like an old foam-rubber doll.

'How ya doin', kid?' he asked and without waiting for a reply he patted the edge of the bed. 'Sit. Take the weight off 'em.'

On the wall above the bed was a framed slogan, hand-painted on wood. It said: 'If you can get it up, I can get it in.'

'You like that, huh?' said Angell, as William read it. 'Know who painted that? Me. Not bad, huh?'

'No. Very good,' said William. 'The message has a rather desperate ring to it, though, don't you think?'

'It's the truth,' said Angell, simply. 'Goddammit, I haven't been able to get it up in years. In here,' he tapped the side of his head, 'I'm as horny as hell. Down there,' he pointed to his crotch, decently concealed beneath the bedspread, 'I'm like one of them goddamn enochs.'

William nodded. 'No fun being an enoch,' he agreed.

'Damn right. I tell ya, kid, don't ever grow old. It ain't worth it. You know something, old men are always horny. It's a little-known fact but, by God, it's true. You get a bunch of old guys together and all they talk about is how friggin' horny they are and how they ain't had it in like fifty years or something 'cause they can't get it up any more. Don't laugh, it's true and I'm like the rest of them. I have a horny heart. I don't have a horny peter, goddammit, but I sure as hell have a horny heart.'

'And a horny mind,' said William.

'Right.' He tapped the side of his head again. 'I got a whole hard-core porno movie going on in here. It's a hell of a picture, believe me. It makes *Deep Throat* look like it was made by Disney. I'm the star and the supporting roles are played by all the broads I used to make it with in the good days. Goes on for hours.'

'Used to put yourself about a bit, did you?'

'You better believe it, kid. But you know the real sad part? This movie, it's like a museum piece. All the action stops ten years ago. Ah, what the hell, it's no good even thinking about it. Where's your crew?'

'Well, they won't be here till this afternoon,' William said. 'They're doing another interview this morning with an actress who made a few films with Willard Kaines. Well, I expect you know her. Kate Goodenough?'

'Kate Goodenough? That ole whore?'

'Pardon?' The description hardly seemed to suit the little old lady whom William had interviewed only the previous morning. She, too, had been tiny – indeed William's researches among the senior citizens of Hollywood were fast leading him to the conclusion that back in the 1930s there hadn't been a star of either sex who was much more than five feet tall – and she had most certainly not looked like a whore. She was demure and pretty, with fluffy white hair and round, innocent eyes and she looked like America's ideal grandmother. In fact she played America's ideal grandmother in an instant-coffee commercial.

'Sure,' said Rex Angell. 'We used to call her Caint Getenough. Jeeze, I could tell you stories about her that would set your shorts on fire. Why, I remember one night when she and I . . .' He stopped and a faraway look came into his eyes. It occurred to William that the old man was just adding another reel to his mental-porno movie. 'Jeeze, Kate Goodenough. Is she really still alive?'

'Oh yes,' said William. 'She's been alive a long time.'

'What? Been alive a long . . .? Hey, I like that. She's been alive a long time, huh? That's good.' He broke into an appreciative and surprisingly youthful chuckle and then he said, 'Get the hell outa here, kid. I wanna put my pants on.'

Ten minutes later, William and Angell were drinking beer at the bar in the western ranch-house and the old man said, 'You wanna know about Willard Kaines, right?' Dressed in black slacks and a western shirt with pearl buttons he looked considerably less plump and doll-like. He was short, certainly, but he was broad and muscular around the chest and shoulders and something of the quality of suggested menace that had made him one of the best-loved heavies of Hollywood still remained.

He said, 'First off, lemme tell ya that Willard Kaines was the meanest son of a bitch I ever knew. Mean, like with money, you know? He didn't give a fart for Hollywood or the movies or any goddamn thing except the bread. In all the years I knew him I never saw him pick up a check in a restaurant or even buy a drink. He wanted a hooker even, he got the studio to pay for it. When he was making a movie, three times a week a hooker was brought into his dressing-room after we finished shooting and she went down as a production cost. Jeeze, he was one tight-fisted son of a bitch.'

'Was?' William said. He made a small adjustment to the volume control on his cassette-recorder.

'Yeah, well, he probably still is. I've not seen him for twenty years. Since we made that last picture together. You remember? I was the old bank robber and he was the old retired cop who tracks me down. God, what a load of horseshit that was. It was supposed to be a comedy. Comedy! Jeeze, I had more laughs at Jean Harlow's funeral.'

'You didn't like him much, I gather.'

'You could say that.' The old man produced another couple of beers from the refrigerator.

'And yet you made umpteen films together.'

'Yeah, well that was the studio. We made good chemistry, Kaines and me. Not great chemistry, but good chemistry. All our pictures, 'cept that last bastard, made a little money, not a lot but enough. He was a good-looking guy, you gotta hand him that. The women liked him – not as they liked Gable or Flynn or Colman but they liked him. And I was the guy everybody loved to hate so it made sense to put us together. Mind you, I did better later on when I made fewer movies with him and more on my own. Like, I'd never have got my Oscar if I'd stayed with him all the time. They didn't hand out

Oscars for the kinda stuff we made together.' He took a swig from his can of beer and William, fretting slightly, began to wonder how all this information could possibly be rearranged so as to present Willard Kaines in the soft and flattering light that was necessary if he was to be passed off as a Great Man of Our Time.

Angell said, 'Hey, I ever tell you about my Oscar?'

'No,' said William. 'Look, I'd love to hear about it sometime, really I would. It's just that right now . . .'

'You saw the movie? *Death on the Run*, right? I'm the Mafia boss, the *capo di capi*. Usual plot, load of horse-shit. What makes it special is me and you know why? We shot the whole damn film in a month and while we're doing it I'm banging three different broads. Sometimes two of them in the same night, once all three of them. My wife – lemme see, that musta been my third wife, or maybe my fourth, who remembers? – my wife and two other girls. I never got more than three hours sleep in any one night and when the film comes out, you know what the critics say? They say this is the finest study of dissolution they ever seen. Study? Listen, I *was* friggin' dissolute. I was exhausted. I went through that whole picture sleep-walking and they gave me a goddamn Oscar for it. I'm the only guy you ever met who truly screwed his way to an Oscar.'

William laughed, dutifully. 'Good heavens,' he said. 'Amazing.' Then, seeing the old man about to embark on another chapter of his reminiscences, he added swiftly, 'Could we, I wonder, just get back to Willard Kaines for a moment? Isn't there anything . . . anything nice you can find to say about him?'

'No,' said Angell, 'not a friggin' thing.' He thought for a moment. 'Well, okay, I could say something nice about his acting, I guess. I mean, he was a lousy actor. I was a lousy actor. We were all lousy actors, except maybe Tracy, but what the hell, Kaines was no worse than the rest of us. Okay, I'll say something nice about his acting.

Oh, and his wife. He was very good to his wife.'

'His wife?' William said. 'Ah yes. She's dead, of course.'

'She is now, right. Died, oh a hell of a long time ago. But for a spell there, when she was sick, just before she died, he was pretty good to her. Wouldn't have a nurse for her, looked after her himself. Went on for months, that did. Naturally, I'm talking about his first wife.'

'Naturally,' William said. 'This is very interesting, Rex. I didn't know any of this stuff. If you'll say it on camera this afternoon, it'll be just the kind of thing we want. But now, what about his second wife? She seems to have been very much a background figure. I can hardly find anything at all about her in the records. Was he just as nice to her before she died?'

'Died?' said Rex Angell. 'What the hell you talking about? She ain't dead. They ain't even divorced. She left him, like fifteen years ago. She's still around someplace – got a house in the Valley, I think.'

'San Fernando Valley?'

'Where else? How'd you get this idea she was dead? Ida ain't the kind that dies.'

'But I thought . . .' William looked through his note-book. 'I don't know. Just the impression I got from everything I read seemed to suggest that she was dead.'

'No way. You wan' another beer? No, Ida was his secretary, looked after the fan mail and like that, during his first marriage. She was there the whole time his first wife was sick. He married her . . . what? . . . not a year after the first Mrs Kaines died. Don't ask me why. Ida was never much to look at, believe me. Well, not bad but nothing special. You know? Maybe she was good in the sack. I guess she musta been good in the sack. Why else would he have marrried her, for Godsake? Listen, you wanna find out how good he was to his first wife, go see Ida. She knows all about it. I got the address here in one of my old books. Maybe she's moved, maybe not. It'll

give you someplace to start anyways. Tell you something, though – this is one very weird lady, believe me.'

He put down his beer can and yelled, 'Hey, Maria.'

The Mexican maid came into the room and stood,
silent, just beyond the threshold. 'Listen, Maria,' said
Rex Angell. 'You know that filing cabinet I got in the
den? Well, look through it, will ya, see if you can find an
address for Ida Kaines. Not Willard Kaines – Ida
Kaines. Oughta be somewhere in the Valley.'

Maria went out and the old man pushed his can of beer
to one side. 'Enough of this piss already,' he said. 'Let's
have some bourbon . . .'

Ninety minutes later William gathered together his
notes and his cassette-recorder preparatory to leaving.
Somewhat to his astonishment he realized that, despite
the beer and the bourbon, both he and Rex Angell were
still very sober. 'I'll be back this afternoon,' he said 'with
the crew.'

'Yeah, okay. What's he like, this interviewer, this
Mark . . .?'

'Payne? He's all right. I mean, he's fine.'

'Big star in England?'

'Pretty big, yes.'

'Pity you're not doing the interview. I like you, kid.'

William mumbled something, bashfully. He wanted
to say, 'I like you, too,' but it sounded like too much of
an emotional commitment. He did indeed like the old
man but, being English, and thus reserved, he could not
bring himself to say so.

'What do you think of this?' said Rex Angell. He
handed William a letter. 'Came this morning.'

William looked through it swiftly. It was from a large
and important publishing house in New York and it was
an offer to the old man to write his memoirs. The figure
quoted for an advance against royalties, merely an
opening figure, after all, a basis for negotiation, nothing
more, was to William quite staggering; he had no idea

that any book of memoirs could be worth so much.

'Maybe I am older than God but they ain't forgotten me, kid,' Angell said. 'Okay, so I haven't made a movie since that turkey with Willard Kaines but they still remember Rex Angell.' And that, William realized, was why he had produced the letter. Hollywood lived on fear – the fear of failure and the fear of being forgotten – and its inhabitants died of fear. Angell, however, was not forgotten and he had this fat offer from a big New York publisher to prove it. William found the old man's obvious pride rather touching.

'Fantastic,' he said, and meant it. 'You'll accept, of course.'

'Like hell,' said the old man. 'Listen, I don't need the money. I'm pretty well fixed, thank God. Mind you, they're goddamn shrewd these publishers. They know, like I know, that if I really opened up I could blow some dandy reputations in this town twice around the world and back again.'

'Then why not?' William said.

'On account of where they say "We'll send a writer to help you." Know what that means? It means they send some smartass college kid, who don't even know why his nose is dripping, to sit on my back for six months and then write *my* memoirs in *his* words. Screw 'em. Who needs that?' He threw the letter with its offer of, to William, unimaginable wealth carelessly onto a coffee-table and escorted William to the door. 'See ya later,' he said.

'Yes,' William said. 'Indeed.' And he went away to find a phone and call Ida Kaines.

5

'Camera running,' said the cameraman.

'Sound running,' said the soundman.

'Rex Angell. Roll 6, take one,' said the assistant cameraman and banged down the arm of the clapper-board.

'We on now?' said Rex Angell. 'Okay? Right, well lemme tell you about Willard Kaines. See, I know that old son of a bitch from, like, way back. Musta been 1926 I first met him. Yeah, '26 – maybe '25, who remembers? Anyway, that time we were both laying the same broad only neither of us knew it.' He broke into a low, salacious chuckle and William, sitting in the corner of the ranch-house room, decided they must be somewhere in the middle of reel two in Rex Angell's mental-porno movie. 'How it happened was like this . . .'

'Just a minute, just a minute,' said Mark Payne. He was sitting opposite his interviewee with a pad of questions on his knee. 'We don't want any lengthy reminiscences. This is a question-and-answer interview and besides we haven't got the establishing two-shot yet.'

'Is that absolutely necessary, Mark?' said Geoff Warbottle.

'Of course it is. Without the two-shot my viewers won't know I'm here.'

'Yes they will. We'll do the noddies later. They'll see you on them.'

'Noddies aren't enough,' said Mark, angrily. 'My

57

viewers like to see me at the very beginning of an interview.' He delivered his sincere sniff, nostrils dilating, mouth turning down at the corners. 'It reassures them.'

Warbottle shrugged. 'All right. Let's do the two-shot.'

The cameraman rearranged himself and his equipment for the two-shot. 'Rolling,' he said. Mark turned slightly to his right so that his profile, while not obliterating Rex Angell's face, would certainly dominate the picture, and flashed a brilliant smile at William. William was rather gratified. Mark's morning coldness towards him had lasted throughout lunch and the briefing session on Rex Angell which had followed it and he could only assume from this brilliant smile that Mark had decided to forgive him for whatever it was he had done wrong and that they were to be friends again.

'All right, cut,' said Warbottle. The smile vanished immediately and Mark turned back to his question pad.

'You want me to start now?' said Rex Angell.

'No, I don't,' said Mark. 'Kindly wait till I ask a question.'

'So ask a goddamn question and quit friggin' around.'

Mark took a deep breath and stared with great loathing at the little old actor in the sunburst sports shirt and black, sleek toupee. 'Mr Angell,' he said, 'tell me in your own words, what were the qualities that made Willard Kaines great?'

'What?' said Rex Angell.

'Christ,' said Mark, *sotto* – though not very *sotto* – *voce*. He took another deep breath and repeated loudly and slowly, 'What were the qualities that made Willard Kaines great?'

'Hey, you don't have to shout at me. I'm not deaf, goddamn it. You wanna know why I said, "What?" I said "What?" not because I couldn't *hear* the friggin' question but because I couldn't *believe* the friggin' question. What are you talking about – great? Willard Kaines is strictly second-rate.'

'Cut,' said Geoff Warbottle. 'We don't seem to be getting along too well here, Mark. Perhaps a different line of quest . . .'

'It's his fault,' said Mark, glaring at William.

'No, it's not,' said William. 'There was nothing on that list of questions I gave you about Kaines being great. That was your own idea.'

'Well, I was badly briefed,' said Mark, 'Very badly briefed.'

'Are you guys always like this?' asked Rex Angell. 'Listen, why don't you let the kid ask the questions? He's a helluva lot better at it.'

'You shut up!' said Mark. He was aware, as William and Alice Flitton were aware, that the entire crew were staring up at the ceiling with smiles of quiet joy.

'What?' said Rex Angell. 'Where the hell do you get off, telling me to shut up in my own apartment? I didn't take that kinda talk from Louis Mayer, so I'm sure as hell not taking it from a friggin' jerk like . . .'

'Gentlemen, please!' said Geoff Warbottle. 'We seem to have got off to a rather bad start here. Can we not begin again and . . .'

'No,' said Rex Angell. 'I'm up to here with this bum. Get him outa my place.'

William got up from his seat in the corner and walked over to the ancient and irate actor. 'Please, Rex. This is very important for us. We can't do the programme without you. I'm sorry you've been upset but if we could just start all over . . . If Mark asked a different question . . . If he asked, perhaps, what you thought of Willard Kaines as an actor . . .'

'Like you and I discussed this morning?'

'Yes, exactly that.'

The old man stared coldly at Mark. Then he sighed. 'Okay, kid, since you're the one who's asking. But he's gotta apologize first.'

'Mark?' said William.

Mark looked at William for a long time with thoughtful and sincere hatred. 'I apologize,' he muttered, sulkily.

'Okay,' said Angell. 'What are we waiting for?'

'Rex Angell. Roll 7, take three,' said the assistant cameraman.

'Mr Angell,' said Mark. 'Tell me, in your own words, what did you think of Willard Kaines as an actor?'

Ida Kaines lived in a small, one-storey wooden house in a street of small, one-storey wooden houses in the San Fernando Valley. It was a long, straight, dusty street and the scraps of coarse lawn outside each home were in various stages of incipient baldness. Ida Kaines's lawn looked better than the others; it looked as if it had been cut recently and watered quite often. At the back of her house was a small patio and a tiny swimming pool, not a great deal bigger than a hip bath. It was only there at all, William thought, staring out at it from Mrs Kaines's tidy sitting-room, because no home in southern California is complete without a swimming pool, however minuscule.

'So how was Rex?' asked Mrs Kaines, emerging from the kitchen with a tray containing coffee cups and a plate of cookies.

'Fine,' said William. It had been a fairly dreadful afternoon. The animosity between Mark and Angell had been evident in every frame of film and though, carefully edited, much of what the actor had said could be used to promote the image of Willard Kaines as a Great Man of Our Time, none of it had been said with any degree of enthusiasm.

To make Angell's testimony work at all, William thought, Geoff Warbottle would have to cut it up into very short takes. And if this was not bad enough, Angell had refused to allow the crew time to do the noddies – the reverse shots, taken from over the interviewee's shoulder, in which Mark would nod and smile and grimace and express surprise and delight and intense interest and would also repeat some of the questions he had asked during the interview itself. As far as Mark was concerned the noddies were the most important part of the interview because without them the most that would be seen of him was the back of his head in the opening two-shot. But their purpose was not merely to feed Mark's ego; they were also vital if the interview was to be edited into the shape of a conversation, rather than a series of answers to off-camera questions. Angell had said he was too tired for all that crap and – even though Mark would have happily nodded and grimaced at, and asked questions of, an empty chair – he wanted everybody out fast because he had someone coming round for an early dinner. Mark had swept out in a huff without even saying goodbye to his host and had, inevitably, blamed William for all that had gone wrong.

'A great guy, Rex,' said Mrs Kaines. She was a small, lean woman in her late sixties with dark, sun-wrinkled skin and grey hair.

'Yes, he is,' William said.

'Is he still . . . er. . . as bad as ever?'

'You mean, sort of mildly sex-crazed?'

Mrs Kaines laughed. 'That's exactly what I mean.'

'Well,' said William, thoughtfully, 'I don't know what he can have been like before but I doubt if he could have been any worse than he is now.'

'That's my Rex,' said Mrs Kaines and handed over coffee and cookies. When they'd both sipped and crunched for a bit she said, 'Well, young man, what can I do for you?'

William got out his cassette-recorder and set it up on the brightly polished table. 'I just want to know about your life with Willard Kaines.'

'My Life with Willard Kaines.' She smiled, shook her head slowly. 'It sounds like a chapter in one of those magazines. You know, *True Horror Stories*, that kind of thing?'

'Pardon?'

Mrs Kaines looked at him in silence for quite a long time. William found the silence and the faint smile she wore slightly disconcerting. 'You don't really know a lot about Willard Kaines, do you?'

'Not enough,' he said.

There was more silence. William fidgeted and, for want of anything else to do, ate another cookie. 'I wonder,' said Mrs Kaines. 'I wonder just how much I should tell you.'

'Everything,' said William brightly.

'Everything?' She shook her head again. 'Are you ready for everything, young man? I doubt it. I really doubt it. But . . .' She looked slowly around the neat, bright little room. 'What the hell, I'm getting out of here anyway so . . . So okay. Turn on your machine. Let's see how we get on.'

Somewhat mystified, William switched on the recorder. 'I think the best thing,' he said, 'would be if you just sort of started from the beginning . . .'

'Okay,' said Ida Kaines and began to unfold her tale.

She had met Willard Kaines some years after he had won his first Oscar and just as she was coming to the conclusion that she wasn't going to be a big star after all. She had intended to be one; indeed she had come to Hollywood as a promising young singer and dancer and for a few years had done quite well.

'I played in a lot of movies. Not the star, not even the best friend but certainly the best friend's best friend.' William studied the neat, lean, nut-brown woman and tried to imagine her singing and dancing and kicking up her legs in a chorus line and exuding girlish enthusiasm and optimism as a best friend's best friend. He found it hard to do . . .

Anyway, said Ida Kaines, things looked okay for a

while but then, as she surveyed the competition around her, she realized that stardom was out of her reach and even permanent best friend's best friendship was barely within it. She had been quite a pretty girl – and she produced photographs to support this claim – but pretty in a way that thousands of American girls were pretty: it was a question of teeth and eyes and pert eagerness. Hers was a prettiness that would never entirely disappear but was unlikely to mature into beauty. Of course, she did have talent – she was a good dancer and a pretty fair singer, but Hollywood in those days was passing full of good dancers and pretty fair singers and barely one in a thousand of them would emerge from the crowd to reach even the comparatively modest status of best friend. All in all then, she came to understand that she was simply average – chorus line and casting-couch fodder. But here she suffered an additional handicap; she refused to play the casting-couch game or to 'entertain' the money men from the New York office when they came to town for what were euphemistically called conventions. This gave her a very bad reputation as a girl who didn't do anything much except sing and dance and act a bit and was no fun to have around.

It was about the time that this reputation was becoming widely established and casting directors were going about ruining her good name in Hollywood even further by suggesting that she was very probably still a virgin that she met Willard Kaines. He was starring, as a theatrical impresario, in an indifferent film musical and Ida had been cast as his co-star's best friend's maid. It turned out to be her last appearance in the movies, as a result of the fact that one night after work Kaines had invited her into his trailor for a drink and, before she had finished her first martini, had seduced her. She told this part of her story very softly because, after all these years, she was still, she said, a little ashamed of herself for allowing it to happen. Kaines was a married man and she knew it.

But she was also in love with him.

'You have to remember,' she said to William, 'that Will was a marvellous-looking man. A lousy actor, if you want to know the truth, but beautiful. If only . . . You know the thing that stopped him being a really big star?'

'The fact that he was a lousy actor?'

She smiled sadly. 'Innocent boy,' she said. 'Ninety-nine per cent of all big stars are lousy actors. No, the thing that stopped Will was he just didn't look mean enough. Gable now, he was another lousy actor but he looked mean. Women like a streak of meanness in a man. But Will . . . well, he *was* mean but he didn't look it. Women thought of Will as a beautiful partner on the dance floor or an escort at the theatre, something gorgeous to wear on their arm. But they never thought much about, well, about what he'd be like in the bedroom.'

'Oh,' said William. Surprisingly, he felt a little uncomfortable to hear her talking about sex, even in such veiled terms. She sat straight-backed with her hands folded primly in her lap and – he couldn't be sure because of the leathery, sun-beaten texture of her skin – but he wouldn't have been at all surprised if she were blushing.

She had told him this, she said, referring to the seduction, because it was necessary if he was to understand what happened next. If she had been in love with Kaines before he seduced her, she was doubly so afterwards. Oh, she knew it was wrong but . . . well, she was lonely and a little frightened about her future and he was kind, then, and gentle, so the affair continued and developed, the strong cement binding them together being (she realized now) their mutual adoration of Willard Kaines.

When the film was completed Kaines had suggested that she move into his home in Beverley Hills as his secretary. She had demurred at first, not because it meant giving up her career (she was already prepared to do that) but because there was, after all, an incumbent

Mrs Kaines firmly installed under the same roof.

William said stoutly that he was not surprised at her reluctance and Ida smiled and said, yes, but it wasn't quite as simple as that. This incumbent Mrs Kaines was an invalid, more or less bedridden with chronic heart trouble and more than a touch of hypochondria. She was fifteen years older than her husband and the marriage had always been one of convenience. He had married her because she was rich and she had married him because he was so good-looking, a notable addition to her already considerable collection of pretty *objets d'art*. The relationship (so Kaines maintained at least) had barely been consummated, his appetite for sex being evenly matched by her repugnance for it.

Before going to Hollywood, Ida said, Kaines had been a gigolo in New York . . .

'Did you know that?' William asked. 'At the time, I mean.'

'Oh yes,' she said. 'Everybody did. And I still loved him. Strange, isn't it?'

Anyway, she went on, Willard had no aversion to servicing elderly ladies. His wife, however, had made it clear that she hardly ever needed servicing and merely wanted him around to complete the decor of her home. So an agreement had been arrived at: he was free to satisfy elsewhere what Mrs Kaines regarded as his animal needs, but discreetly and only so long as he presented the public appearance of a perfectly happy spouse.

Willard Kaines had indeed been as discreet as possible about his extra-marital relationships but he had also been rather more prolific in them than his wife had anticipated. When Louella Parsons printed a paragraph that read: 'Which handsome leading man leaves his elderly wife at home while he goes dancing and romancing with a different starlet practically every night?' Mrs Kaines, realizing that scandal lurked around the corner, blew the whistle on him. By the simple expedient of restricting his access to her fortune she frightened him into curtailing his amorous activities. Such was the position when he made the film on which he met Ida, and Kaines, being by now seriously frustrated, had come dangerously close to returning the love which the young actress felt for him.

All this, too, Ida knew or at least suspected and yet still she loved him, though not enough to move into his home. But at this point Mrs Kaines herself took a hand.

'She invited me to tea,' Ida said. 'It was a very weird experience. We sat in this little parlour where she had a load of 1930s English furniture? You know the stuff? Lots of huge armchairs and glass tables with tubular steel legs. It was horrible. And she was kind of horrible, too. She was fat and white and she looked older than she was. Anyway, she told me all about herself and Willard – I mean, she really laid it on the line – and in the end she said she was tired of him running around with what she called little whores all the time and if he really had to have sex she'd rather he had it with me, right there in the house where she knew what was going on. And then she offered me a job as *her* secretary.'

'And you accepted?' William asked.

'God forgive me, I did. It's hard to explain but . . . well, I was just obsessed by the guy. It's not easy even for me to understand now but I was. I must have been because, boy, she was a frightening lady. All the time she was talking to me she kept eating chocolates and staring at me with those cold eyes.'

So Ida moved in and for quite a long time the arrangement appeared to work very well. Indeed, it worked too well because suddenly, unaccountably, Mrs Kaines began to grow jealous. Her heart condition had become worse and she spent more and more time in bed, eating more and more chocolates and growing whiter and fatter by the minute. She also started to feel sorry for herself, to believe herself shamefully neglected by her unfaithful husband and his paramour. And so, one day, she ordered Ida to leave the house and told her husband she wanted a divorce.

(William had listened to all this – surreptitiously checking from time to time that the recorder was still working – with increasing excitement. If only Mark could get the same kind of stuff out of Ida when the camera was rolling they would have an absolutely sensational documentary.)

'A divorce!' he said. 'Crikey. What did Willard do?'

'Well, he killed her,' Ida said.

'What?'

'He killed her.'

'You're not serious?'

'Yes, I am. The doctors had prescribed all kinds of drugs for her and one night Will just mixed up a whole mess of this stuff and fed it to her and she died.'

'But . . . but this is appalling,' William said and indeed he was appalled though the journalist in him was thrilled too. He felt ashamed of the journalist in him. 'I can't believe it. I mean, Rex Angell said that Kaines looked after her like a child when she was ill. He says everybody knows that and . . . and all Hollywood was so touched by his devotion to her that it sort of revived his career.'

Right, Ida Kaines said. His career was on the skids. The musical they had appeared in together was a box-office disaster and Kaines was increasingly dependent on his wife's money. At most Hollywood studios he couldn't even get arrested and at one they had told him he *would* be arrested if he set foot in the place, uninvited, again. In Hollywood nobody likes a loser and Kaines had been a loser three times in a row, both commercially and critically. He was a freelance and nobody wanted him, so he had let it be known that he had temporarily retired from acting to look after his sick wife. He had been, to all appearances, so engaged for more than a year when Mrs

Kaines announced her intentions of divorcing him and by then Hollywood, which always prefers to believe the legend rather than the truth, had convinced itself that he was truly a devoted husband who had sacrificed his career for his wife. Kaines did not particularly mind being unemployed. He missed the adulation and probably he missed the willing starlets but, so long as he still had access to his wife's money, he was not too perturbed. A threat of divorce, however, changed the situation entirely. A divorce would leave him penniless. So he decided to make himself a widower.

William, still unable fully to comprehend what he was hearing, said, 'But how do you know?'

'Because on the day she died he was supposed to be with me. By this time he'd got me a little apartment on Wilshire Boulevard. He told everybody it was his office and that he and I were working on a script there.' She shrugged. 'People believed him. Why not?'

Anyway, on the day Willard Kaines became a widower he and Ida had been together in the apartment. At lunch-time they had gone to the Brown Derby where, unusually and on Kaines's cheerful insistence, she had drunk two large, dry martinis as well as a couple of glasses of wine. He'd said, 'Come on, let's have a few drinks, enjoy ourselves. We won't be able to afford this if she divorces me.' A newspaper columnist had stopped at their table and asked Kaines when he was going back to work and he'd said not until his wife was better, though of course he was working on this script . . . The newspaper columnist had patted him on the shoulder and said Jeeze, it was a tough break, the wife being ill and all and they didn't make guys like Willard Kaines any more . . .

After lunch, Ida and Kaines had returned to the apartment and made love and then – again unusually – he had brought her tea and she had drunk half of it and fallen asleep. When she awoke an hour later Kaines was coming back into the apartment. Thirty minutes after that the phone had rung and an hysterical maid at the Kaines' house had announced that Mrs Kaines was dead.

Kaines had then returned to his home just ahead of the doctors, the police and the ambulance and, according to Ida's account – based on second-hand information from the various servants who had been present – had given the performance of his life, tearing his hair, weeping and shouting that he'd never forgive himself for being away working on his stupid script while his wife was killing herself.

For in the end suicide was what everyone agreed it must have been, though they might not have come so easily to that conclusion had not Ida testified that Kaines had been with her, working on the script, from the time they left the Brown Derby until the maid phoned. The crucial time, according to the autopsy, had been around 3.30 p.m., which was when Mrs Kaines had apparently imbibed the overdose that killed her. And 3.30 p.m. was about half an hour before Ida woke up and Kaines let himself back into their apartment.

William said, 'But surely . . . Didn't you tell anybody that he hadn't actually been with you all day?'

She shook her head. 'No. I didn't . . . I didn't want to believe he could do anything like that. I asked him where he'd been and he said he'd just gone out for a few minutes to get some cigarettes. And . . . oh and then he asked me not to mention the fact that he'd left the apartment at all.'

'And you agreed?' William said, incredulously.

'Yes. Because . . . because I loved him. I don't know . . . maybe you've never been in love, young man, but if you have you'll know that when you're in love, really, deeply, infatuatedly in love, you believe what you want to believe.'

Kaines had been particularly nice, particularly solicitous, towards her in the months after his wife's death.

For a while, inevitably, he had been under suspicion, especially as he was the sole heir to a considerable amount of money and property. But Ida had steadfastly maintained that they had been together the whole afternoon, working on the script – and indeed there was a script, or at least part of one, an awful one, which he produced as corroboration. Ida had never seen it before and when he showed it to her and asked her to read it so that she could give plausible answers to any questions the police might pose, her doubts about him deepened into suspicion.

But, in fact, the police asked her no questions because Mrs Kaines's doctors staunchly insisted that suicide was the most probable cause of death. They, of course, were merely protecting themselves. Mrs Kaines had been a very rich woman and they had supplied her rather too liberally with various pain-killers and sleeping-pills. When the house was found to be overfull of such things, the doctors had declared that she must have been stockpiling them with the intention of taking her own life.

Six months after his first wife's funeral, Willard Kaines had married Ida. He informed the press that they were marrying for companionship and because it was what the late Mrs Kaines would have wanted, for she and Ida had adored each other. Ida had been very surprised to learn this fact but the whole improbable tale was accepted because Kaines, the gorgeous, grieving, loving widower, had been signed by one of the major studios and this studio had exerted considerable muscle to ensure that the right kind of publicity attended the wedding.

On the first night of the honeymoon, Kaines, drunk and boastful on champagne and secure in the knowledge that a wife could not testify against her husband, had confessed to murder. He had also confessed that on the significant afternoon he had put a sleeping draught in Ida's tea and claimed that if she had only drunk it all she would have slept twice as long, would have believed – as in fact she did anyway – that it was the lunch-time booze that had made her drowsy and would never have known that he had left her. The admission had horrified her and yet had not really surprised her. Deep down she had probably always known and had come to accept the knowledge because, well, because dammit, she really loved him still.

So that was the beginning of their marriage, Ida said, and it was also virtually the end. Within a few weeks he was back at work, making the first of his films with Rex Angell, and within a few months it became obvious that he was once again sleeping with other women. Soon after, as a defence mechanism against the pain his infidelity caused her, Ida herself had developed other interests, not in men but in travel. She had spent much time in the East, in Africa and finally in South America. There was a village, deep in Brazil, virtually untouched by civilization even now, where the people loved her and she loved them and soon, very, very soon, she was going out there to stay. 'And I mean that,' she said, 'when I get there I will stay. I'll never come back to America.'

William looked curiously at this small, elderly woman, who for years had covered up a murder, and said, 'Why are you telling me all this?'

She said, 'I'm not really sure. For a long time I suppressed it, I wouldn't even think about it. And then, when I finally left Will I thought at first I might get a divorce and I wouldn't be his wife any more and I could tell the police and . . . Oh, it wouldn't have worked. Who would they believe – me, a rejected wife, or a guy who owned half of downtown Los Angeles and a chunk of Beverley Hills?' So I didn't divorce Will. I just left him and he gave me this house and an allowance and . . . I did nothing. I'm one hell of a person, aren't I?'

'Well,' William said. He tried to think what he would

have done in her position but since he couldn't imagine being in her position it didn't help much. 'Who am I to judge?'

'Sure. But you're judging anyway, aren't you?'

'I'm trying not to,' he said. And then . . . 'I still don't understand why you're telling me this now.'

'I guess . . . I guess that as I get older it worries me more. It's strange . . . I don't feel bad about the woman he killed. She wasn't a pleasant person in any way. But I do feel bad about my part in it, about my silence, and I feel that . . . oh, that people should know what happened. I hear they're going to give Will a special Oscar next time around and it's wrong. They shouldn't honour him. He doesn't deserve honour. People should know. So, when I decided to quit here and go to Brazil, I thought I might leave a letter with my lawyer. You know – "Not to be opened until . . .". I was just going to write it when you called and I thought, well, maybe television is better.'

William said, 'Do you mean you're prepared to tell all this on camera tomorrow?'

She nodded. 'Yes. You won't be able to use it, of course, not until Will's dead but at least it'll be on record.' She paused. 'There's one other thing: it'll cost you 5,000 dollars. Not for me – it's for this village in Brazil. They could use the money.'

'Five thou,' William said. 'That's quite a lot of money for us. But . . . It's a hell of a story. I'll talk to my producer. I'm sure he'll be interested.'

'Okay. If he agrees the numbers, we've got a deal.' She put the empty coffee cups and the cookie plate on the tray. 'So I'll see you tomorrow morning, right?'

'Right,' William said. He turned off his recorder and put it away in his briefcase. 'Do you think . . . could I ask you a question? What are you going to do in Brazil?'

Ida Kaines smiled ironically. 'I'm going to be living

and working with this rather primitive tribe in the jungle. I'm going to help them all I can. Can you think of a better way to assuage guilt?'

'No,' said William. 'Not offhand.'

6

William pulled up sharply as he approached the motel to avoid running over a tall, thin man in faded jeans, denim jacket and Mickey Mouse mask who was passing the entrance arm-in-arm with a hippy girl in a short leather skirt. Over one breast on the girl's grubby white tee-shirt was the word Sugar and over the other, Spice. The girl took a hand-rolled joint from her mouth and slipped it lovingly between her companion's Mickey Mouse lips. Then she gave William a lazy, happy smile and arm-in-arm and thoroughly stoned the odd couple continued on their slow, uncertain way.

'California,' William said to himself as he parked the car. 'Hollywood.' Where are they going to, those two, he wondered. Nowhere, probably. And why was the man dressed as Mickey Mouse? For no better reason, perhaps, than that it had seemed a good idea at the time. William shook his head. What a place this was – a dream factory where everyone smiled incessantly because nobody dared look sad in a dream factory. But the trouble with a dream was that it only needed to take an unexpected little twist to become a nightmare and those two, he thought – the Mickey Mouse man and his Sugar-and-Spice companion – had glimpsed the nightmare, had experienced the fiercely competitive in-fighting that waged ceaselessly beneath the unwavering smiles. They were Hollywood's walking wounded and pot was the anaesthetic that eased the pain.

On the T.V. Tina Ling, greenly beautiful, was delivering the news and giving the English language its nightly mauling. Between times the same man with the same haemorrhoids complained to the same chemist who suggested the same palliative. William ignored them all, keeping the set turned on merely as a form of visual muzak, and settled down to transcribing the Ida Kaines interview.

He had tried, as soon as he got in, to contact Mark Payne and Geoff Warbottle to tell them of the afternoon's sensational revelations but they were both out and so was Alice Flitton. The desk clerk seemed to think that Mark and Geoff had gone early to dinner and William was pretty sure where Alice would be – across the road in the coffee-shop admiring the tanned and rounded charms of Larraine Laroux.

Well, he thought, the news would have to wait. He would tell them all at breakfast. He imagined their excitement as he recounted the story; their realization that what had threatened to be an uncompromisingly bland profile of a rather uninteresting old ham had unexpectedly been given a sharp cutting edge. The Killer with Two Oscars. Or possibly three after the next Academy Awards. True, they were only a reward for supporting performances and longevity but they were undeniably Oscars. Hollywood, murder and sex. As a documentary it had every ingredient anyone could desire. Of course, it wasn't a documentary for now – it would have to wait until Willard Kaines was dead but that, surely, couldn't be too long. Kaines was very old after all and when it was finally shown, well, it was bound to be top of the ratings – a position but rarely achieved by programmes issuing from National-Metropolitan – and he, William, had unearthed the vital information. Once this was known his career was bound to take off. Perhaps the company would make him a producer, or a presenter, or . . .

In the middle of this day-dreaming the enormity of what Ida Kaines had told him struck home. He was in possession of knowledge of a murder. He was as guilty as she was; he should do something, tell somebody. Yes, but whom should he tell – the police? Should he go to them and say, 'Listen to this tape . . .'? That would be a betrayal of Ida Kaines and though he could not in any way condone her part in covering up the fact of her predecessor's murder, she had trusted him. And besides, he had liked her and could, at least dimly, comprehend why she had behaved as she had done. She wasn't . . . she wasn't an evil woman but she had committed a crime and if he, William, told the police she would be in nearly as much trouble as Willard Kaines.

He worried over this for some time until, in the end, he decided to wait until he could consult Payne and Warbottle and see what they advised. Thus resolved he carried on transcribing the tapes and roughing out Mark's crib sheet of questions for tomorrow's intèrview with Ida and he had just about finished when the phone rang and the desk clerk said, 'Mr Pen'leton? There's a guy down here for you. A Mr Angell?'

'Rex Angell?' said William, startled.

'Hang in there, I'll ask him . . . Yeah, that's right . . . Rex Angell . . .'

Puzzled, William went downstairs to greet his guest and for the moment he banished the problem of Ida Kaines from his mind.

Rex Angell, dressed for a public appearance in black toupee and electric-blue suit, was perched neatly in one of the deep armchairs in the foyer, wistfully following the progress of a tough-looking blonde as she walked with a provocative sway of the hips across the plastic lawn of the pool area towards her room.

'That's a hooker,' he said by way of greeting as William approached.

'Really? Are you sure?'

'Bet your ass I'm sure. She smiled at me.'

'Well, maybe she liked you,' William said.

Rex Angell patted him gently on the arm. 'Kid, no woman that age smiles at a guy my age because she likes him. The only thing a woman that age likes about a man my age is his wallet.'

'Is that such a bad thing?'

'Ah, who needs hookers? Listen, kid, in my time I laid practically every broad on the M.G.M. lot and I'd have done the same at Warners only my contract expired. I never paid for it in my life and I ain't about to start now.'

At the door of her room the blonde turned, flourished a coquettish smile and then, receiving by way of response merely a bleak stare, put the smile back under wraps for a more deserving cause.

'See?' said Rex Angell, sadly. 'A hooker.'

'Yes,' said William. 'I expect you're right. Only I didn't realize they let hookers into places like this.'

'In this town they let hookers in everywhere. Why not? The place is full of goddamn whores anyway. The producers are whores, the agents are whores, the stars are whores, the . . .'

'Yes,' said William, hastily cutting short this litany. 'Quite. Rex, what can I do for you? It's lovely to see you, of course, but . . .'

'Ah, yeah.' Suddenly Rex Angell looked embarrassed. 'See, what it was, kid, I wondered if, like, you wanna have dinner with me tonight. There's a new place on Rodeo Drive they tell me is good. Well, I say good. Who knows what's good in this town? What they mean, it's less of a rip-off than some of the other joints and . . . Well, you wanna give it a whirl?'

William looked at his watch. To his surprise it was still not quite eight o'clock. 'Yes,' he said, realizing that he was rather hungry. 'I'd love to, only I thought you had dinner guests at home tonight. You told us . . .'

'Forget that. I just wanted to get that schmuck you

work for outa my apartment. Who would I have coming to dinner, for Chrissakes? At my age everybody I know is dead, even the living ones. C'mon.' He led the way outside to where a Mexican chauffeur waited in an old Rolls-Royce.

'This is really very nice of you, Rex,' William said as the car moved out into the traffic of Sunset Boulevard.

'Yeah, well, I was just passing by and thought, hey, that's where the kid's staying. So I called in. It's no big deal.'

Just passing, William thought. From Century City to Rodeo Drive via Sunset Strip was quite a detour. The old man had been lonely and the only person in the whole of Hollywood, apparently, whom he could find as a dinner companion was him, William, who was almost a complete stranger and young enough to be Rex Angell's great-grandson. He felt very sorry for the little, randy old figure whose legs, as he sat back in the comfortably padded rear seat, didn't even reach the floor.

'You like working for that asshole?' Angell asked.

'Mark? No, not much. He's a bit pompous . . .'

'He's an asshole,' Angell said firmly, brooking no argument. 'That's what he is and you can tell him that from me.'

William contemplated the prospect . . . 'Oh, by the way, Mark. Rex Angell wishes to be remembered to you and says you're an asshole.' Or would it be better translated from American English into English English? '. . . and says you're an arsehole.' Either way it was probably true but neither way would Mark react to the information with anything resembling pleasure. Better all round, William thought, if he were kept in happy ignorance of the facts. . . .

The new place on Rodeo Drive turned out to be a species of steak house, not noticeably different, as far as William could tell after a cursory inspection, from any other expensive steak house on this expensive street.

But it was undeniably popular: customers waiting for a table stood five deep at the bar and others, with even longer to wait, stood outside on the sidewalk, chatting animatedly together and trying to pretend they were there from choice and not, as was the case, because they simply couldn't get in.

'What's so special about this place?' William asked.

'It's new. What more do you want? Next week it won't be new and everybody'll go someplace else.'

'Is the food good?'

'I don't know. What the hell's that got to do with anything?' The old man barged his way through the resentful crowd on the sidewalk and into the lobby-cum-bar. The *maître d'hotel* approached him swiftly with the grimly contented look of a *maître d'* who knew he was running the hottest spot in town and was about to have the pleasure of ejecting some aged peasant who didn't know his place and was in need of a sharp lesson.

Rex Angell, however, knew his way around *maître d's*. 'Rex Angell,' he said, 'I booked.'

'Ah.' Swiftly the *maître d'* consulted the list in his hand. 'Oh sure, Mr Angell. Only you booked for eight and it's 8.20 already and like you can see we're real busy and . . .'

Rex Angell slapped a twenty-dollar bill into the man's hand. 'Rex Angell,' he said firmly. 'I booked.'

'So you did, Mr Angell,' said the *maître d'*. 'This way, gennulmen.'

The traditional formalities attended to, he led them into the restaurant. There was another bar here and a tiny dance floor and an even tinier bandstand where four scowling musicians, armed mainly with electric guitars, were smoking morosely. The rest of the space was taken up by tables with red-and-white checked cloths and snug little booths tucked against the wall. The lights were low and palely pink and the place was full. The popular dish of the evening, it seemed to William as he glanced at the tables, was steak with lobster tails, a bizarre combination that he thought could only appeal to a nation whose palate had been irreparably damaged by a lifetime's consumption of junk foods.

He and Rex Angell were making their way across the temporarily deserted dance floor towards their table when a female voice cried, 'Rexie, baby!' and a woman of about fifty with a hairstyle designed for a girl of about twenty and a dress created for a woman of about thirty pounced upon them and hugged Rex Angell to her bosom. It was an ample bosom for she was an ample lady. In her time she must have been a beauty, William thought, and even in his dispassionate view she was still handsome.

Recovering rapidly from his natural shock at being thus encompassed, Rex Angell, his face jammed between two magnificent breasts, administered an enthusiastic love-bite to the left one and only then, as the woman yelped girlishly and relaxed her grip, glanced up to identify his assailant.

'Clara!' he yelled and bit her right breast, too.

'Rex,' said Clara, still giggling. 'You li'l devil! You don't change none.'

'Neither do you, Clara, you just get bigger and better.' And as she hugged him again he dug his fingers enthusiastically into her formidable buttocks.

'My God, Rex,' she said, 'you damn near bit my titties off!'

Tactfully William moved on in the wake of the *maître d'* and waited at the table until the two ill-matched wrestlers on the dance floor had mutually agreed to call the contest a draw and Rex Angell collapsed ecstatically into the chair opposite him.

'Ya see that?' he said. 'Did ya see that? She damn near screwed me right there on the dance floor! I tell ya, kid, if I could only get my goddamn peter to work I could still have every woman in this friggin' town! Hot shit! I damn near as hell got a hard on there!'

'Congratulations,' William said. 'Who is she?'

'Who is she? You mean you didn't recognize her? That's Clara Lafayette. She used to be big in this town.' He fanned himself with his red-and-white checked napkin and readjusted the toupee that had slipped a little over one ear during the recent encounter. 'First time I had her was, oh, thirty years ago. We were making a movie called . . . ah, shee-it, who knows what it was called? Anyways, she was new in town and we made some sweet music together, believe you me. Jeeze, I remember it well! Who was I married to then? Musta been my third wife, or maybe my fourth. One of those anyway. But Clara and I, oh boy, did we have some times!'

'Well,' said William, 'she certainly seemed glad to see you again. Maybe you should give her a call. You know, take her out or something.'

Rex Angell's look of ecstasy vanished. 'No good, kid. She's married. Got her husband with her right now. Must be her third husband, I guess. I asked her for a date but she says she don't play around no more, on account of her old man owns the rest of Rodeo Drive that ain't owned by Greta Garbo and the Arabs. Can't blame her, I guess. Lady gets to her age, she can't take too many chances.'

He fell silent, smiling reminiscently, as another reel of the longest-playing hard-core porno movie in the entire history of the world rolled through his mind.

What remained of the English Puritan in William felt it ought to be shocked by the behaviour of this sexually obsessed old man but another, gentler and more liberal part of him felt pity and wondered what it could do to help. What the hell, said the gentler, liberal William, what the old boy wanted was love. He disguised the need with dirty talk but that was really what he wanted. It was a shame that he should be deprived of this most basic of

81

human comforts simply because he was old and his peter wouldn't work any more.

And while each of them was musing on their different, though parallel, lines another female voice said, 'Excuse me. I'm sorry to interrupt but it is Rex Angell, isn't it?' This was a very different female voice, a softer, huskier female voice with the lilt of the Orient in it and glancing in the direction whence it came William recognized Tina Ling.

He would have known her anywhere, even though she wasn't green any more. In fact, she looked even better not green. Her skin was a sort of warm olive colour and her eyes and her hair were deeply black. She was taller than William had expected, with a trim figure and surprisingly long legs that were thrust into a pair of tight, white Fiorucci jeans. He fell in love with her immediately, even though she wasn't looking at him but was, in fact, staring with obvious hero-worship at Rex Angell.

'That's right,' said Rex Angell. 'Who are you, honey?'

Before she could answer, William burst in hoarsely. 'Don't you know?' he said. 'This is Tina Ling.'

For the first time the girl glanced at him and – surely it wasn't wishful thinking; no, dammit, it certainly wasn't wishful thinking – there was an appreciative look in the wide, dark, almond eyes. 'You know me, huh?' she said. 'Seen me on television pro'lly.'

At the delicious sound of that well-remembered, and already well-loved 'pro'lly', William's heart turned over. No, in fact it did nothing so prosaic as simply turn over; it leapt into the air with a joyous yelp and executed a lightning series of perfect back-flips.

'Sure I know you,' Rex Angell said. 'Sure. T.V. newscaster, right? Siddown, honey.'

So she sat down and William poured her a glass of wine and she apologized once more for interrupting Rex Angell's dinner but, she said, she had recognized him at once and simply had to come over and introduce herself because he was her all-time favourite film star and she'd seen all his pictures and, God, why weren't there movie stars like him any more? And Rex Angell said why didn't she join them for dinner and she said she'd love to only – and she waved towards a dim corner of the room – she was with a whole bunch of people from the T.V. network and she couldn't walk out on them. And from the dim corner a whole bunch of sharp-looking T.V.-network-looking people bowed and nodded affably in their direction and Tina Ling said, oh gosh, she knew it sounded kinda screwy but would Mr Angell please sign his name on this napkin and she snatched William's napkin away and gave it to Rex Angell who wrote upon it: 'To Tina – if only I was twenty years younger, oh boy! . . . Love, Rex Angell'. And while this was going on and Tina Ling was uttering little contented sighs over the autographed napkin, William kept clearing his throat in such a meaningful way that at last, emerging from the warm cocoon of adulation in which the beautiful girl had wrapped him, Angell effected the desired and necessary introduction.

And Tina Ling turned her big, almond-eyed, appreciative gaze on William once more and said, 'Gosh, you're pretty.'

William's heart then followed up its back-flips with an even more spectacular series of intricate double somersaults, while Rex Angell explained that, by coincidence, his young friend was also in television and told Miss Ling exactly what his young friend was doing in California and Miss Ling smiled meltingly at William and said, gee, wasn't it a small world and then said, 'I love your hair. Is it real? I mean, is it really blond? Is it really curly?'

And William said, certainly, it was both of those things and she could examine it more closely if she didn't believe him and she leant forward and ran her small, slim fingers over his head to such effect that he thought he would die.

And then she said, 'Well, I'm really pleased to meet

you, William,' and held his proffered hand just a beat or two longer than was strictly necessary before standing up and announcing, with what seemed to him genuine reluctance, that she must get back to the rest of her party. But, gee, she said, it had been such a thrill to meet Mr Angell and she really hoped they might meet again and . . .

'Say, listen,' said Rex Angell, 'whaddya doing Sunday, honey? I mean, why not come over to my place for brunch? Like midday, know what I mean?'

She hesitated, just for a moment. Then . . . 'Will he be there?' she asked, nodding and smiling towards William.

'Sure he will,' said Rex Angell. 'Won't you, kid?'

'Sure I will,' said William fervently and so it was agreed and Tina Ling made a note of the address on the autographed napkin and tucked it carefully into the back pocket of her jeans and as she did so the jeans bulged out roundly and enticingly towards William who moaned softly at the sight. Then she kissed Rex Angell lightly on both cheeks, ran her hand once more over William's blond curls, murmuring, 'Gee, I love it,' and said goodnight and 'See you Sunday' and left.

'Wow!' said William.

'Shit!' said Rex Angell. There was a contemplative silence for a while as the waiter brought their main courses – peppered steak for William; steak and lobster tails for the determinedly American Angell. Then William spoke . . .

'I've got to hand it to you, Rex' he said. 'You're the best bird-puller I've ever met and I don't care how old you are. I mean, to attract a girl like that . . .'

'Kid,' said Rex Angell, shaking his head slowly. 'Kid. Let's not fool ourselves. She didn't come over here to meet me; she came over here to meet you. Jeeze, you're the one with the golden curls, goddamn you. I hate your lousy golden curls. It's like sitting here with friggin' Shirley Temple.'

'She thinks I'm pretty,' William murmured. 'She said so. She said I'm pretty.'

'Pretty!' Angell snorted with macho disgust. 'When I was your age any broad said I was pretty I'd have belted her in the mouth. Jeeze, what's the world coming to when guys wanna be pretty? You sure you're not gay?'

'I'm sure,' William said. 'I'm really, really sure. And even if there'd been the slightest shadow of doubt before tonight it would all have gone now. I'm in love, Rex. I'm truly in love.'

'Up yours,' Rex said sourly. 'Goddammit, you're all fixed up for Sunday and I'm the friggin' pimp. I've never played the pimp in my life before . . .' He swallowed his last lump of lobster tail, sighed deeply and leaned across to pat William on the cheek. 'What the hell. I wish you well to wear her, kid.'

Around half-past ten Rex Angell and his Mexican chauffeur dropped William off at the King and Queen. Angell said he wouldn't come in for a nightcap because at his age he needed all the beauty sleep he could get. His intention, he said, was to go home and lull himself to sleep by counting all the times he'd humped Clara Lafayette. 'Keep in touch, kid,' he said. 'And if I don't see ya before, I'll see ya Sunday.'

William was quite glad to be alone. He wanted to sit at the bar with a Jack Daniels on the rocks and think erotic thoughts of Tina Ling. 'Pro'lly,' he kept saying to himself, exulting in the magic of the sound. 'Pro'lly.'

He was already at the bar with the first deep mouthful of bourbon trickling down his gullet before, his eyes having grown accustomed to the sepulchral gloom, he looked around and recognized on the stool beside him the burglar of the night before.

'Good Lord,' he said. 'Well, well, it's you.'

'Parme?' said the burglar.

'It's you,' William said. 'The Burglar.'

'Watch your mouth, man,' said the burglar, menacingly.

'Oh yes, of course. Sorry. Didn't mean to speak quite so loudly. Keep my voice down from now on. It was just that I was rather surprised to see you again . . . '

'What you mean – agin? I ain't never seen you afore in my life, man,' said the burglar. He had half turned towards William and was looming over him like the shadow of death. He had the build of Muhammed Ali in his prime and the face of Joe Frazier after it.

'Rubbish,' said William gaily – in the strict, rather than the modern, meaning of the word. The gaiety was due entirely to the warm memory he still held of Tina Ling's smile and gentle curves. 'Of course you've seen me before. You saw me last night. You broke into my room and I lent you ten dollars.'

'What is this, man? You tryin' to hustle ten bucks off'n me?' said the burglar. It dawned upon William that the barman had vanished into some barman's hell-hole in the depths of the pub and that he and this enormous burglar were the only two people in the place. As a bar it didn't seem too well frequented on non-gay nights. Prudence appeared to be the order of the day.

'A hustle? No, no,' he said. 'Forget the ten dollars. I was glad to help you out.'

The burglar got up, went to the door, opened it a fraction and peered out into the night. Then he returned to the bar and hauled himself back onto his stool. 'You brought the fuzz with you, man?' he asked.

'Fuzz? Good heavens, no,' said William hastily. 'Certainly not. Look, I'm sorry if I made a mistake . . . '

'You didn't make no mistake, man,' the burglar said. 'I knows you and you knows me. You wuz good to me last night, man. I figure I owe you a drink.'

'Well, ten dollars actually,' William said in the interests of strict accuracy. The burglar frowned.

'I owes you a drink,' he said in a tone that brooked no argument and William decided to offer him none.

'Right,' he said, 'right.'

The barman returned from his lair and the burglar summoned large bourbons on the rocks. 'You he'ped me out las' night,' he said. 'Here's lookin' at you, kid.'

'It was a pleasure,' William said. 'A real pleasure.' The bourbon he had drunk while transcribing the Ida Kaines interview had got together with the wine at dinner and the bourbon now to promote in him a mood of jovial bonhomie. 'Any time.'

'Well, I appreciate that, man.'

'Think nothing of it,' William said. 'I regarded it as a privilege. You are quite the nicest burglar I have ever met.' He said this carefully, on account of the alcohol, and sincerely, on account of the fact that the burglar now in his midst was the only burglar he had ever met.

'I ain't no burglar, man,' said the burglar, affronted. 'Hell, how'd ya get that idea, man? I ain't no burglar. I'm a pimp.' The latter statement was delivered with a certain degree of modest pride.

'A pimp?' William said. 'Golly.' He turned the thought over in his mind: was a pimp more or less impressive than a burglar, especially if one had never knowingly met a member of either profession before? He decided there wasn't much in it either way.

And then he thought, 'A pimp? A *pimp*?' And incredulity, an emotion which, generally speaking, he felt but rarely, visited him for the second time that day. First an accessory after the fact of murder and now a pimp. What kind of company was he getting into here?

'Do you mean you live on immoral earnings?' he said and, though he tried to sound casual and worldly, he was unable to keep a note of disapproval from his voice.

The pimp sneered at him. 'Immoral earnings? What kinda shit's that you talkin' man? I'm in the service industry, man. I'm a businessman.'

Well, thought William, perhaps he was. It wasn't necessarily a business that he, William, approved of, but who was he to judge?

He said, 'Then what were you, a pimp, doing in my room last night pretending to be a burglar?'

By way of reply the pimp or burglar pulled William towards him by the lapels of his jacket and, with their faces only inches apart, sought further reassurance that the fuzz were not even remotely among those present in the immediate vicinity. William announced, breathlessly, that if he were only free to do so he would cross his heart and hope to die and, apparently convinced, the burglar or pimp slowly released him.

'Well, I'll tell you, man,' he said. 'I was in big trouble last night. Real big trouble . . . Buy me another bourbon and I'll tell you about it, man.'

William did as he was bade and the pimp/burglar told his tale. His name, it transpired, was Stack – though whether he had been so christened or whether he had merely assumed the name for reasons of professional anonymity was not explained – and generally speaking he was regarded hereabouts as a quite respected pimp in a fair way of business. Of late, however, fate had conspired against him and by the previous night his fortunes had sunk to a low ebb. At that time, so far as William could gather, two of the five hard-working girls on his books were helping the police with their enquiries and two others were sick.

'Oh dear,' William said. ''Flu, was it? Something going around?'

'What they got, man,' Stack said, 'goes around all the time. The sickness they got was an occupational hazard, man. They clear now, man. They got cleared this morning but last night they wuz still laid up . . . '

And last night, it seemed, with four of his team of five having been *hors de combat* for several days and the fifth being, at the best of times, a slow-moving veteran at the game, Stack had found himself down to his last few hundred dollars.

In an attempt to double, triple or even quadruple his modest roll he had been unwise enough to allow himself to be inveigled into an illicit poker game on Sunset Strip where he had been coolly fleeced by experts and found himself, late at night, without even a cab fare home. At that point he had gone looking for his fifth hooker to relieve her of her night's takings but she had been nowhere to be found and the unworthy thought had occurred to Stack that she had been skimming on him – that she had taken the money she had made, *his* money, after all, and had run out on him. Brooding resentfully over such disloyalty he had remembered that before she had come under his protection she had operated as a freelance out of William's motel – out of, indeed, the very room that William was now occupying. Perhaps, he thought, she had gone back there to resume freelance operations and so it was that he had made his way into the room through the window with honest intent, if he found her at work, to beat her senseless and relieve her of all her money as a kind of disciplinary measure.

William accepted this story. It didn't quite explain why Stack had been making his way across the floor to the wardrobe and the wallet in such a purposeful manner but perhaps he had simply wanted to get his hands on whatever money happened to be lying about – whether it were the girl's or the john's – before beginning his chastisement. In any event it seemed more tactful not to mention the matter. Instead he ordered another round of drinks and reflected on the curious frequency with which pimping and pandering seemed to be cropping up in his life.

The long arm of coincidence – and yet, perhaps not. Hollywood society was founded on money and sex and where there was money and sex there were sure to be pimps and panders. The chances were, he thought, that anyone who ever went to Hollywood for any length of time was bound to meet a pimp, either amateur or professional, sooner or later and he just happened to have met one sooner.

'But if you thought she was, er, skimming,' he said, 'why did you assume she would go back to her old place? Dangerous thing for her to do, surely?'

'Whores is creatures of habit,' said Stack with the wisdom of one who knew. 'Also they stupid, man.'

'And was she skimming?'

'Nah. She called me this morning. She been at a party with a couple of johns down on Wilshire. She done real good, man. I was proud of her.'

'All's well that ends well then,' William said and Stack said, 'Yeah,' and finished his drink and looked at his watch and said, well, he couldn't sit around here chewing the fat all night, 'cause he had to get on his rounds and see to his business.

'Good luck,' William said and then, to his surprise, Stack said, 'You wanna come with me, man?'

'What? Good Lord, no. I mean, well, thank you awfully but . . . '

'Why not, man? You ever seen a pimp at work?'

'Well, no, but . . . '

'So come on.'

William said, 'No, hold on. I really don't . . . I don't . . . '

Stack nodded grimly. 'You don't wanna be seen with no nigger, right? You jes' like all the other white mother-fuckers, man.'

'I'm not!' William said indignantly. 'I'm not like the other white mother-fuckers at all. I simply . . . ' He sought desperately for a plausible excuse for declining the invitation. 'Won't it be dangerous? I mean, what if the police stop us?'

'The heat? Hey, man, you don't have to worry about the heat. They won't stop us – not if you with me. Even if

90

they pass by while we talkin' to one of the girls they jes' gonna think we a coupla johns. I need you, man – you my protective coloration. Like I told you, I can't afford to get busted right now.

'Well, thank you very much.' William said, indignantly.

Stack put a huge, heavy arm around his shoulders. 'Sides,' he said, 'I wouldn't want to go away from here thinkin' you jes' another nigger-hater. A racialist, you know what I mean? Jes' another asshole who don't wanna have nothin' to do with his black brothers, who don't wanna even find out how a black brother earns his livin'. You come with me, man, it'll be an education for you.'

And William, frankly intimidated by the heavy arm but also intrigued at the prospect of watching a pimp at work – a prospect, after all, that was unlikely to occur too often in his life – succumbed. At the very least, he told himself, it would provide an anecdote with which to regale the rest of the team. 'All right,' he said, 'but any sign of the cops and I'm off.'

Stack's car was a rather nondescript dark-blue Chevrolet for which he apologized profusely. While he was about it he also apologized for his sober appearance. He was wearing black cords, a black bomber jacket and a white, polo-necked sweater. These, he explained, were his professional clothes and this was his professional car. Back home, he went on, waving vaguely in the direction of the Hollywood Hills, he had this real cute Lincoln Continental, and fur coats and diamonds and 'gator-skin boots but if he drove around in that car and those clothes while attending to his business the heat would be down on him, sure as shit, and while they would have nothing on him they could still hold him for questioning and while that was going on who could tell how much his whores would be skimming from him?

'You can't trust nobody these days, man,' he said sadly. 'Least of all whores. They'd rob you blind.'

He gave William instructions to keep his eyes peeled for the heat, the Metro Division of the Los Angeles Police Department, who at this time of night would also be on the prowl, looking for whores. 'They bad news, man,' said Stack. 'They bust one of my girls, she gets like forty-five days in the slammer. For her maybe that's okay. She got the sickness, they cure it and she come out all rested and lookin' good. Meanwhile, I'm losin' money, man. See, if each of my girls does ten tricks a night that's 400 dollars an' if I lose forty-five times 400 dollars I feels the hurt, man. I gotta lotta overheads.'

He was, he said – driving slowly and keeping a careful eye out for the heat – fairly new to the pimping game but he had drive and ambition. Three months ago he had had only two girls working for him; six months hence he expected to have ten and after that, who knew?

They cut across from Sunset to Hollywood Boulevard and drove up towards Highland. It was around midnight and the traffic had eased a little. There were very few pedestrians about.

'These overheads of yours,' William said. 'What are they exactly?'

'Well, hey, man, these whores gotta eat, right? They gotta sleep, they gotta have a little drink, get high from time to time. It all comes outa my pocket, man. I don't,' said Stack, with the modesty of a true philanthropist, 'keep all that bread to myself, man.'

William commended him for his generosity but was about to suggest, nevertheless, that the money was actually earned by the girls and surely they would be better off without a pimp, when Stack said, 'Hey, there's one o' my ladies now.'

Up ahead a trimly built black girl was making leisurely progress in the general direction of Mann's Chinese

Theatre, staying close to the kerb, her very walk advertising her profession. As William watched, a car cruised up alongside her and the driver leant over to talk to her. The girl smiled and stopped and the car stopped, too. The driver leant over again and opened the passenger door. The black hooker moved closer and said something to the potential john and a brief discussion ensued.

'That's my girl,' said Stack, approvingly. 'She talkin' turkey now. Here come another forty bucks for ol' Stack.'

But suddenly there was a change of mood in the brief encounter ahead of them. The black girl stopped smiling and started to scowl; the driver, still holding the passenger door open, spoke to her again, whereupon the hooker took one pace backwards, emitted an irate scream so loud that householders as far away as Beverley Hills probably peered anxiously out of their windows to see who was being murdered beside their swimming pools or on their tennis courts, and administered a vicious kick to the car door. Then she kicked it again and for good measure snapped off the wing-mirror.

William watched all this with awe, wondering what obscene suggestion anybody could possibly make to a hooker to upset her so much. 'Oh, oh,' said Stack. 'Here come trouble.'

The car owner, now no less irate than the whore on account of the assault and battery to which his vehicle had been subjected, had leaped out and was approaching the girl with clear intent to exact retribution. 'C'mon, man,' said Stack and got out of his car, followed slowly and with reluctance by William.

The potential john, a stout, white, middle-aged man, who looked as though he was normally a pillar of his community and the kind who wrote indignant letters to the press complaining that the mere presence of prostitutes on the streets was a public nuisance and an insult to American womanhood, had grabbed the girl by the scruff of the neck and was insisting that she (a) examine

93

and (b) make restitution for the severe damage to his car. As far as William could decipher the almost incoherent babble of rage that poured from the man's lips, the problem uppermost in his mind was what on earth he was going to say, by way of explanation, to his wife.

Approaching, swiftly and unheard, from the rear Stack eased the startled man and the relieved girl apart. 'You got trouble, my man?' he asked courteously.

'I'll say I've got trouble,' said the man. 'Look what this bitch has done to my car! My wife's car, dammit.' He wrenched himself free of Stack's gently restraining grip and swung a wild punch at the girl's face. 'I'll kill the bitch.'

'No, you won't, man,' said Stack and, almost dreamily, hit him in the stomach. The man said, 'Hurrff!' and fell back against the car. Stack caught him neatly before he could drop from there to the pavement, opened the passenger door and bundled him, quite gently, inside.

'There you are, my man,' said Stack. 'Now you jes' sit there for a while and when you feelin' better you go home an' have a good night's sleep. Come the mornin' you'll be laffin' about this.'

The retired potential john stared at him with bulging eyes from which all mirth had fled, possibly never to return. 'Hurrff!' he said again, though whether or not by way of thanks for Stack's solicitude William found it hard to tell.

'Lulu-Belle,' said Stack to the hooker, 'let's you an' me go have a little talk.' He led her back to the Chevrolet and sat her in the back seat.

'Gee, thanks, Stack,' said the girl. 'You hadn't come along, he'da kill me for sure.' Then she noticed William and scowled suspiciously. 'Hey, Stack, who the honky?'

'This heah honky,' said Stack, 'is my friend. Don't you worry none about this honky, Lulu-Belle. This a good honky. They ain't many of 'em around but he one of 'em. Now then, girl, what the hell wuz all that about? What the john say to you?'

'That asshole,' said the girl, forgetting William in a renewed rush of anger against the john, 'he say to me, hey, li'l girl, how much? An' I tell him forty dollar an' he laff an' he say, forty dollars! Why, I wouldn't pay you forty dollars for a gang-bang at an Elk's Convention. He say, I'll give you ten and you give me any argyments and I cut the price to nine. Well, hell, Stack, a girl cain't take that kind o' shit from a john; a girl's got her pride.'

So that was it, William thought: that was the sort of obscene suggestion that would enrage a whore. Though he would not, personally, have paid her – or any other hooker – forty dollars for her professional services, he rather sympathized with the girl. After all, to indicate that she was worth barely a quarter of her asking price was highly insulting.

'You done right, Lulu-Belle,' said Stack, soothingly. He leant over and kissed her absentmindedly on her forehead. 'How many tricks you turned tonight, honey?'

The girl looked anxious. 'Why, only three so far, Stack.'

'Three!' said Stack with the righteous indignation of a works' manager who had glanced into the machine-room only to find the labour force taking an unscheduled coffee break. 'What the hell you been doin' girl?' He grabbed her chin in his hand and yanked her face towards him. 'You been skimmin' me, Lulu-Belle?'

'No, Stack, honest,' she muttered through compressed and screwed-up lips. 'Trade kinda slow tonight, is all. I'll do better for you, Stack, I promise.'

'That's good, honey, 'cause if I catch you skimmin' you know what I gonna do?'

'Yes, Stack.'

'Okay, then get out there and start hustlin' your little black ass.' He opened the rear door and heaved the girl out. 'I be round for the bread in the mornin', same as usual.'

95

'Sure, Stack. Have a nice day.'

'Have a nice friggin' day,' said Stack derisively as he drove off again. 'That's all anybody says in this suckin' town. How's a guy supposed to have a nice day when he works as hard as I do? You tell me that, man.'

William murmured sympathetically. The recent encounter had impressed upon him that, unless one had a vocation for it, a pimp's work could indeed be somewhat arduous and even dangerous. Suppose the john had pulled a gun, for instance? Even so, the pickings seemed to be high. Five girls turning ten 40-dollar tricks a night each came to 2,000 dollars a night and after making due allowance for Stack's overheads the profit margin from his commission was surely considerable.

'What do you do, Stack,' he asked, 'if you catch one of them skimming?'

'Why, I bust her in the face, man,' Stack replied, genially. 'It gotta be in the face so's all the other whores can see the damage an' take note. Never fails, man. You give one whore a coupla black eyes an' a fat lip an' all the other girls goes skeeterin' out like scared rabbits and hustle like there's no tomorrow.'

'And they don't mind?' William asked. 'I mean, they don't bear a grudge? They don't leave you?'

Stack chuckled at such naïvety. 'Course not, man. Why they wanna leave me? They love me, man. I'm their daddy. They come home with a great big wad of dollars and there's ol' Stack to love 'em and pet 'em and get 'em a little high and tell 'em what good little girls they are. An' that's what they are, man – jes' little girls at heart. That's the whole psychology of pimping, man, to reckernize that whiles they looks like women they jes' little girls who wants their daddy to love 'em and give 'em candy.'

He stopped the car outside a coffee-shop near the intersection of Hollywood and Vine. Once this had been one of the most glamorous spots in all Hollywood; in the old hotels around here the budding stars of the future had been wont to put up when they first arrived in tinsel town. But over the years the district had come down in the world. There was a seedy, shifty look about it and the people who hung around the corner were freaks and mobile disaster areas – junkies and pushers, pimps and prostitutes of every imaginable age and sex.

Stack led the way into the coffee-shop. Inside it was shabby but surprisingly clean. At one of the tables against the wall sat two girls, one black, the other white. Both were pretty, the white one particularly so. She was slim and blonde and though her dress proclaimed her a hooker, her face was gentle and there was a pleasing glint of humour around her eyes and mouth.

Stack, with William beside him, sat at the table next to the girls, ordered coffee from the thin, depressed waitress, and looking straight ahead and barely moving his lips addressed his two neighbours.

'You celebratin' somethin', Mary-Jane? Like your birthday, maybe?'

'No, Stack,' said the black hooker, also staring straight ahead and barely moving her lips. 'Ain't my birthday.'

'Then maybe it's Jenny's birthday, huh?'

'No, ain't Jenny's birthday neither, Stack.'

'Your poppa die an' leave you a fortune?'

'No, Stack, my poppa ain't dead.'

'Well, well,' said Stack, apparently puzzled. 'It ain't nobody's birthday and it ain't Christmas and it ain't the Fourth of July and it ain't Thanksgiving and it sure as hell ain't Mardi Gras, so what you two girls doin' sittin' here takin' a vacation on my time?'

'The heat's on, Stack,' said Mary-Jane, the black girl, anxiously. 'They's fuzz all over the streets, man. I don't wanna get busted again.'

Stack was not to be placated by such an argument, reasonable though it seemed to William. 'Okay, so gettin' off the streets maybe ain't so stupid but what you doin' around heah in a dive like this? You ain't gonna turn no forty-dollar tricks up here, baby. This strictly two-dollar whore country.'

Mary-Jane looked even more anxious. 'We jes' happen to be passin', Stack . . .'

'Don't you feed me no horseshit, baby,' Stack said, as sternly as any man could whose lips were hardly moving. 'I know why you up here. You up here because your boyfriend is the short-order cook and don't you give me no jive. Now you git out there and hustle – both of you.'

The two girls rose hastily, Mary-Jane looking frightened, Jenny, the white girl, smiling in a faintly amused manner.

'One more thing, Mary-Jane,' Stack said softly, and this time he looked directly at the girl. 'I find you been skimmin' from me and givin' to this boyfriend of yours I'm gonna bust your face up and cut his heart out, you hear me?'

'I hear you, Stack,' said the girl. 'I sure as hell hear you. Have a nice day, Stack.' She scuttled out after her friend.

Stack sighed and yawned. 'You see the trouble I have with these wimmin? Man, sometimes I ask myself whether it's all worth it. You look away for one minute, they cheat you blind, man. Shee-it.' He allowed William to pay for the coffee and offered him a lift home.

And on the way . . . 'You ain't the worst honky I ever met, man,' he said. 'An' I owe you for the other night.'

'No, no,' said William. 'Please, think nothing of it.'

Stack frowned thoughtfully, his pimp's pride doubtless hurt by the fact that he was in somebody's debt, and was silent until they pulled up outside William's motel. Then he said, 'You like those girls, man? My girls?'

'Well, yes,' William said. 'Of course, I didn't have a lot to say to them but they certainly looked most awfully nice girls.'

'They is nice girls, man. Clean, too. So what I'm

gonna do, man, I'm gonna make you an offer you can't refuse – any one of 'em, the whole night, fifty bucks, okay?'

William said, 'Well, gosh, that's terribly nice of you, Stack, but you see . . .'

'You don't like hookers?'

'No, no, it's not that. Honest. Good heavens, I'm sure hookers are the salt of the earth – pimps, too, naturally. It's simply that . . .'

Stack gave him a hard stare. 'Don't you go turnin' me down now, man. Like I said, I owe you. You done me a favour an' I'm doin' you one. You throw my favours back in my teeth and you gonna hurt my feelings. You hear me, man? You wouldn't want to do that now, would you?'

'Good Lord, no. Certainly not. I just . . .'

'Okay. So you jes' think about it and let me know when you decide. An' I'll tell you, man, they all good at their job but that Jenny, the white girl – she really special. She could make a corpse turn tricks he didn't even know when he was alive. Anyways, you choose an' when you decide which one you want and when you want her, jes' let me know, okay? You know where to find me – right where you found me tonight, 'cept on gay nights. I hate gays. They ruin my business, man. Okay? See ya, man.' And he drove away, the traditional Californian benediction trailing behind him . . . 'Have a nice day.'

7

William was awakened the following morning by the sound of the Mexican gardener Hoovering the grass round the swimming pool. The many and varied events of the previous night buzzed around in his mind, leaving him with a sensation that was part anxiety and part exhilaration. The latter, of course, was due entirely to the meeting with Tina Ling and the prospect of seeing her again on Sunday; the former had much to do with the problem of Ida Kaines and also with the strongly-implied threat behind Stack's generous offer of a cut-rate hooker. He didn't want a cut-rate hooker; he didn't want any kind of hooker, but what he wanted even less was an insulted Stack coming around to cut his heart out.

He shaved and showered and, while he was dressing, tuned the television set to 'Good Morning, America' to catch up on the world's news. Satisfied that the haemorrhoid situation was much as it had been the previous night and that not a lot else seemed to have happened save that there was some unaccustomed activity on the acid-indigestion front, he went down to the coffee-shop for breakfast.

Mark was already there, clad for interviewing in the casual Yves St Laurent suit that had been whipped up for him by a back-street tailor in Kowloon while the back-street cobbler was making his Gucci shoes. He greeted William with what had already become his traditional glare of cold disdain. 'Where were you last night?' he asked.

'I went to see Ida Kaines. I told you. When I got back you and Geoff had shoved off. Where did you get to?'

'Restaurant up the road,' Mark said, snapping his fingers with irritable nervous energy. 'Frightful place. Purported to be French. French! My God, any self-respecting Frenchman who wandered into that place would have gone after the chef with a knife. You won't believe this but they served me broccoli with a sweet sauce. I ask you – a sweet white sauce. I've never tasted anything so disgusting.'

'Not much of a night then,' said William, ordering his customary eggs, bacon and hash browns.

'A dreadful night. Warbottle drank himself stupid again and offered the waitress twenty-five dollars to go to bed with me. In front of my face, mark you. Drunk as he was you'd think he'd have had enough sense to conduct such an enterprise behind my back.'

'Did she bite?'

'Don't be stupid. For twenty-five dollars? Would you?'

'Not for twenty-five million,' said William, 'I'm not that sort of boy.'

Mark gave him a look of sincere hatred. 'Don't get smart,' he said. 'Have you seen Warbottle this morning? No, of course you haven't. I expect he's up at the liquor store buying his breakfast. I really don't know what the company was thinking about to send me off with a Fred Karno outfit like this. The entire technical crew views me with unveiled hostility, the producer's pissed out of his mind all day long, his assistant turns out to be a raging dyke and the researcher . . . ' He stopped abruptly, as if suddenly remembering that the man sitting opposite him munching bacon and eggs was the researcher himself. 'Well, never mind,' he said.

William gulped down some coffee. 'Do you want to hear about Ida Kaines?' he asked.

Mark sighed. 'Might as well, I suppose. I only hope it's

101

good. Everything else so far has been rubbish. I really don't know which was worse – that dreadful, dirty old man yesterday afternoon or the barmy old woman in the morning. My God, William, where did you unearth these people? That woman yesterday morning could hardly remember Willard Kaines. We'd shot two rolls of film before we realized she wasn't talking about Willard Kaines at all: she was talking about John Gilbert. I ask you – bloody John Gilbert. Silly old cow.'

'Sorry about that,' William said. 'But I think I have something here that will really interest you. I suspect it's going to change the whole focus of what we're doing, but . . . Well, look, read it for yourself.'

He handed over the Ida Kaines typescript and concentrated on his breakfast while Mark read slowly and twice uttered some wordless exclamation of surprise. William smiled contentedly to himself, enjoying the warm self-satisfaction that is due to one who knows he has delivered the goods.

Finally Mark laid aside the last page and stared at William. 'Are you serious?' he said. 'I mean, this isn't some bizarre practical joke, is it?'

William had not expected anything like this; he had expected congratulations, a slap on the back, followed, perhaps, by some expression of the kind of concern he felt about the legal and moral aspects of the knowledge in their now joint possession. 'What?' he said.

Mark gave a deep, sincere sniff. 'I don't believe this,' he said, 'I suspect the woman's senile. Everybody else you've found for me has been senile and I have little doubt that she is, too.'

'Of course she's not senile,' William said.

'Then she's almost certainly conning you. Does she want money for this preposterous tale?'

'Well, yes she does, actually. She wants 5,000 dollars . . . '

'Aha!'

'No, it's not like that. She doesn't want it for herself. She wants it for this tribe in Brazil . . . '

'In Brazil? Oh, yes. Conveniently far away.'

'Listen, will you? She's going to live in Brazil. With this tribe. And she wants money to help them.'

'Help them do what? Start a nut farm? Really, William, have you any idea how much legal excrement would hit the fan if I interviewed this woman on these lines and the network put it out? Before the closing credits had stopped rolling we'd be up to our eyes in libel writs and by then our chief defence witness would be . . . Where the hell's she going?' He consulted the typescript. 'Borneo, is it?'

'Brazil,' William said, dully.

'Yes, Brazil. And while Willard Kaines is suing us for an arm and a leg and both knackers your precious Mrs Kaines is shacked up in the Brazilian jungle with some bloody head-hunter.'

William said, 'I don't think they have head-hunters in Brazil and anyway that's not the point. Look, I understand the legal problems and I know there are moral problems but this is a marvellous story and . . . '

'Oh, indeed,' Mark said. 'Absolutely marvellous. Meanwhile, what do we do about the programme we're here to make – Great Men of Our Time? Remember? That's the title we're working to – not The Californian Crippen.'

'Well . . . well, obviously we'd have to abandon the original idea. We couldn't possible carry on with that.'

Mark uttered another of his disdainful sniffs. 'The company and indeed the whole network would love that, wouldn't they? A bloody great hole in their schedules and 5,000 dollars' worth of dubious revelations locked up until God knows when. We couldn't put it out with any safety until old Kaines was dead.'

'But . . . ' William said and at this point Geoff War-bottle appeared, looking dreadful. Ever since his arrival in Hollywood his appearance had been deteriorating even as one watched and now, several bottles of wine and an immeasurable amount of bourbon having elapsed since William had seen him last, he had reached a new low. His clothes had certainly been slept in and in his efforts to shave – noble efforts, William had to concede, considering the man's disastrously hungover condition – he had cut himself several times and had staunched the wounds with strips of lavatory paper, which now fluttered gently like tiny, blood-stained flags from his cheeks and chin.

'Oh my God,' he said. 'Where's that girl with the coffee?'

'Never mind the coffee,' Mark said. 'Read this.' Warbottle winced at the sudden noise of the typescript being laid in front of him. 'Read?' he said, as if trying to divine the meaning of some word hitherto unknown to him. 'Read?'

'Read,' Mark said and resignedly Warbottle fished his glasses from his pocket and, while William summoned coffee for him, read through the interview, his lips moving rather more than Mark's had done.

'Well?' Mark said, when he had finished. 'I say the woman's either senile or lying.'

'Do you think she's either senile or lying, William?' Warbottle asked.

'No, I don't. I truly believe she's telling the truth.'

'Assuming you're right,' Warbottle said, 'we could be in a very difficult position.'

'I'm in a difficult position already,' said William. 'I mean, in a sense this is confidential information she's given me but even so if a crime has been committed . . .'

Warbottle nodded. 'Exactly. But it would be even more difficult if she were to say all this on camera. We'd have to tell the police.' He raised his shaking coffee cup to his lips and drank deeply.

'The police?' Mark said, sharply. 'Whatever for?'

'We're talking about murder,' William said. 'It would be our duty.'

'Bugger that,' said Mark. 'Oh yes, that's all we need, isn't it? To get mixed up with the L.A. police department. Charming, that would be. Can you imagine getting in touch with Nat-Met and saying, oh, sorry, we can't go on with this documentary. We're helping the local Filth with their murder enquiries?'

Warbottle nodded. 'That's more or less it. Assuming, of course, that Ida Kaines really is telling the truth. Does she want money for this tale, William?'

'Five thousand dollars,' William said.

'Aha!'

'No, no.' Mark's tone was deeply sarcastic. 'You misunderstand. She doesn't want the money for herself, good heavens, no. It's for a tribe of Brazilian pygmies.'

'They're not pygmies,' William cried.

'Even so,' Warbottle said, thoughtfully. 'It makes a difference, you know. The company doesn't approve of paying criminals for their true confessions and that's what it amounts to.'

'But he ought to be exposed somehow,' William said. 'The man's a killer. This woman is telling the truth – I *know* she's telling the truth . . . Look, why don't we call London and ask what they suggest?'

'Early evening there now,' Warbottle said. 'Anyone with any authority will have pissed off home.'

'So what are we going to do then?'

There was silence for some time while they all pondered the question and then Warbottle said, 'Well, we could make an arbitrary decision to pay her the money, knowing that we couldn't use the interview while Kaines was alive . . . '

Mark cut in sharply. 'No! I say we forget it, forget we ever knew about it. If we go off chasing this particular hare the company is sure to tell us to abandon the present programme and there's no time for us to find an alternative Great Man. Now that's all right for you lot because you're either on the staff or on monthly salaries but if I lose a programme it'll cost me a lot of money.'

For the third time in less than twenty-four hours William was incredulous. 'But you can't be that hard up, Mark!'

Mark glared at him sincerely. 'It's not a question of being hard up. My contract stipulates a certain fee for a fifty-minute documentary. What's this Ida Kaines interview going to amount to, even padded out with old film clips? Thirty minutes at best. So that means the company will have 5,000 dollars and I'll have my fee – and a smaller fee at that – tied up in a piece of film that nobody will be able to show for donkey's years.'

'Well, only until Kaines dies,' said Warbottle. 'It'll be perfectly safe to put it out then. The only one the law could get at would be Ida Kaines if we waited until the old boy was dead.'

'Ah, right. When he's dead. But who knows when he'll die? I could be dead before he is.'

'Even so,' William said, desperately, 'I still think we should go ahead. Look, putting it out when he's dead is a bit underhand, if you ask me, but if that's the only way the truth can be told, let's do it. It's better that the truth comes out sometime than never at all.'

'You,' said Mark, coldly, 'are gullibly assuming that this woman is telling the truth. Personally, I have very grave doubts. Furthermore if, as you suggest, Warbottle – though I can't say I agree with you – we have some obligation to tell the fuzz about it, I feel even more strongly that the whole thing is better ignored.'

Warbottle said, 'You have a point, Mark. We only have Ida Kaines's word and, short of a confession from the old man, which seems most unlikely, we're not going to find any corroboration. Tell me, William, how would Ida Kaines react if we told her we'd have to take the filmed interview to the police: would she agree to that?'

William shook his head. 'No, I'm pretty sure she wouldn't. She can't offer any proof and besides she wants to get away to Brazil.'

'Oh yes,' Mark said, 'the pygmy head-hunters. Well, that settles it. If she doesn't want to get mixed up with the cops, neither do I. And don't suggest phoning London again, William, because they'll simply toss the ball back at us and tell us to make up our own minds. And if we go ahead and it turns out later, as I predict, that she's senile we'll have to carry the can. The whole thing is far too hazardous and I think if you can shake last night's alcohol from your brain, Warbottle, you'll agree with me.'

Warbottle's already pale face turned a shade paler. 'What can I say?' he said.

Mark threw the Ida Kaines typescript across to William. 'Good,' he said, 'that's settled. Go and write me some more questions, William. And when you've done that go and tell this woman we're not interested in her muck-raking. Meanwhile, I shall compose another piece to camera. A summing-up of the man's career, I think. With the quality of interviewee that you appear to be arranging for me, William, I can see that this programme is going to be held together entirely by my commentary and pieces to camera. I may tell you that I have never, never had such appalling back-up from a production team.' And having worked himself up into a fairly impressive temper he swept away, oozing wrath and indignation.

William sighed and sat back in his chair, riffling sadly through the typescript. 'She's telling the truth, Geoff,' he said

Warbottle looked away, embarrassed. 'I believe you, William. But . . . I had to back Mark up. He was quite adamant – well, you could see that and . . . and he has the ear of all the right people at the company.'

'Yeah,' William said. 'Forget it.'

'Drop the subject, shall we?'

'If you like.' William folded the typescript and put it in his pocket.

'Haven't seen much of you lately,' Warbottle said, not merely dropping the subject but changing it for another one. 'Not since yesterday afternoon anyway. How . . . how are you getting on here?'

'I was offered a hooker last night,' William said. 'Cut-rate. Fifty dollars the whole night.'

'Really? Very old hooker, was she?'

'No. Well, there were three of them. All very young and very pretty. I was told I could take my pick.'

'And did you?'

'No.'

'Why? Didn't you fancy them?'

'Not a lot.'

Warbottle mused for a moment. 'I won't ask how this extremely generous offer came about but . . . '

'No. It's all right, I'll tell you. See, I met this burglar again . . . '

'What burglar?'

'The one who was in my room the night before last. Only it turns out he wasn't a burglar really. He was a pimp and . . . ' William paused. 'It's a very long story, Geoff. I don't think I'm up to it at the moment. Perhaps I'll tell you later.

'As you wish. Though I must say you seem to be leading a very active social life in this town. There's obviously a lot more to you than meets the eye, young William.'

'Well,' William said, modestly.

'Just one thing before we abandon the topic. If this offer is still open, keep it open. Worst comes to the worst, we might shove this girl off on Mark. We can always lose the fifty dollars in the production budget.'

William said, 'Look, Geoff, let's not go into that again. I've told you – I'm not doing that kind of thing for Mark. Ever.'

'We'll see, William,' Warbottle said. 'Take my advice, lad – always keep your options open. It's the only way to survive in this ridiculous business.' He heaved himself to his feet. The coffee had made a certain improvement in his condition and the redness was beginning to fade from his eyeballs. 'Ten-thirty rendezvous at Ida Kaines's place, is it? Good. Gives me time to have a shower and change my shirt.'

He headed back towards the shower and the shirt and the bourbon bottle in his room.

Alice Flitton went with William to see Ida Kaines. The alternative for her was to arrive later in the same car as Mark and Geoff Warbottle and she found the prospect displeasing. The strength of Warbottle's morning breath was such that after half an hour in a closed car with him anyone with such a low tolerance of alcohol as herself stood a very fair chance of ending the journey tipsy. And Mark's humiliation at having been measured against a producer's assistant – and a female assistant at that – by a mere waitress and been found wanting had caused him to develop such an intense dislike of Alice that he was unable even to look at her civilly.

Several times the previous day she had caught his baleful stare upon her and had fancied she could read in it a mixture of puritanical horror at her sexual predilections and animal jealousy that Larraine Laroux's sun-bronzed body should be wasted on her, Alice, when, if there were any justice in the world, it should have been offered adoringly to him.

Not that Alice Flitton was too worried. Generally speaking she had never in her life had such a nice time as she was having now; she had never enjoyed such a physically attractive bed partner as Larraine nor such a genuinely happy and cheerful one. It was true, of course, that when they were handing out the brains the poor girl had been so far back in the queue that she only just got in ahead of the beasts of the fields, but what did that matter? Intellectual stimulation was not what she and Alice sought from each other. And besides Larraine had a delightfully sunny nature.

'She's so . . . so optimistic,' she said to William.

William nodded. 'I think it's a Californian characteristic. It doesn't seem to matter how often fate crept up and goosed them yesterday, they always believe today is going to be better.' This had been impressed upon him by a brief conversation he had had with an underground car-park attendant a couple of days after his arrival in Hollywood. She was a stout, black middle-aged woman who apparently spent her entire working life cut off from daylight in an atmosphere of petrol fumes. It seemed to William that her lot was not a great deal better than that of a laboratory rat being used in an experiment to discover the effects of air pollution.

'Have a nice weekend,' he had said to her, falling easily into the Californian conversational style, when he drove his car out of the parking lot.

She had given him a big, confident smile. 'I'm goin' to,' she had said as if there could be no possible doubt about it. It had struck William at the time that what this woman intended to do was take the weekend by the scruff of the neck and shake it into a shape that suited her.

An underground car-park attendant in London, on the other hand, would have given a far more negative response, probably on the lines of, 'Yeah, well, I s'pose it'll be all right if it don't rain.'

It was the difference, William thought, between Californian optimism and British pessimism, the difference between a belief that life was there to be attacked and a deep conviction that it simply happened and there was very little that could be done about it.

'I wonder,' said Alice Flitton, 'if I should ask Larraine

110

to come to London with me.'

'Why not?' said William, with an onrush of Californian optimism. 'You could have a marvellous time together.'

'Perhaps,' said Alice, with congenital British pessimism. 'But I have this nasty fear that I might lose her over there.'

Ida Kaines was sweeping her already immaculate patio when William and Alice arrived. By that time Alice, too, had read the typescript and shared William's indignation at Mark's rejection of the story.

Ida Kaines took them inside and made coffee and when they were all sitting round the kitchen table William said, 'I'm afraid I have bad news. My producer and presenter don't want to interview you about the murder. They just want . . . more innocuous stuff.'

She nodded slowly. 'Is it the money or don't they believe me?'

'Bit of both, I think. Also they said that if you told the story on film they'd have to report it to the police and I didn't think you'd like that.'

'No, I wouldn't.' She smiled sadly at him. 'What about you, William? Are you going to report me to the police?'

He shook his head.

'They wouldn't believe me anyway,' she said. 'I mean, I have no proof. And even if they did investigate you can bet your life that within five minutes Willard's lawyers would be claiming I was crazy or vindictive or both . . .' She sighed. 'So he's going to get away with it after all, alive or dead.'

'Not necessarily,' William said. 'I've been thinking: I've got your story here, all typed out. You could sign it and Alice could witness it and then, well obviously I couldn't do anything with it while he's alive but after

111

he's dead I could make sure it was published some-where.'

She considered this proposition and then nodded. 'All right. I'm sorry it won't be on T.V. though. No money for my poor tribe now.'

'If I sell the story,' William said, 'I'll split the proceeds with them. Give me an address, a bank or something, where I can send the money, though God knows when it will be.'

So she gave him the address and read carefully through the transcript, correcting it slightly here and there and when she had finished she signed each page and Alice witnessed her signature.

'I tell myself,' said Ida Kaines, 'that I'm doing this to set the record straight and in a way to ease my own conscience. But I wonder – am I being vindictive really?'

William and Alice hesitated and then Alice said, 'Well, a little bit perhaps?'

Ida Kaines nodded. 'I think you're right. I don't like myself for it but then . . . I haven't liked myself a hell of a lot for quite a long time.' She handed the signed pages back to William. 'Okay, it's yours. Now then – what kind of an interview do your people want me to give?'

William grimaced. 'You're not going to believe this – but they want to know all about your happy life with the wonderful Willard Kaines. I won't blame you if you want to cry off.'

She said, 'How much am I getting, just for the straight interview?'

'Five hundred dollars,' Alice said. 'That was the figure in the contract you signed.'

She nodded. 'For 5,000 dollars you'd have got the truth; for 500 all you get is a lot of lies. Well, I don't care. What's a few more lies after all the others? And at least 500 bucks will help my Brazilians a little.'

At this point there was a ring at the doorbell and in a moment Mark and Warbottle and the crew came into the room.

The interview with Ida Kaines was long, detailed, gentle and exceedingly dull. Sitting in a corner out of camera-shot and away from the interviewee's eyeline, William compared what the woman was saying with what she could have said and felt gloom settle upon him. In his determination to paint a portrait of a Great Man of our Time, Mark was doggedly presenting Willard Kaines, a man whom nobody seemed to have liked, as a kind of elderly saint, endowed with enormous and generally unrecognised talent, who had devotedly nursed his sick wife to the detriment of his own career.

The truth, William thought, was much more interesting. Rex Angell had described Kaines as a mean son of a bitch; his former co-star had remembered him so dimly that she had preferred to reminisce about John Gilbert; and his present wife had accused him of murder. A documentary on those lines would have been a real rating-topper, while this sugar-coated fiction that Mark was inventing would barely keep the viewers awake between commercials.

Mark, however, was entirely happy. The faintly ironic smile with which Ida Kaines received his questions about her husband's brilliance and inherent goodness passed him by unnoticed. True, he was slightly taken aback at the very end of the interview when he said, 'Ida Kaines, thank you very much,' and she replied, 'You're quite welcome. I never spoke so much – if you'll pardon the word – horseshit in my life but if horseshit is what you want in this world, horseshit is what you're gonna get.'

'Cut,' said Geoff Warbottle.

'Get that last bit, did you, Fred?' asked the camera-man.

'Loud and clear,' said the soundman.

'We're not using that in the programme,' said Mark.

'Be a bloody sight better programme if we did,' said the cameraman.

This slight unpleasantness apart, though, Mark felt he had given a well-judged performance. His tone and his questions had been gentle and sympathetic to give the impression that here was a skilled interviewer subtly extracting information from a shy old lady. And now he was about to add the final gloss to the reverses. With William sitting in for Ida Kaines, Mark went through the gamut of his expressions. He nodded, he frowned, he smiled, he chuckled, he looked interested, he looked concerned, he looked perturbed. He would have been quite happy to carry on doing this all day as the camera peered at him from over William's shoulder but a couple of minutes of this kind of stuff was about all the rest of the unit could take.

'Cut,' said Warbottle. 'We'll do a few questions, now, Mark. William, throw him a question.'

William consulted the question sheet in front of him. 'Would you describe Willard as being devoted to his first wife?' he read in a deliberately flat tone.

Mark put his fingertips together and frowned sincerely. 'Would you describe Willard as . . . ' he glanced away for a moment, conjuring words out of the air, 'as a *devoted* husband to his first wife?'

'And you, Ida, married him because you both felt that this is what the first Mrs Kaines would have wanted?' read William in the same flat voice.

This time Mark leaned forward, his black-rimmed spectacles gleaming with passionate sincerity. 'And you, Ida,' he said, 'you married him because that, that was what . . . ' he threw in a sincere sniff, nostrils dilating, corners of mouth turning down, 'the first Mrs Kaines would have wanted?' His voice throbbed softly with emotion. Willard Kaines himself, William thought, could hardly have sliced the ham more thickly.

'Couple more questions, Mark,' said Warbottle. He had just noticed Ida Kaines waiting at the kitchen door with a tray laden with cold beer. Warbottle was in dire need of a cold beer.

William read a few more questions and Mark repeated them for the benefit of the camera. Then . . . 'Ida Kaines, thank you very much,' he said.

'Oh, you're quite welcome,' said William, cheerfully. 'I never spoke so much – if you'll pardon the word – horseshit in my life, but if horseshit is what you want . . . '

'Shut up,' said Mark. 'Just shut up. I warn you, William.'

'Bloody good,' said the cameraman, laughing heartily. 'I like that last bit, William. Right, that's it then, is it? We have a wrap, do we, a bijou wrapette, unless of course you want to do a couple more party tricks, Mark. Piece to camera on the lawn, perhaps, establishing Willard Kaines's position in the history of the cinematic arts or . . . '

Mark said nothing. He seethed – there could be no possible doubt that he seethed – but he said nothing and William realized that Mark was a little afraid of the cameraman and his sarcasm, his lack of, well, reverence and his air of inviolability. Mark could make life exceedingly awkward for Warbottle, Alice and William but over the technical crew he had no power at all. They were all skilled and experienced men, protected by a strong trade union, and as long as they did their work competently Mark's opinion of them was of no importance, one way or another.

It was odd, William thought. In Britain Mark was a national figure enjoying the curious celebrity that attends people who appear regularly on television. It is not necessary for such people actually to do anything; it is enough that they are there – famous for being famous.

Wherever he went in Britain his appearance would, at the very least, cause passers-by to nudge each other and murmur, 'Oh look, there goes whatsisname.' Strangers stopped him in the streets and requested his autograph; viewers wrote in asking for signed pictures. In Britain Mark was Somebody but here, in America, he was as anonymous as William and treated with even less respect and affection by his own crew. Little wonder perhaps that, deprived of his regular fix of adulation and offered hardly more than sarcasm by way of compensation, he sulked moodily over his cold beer.

Watching him there, cut off from the post-interview chitchat and answering any remark directed towards him with no more than a monosyllable, William was almost moved to pity him. Almost. Not quite.

8

They lunched at an expensive hamburger joint with
pretensions above its station. It was a large place,
gloomily lit and staffed by Mexican waiters in black
trousers and waistcoats and girls of assorted shapes and
colours in mini-skirts. The menu offered more than fifty
different main courses, nearly all of them hamburgers,
hamburgers with eggs, hamburgers with eggs and bacon,
hamburgers with eggs and bacon and cheese, hamburgers
with avocado pear, hamburgers with chili sauce, hamburgers with avocado pear and chili sauce, hamburgers
with . . .

'Don't they do anything but bloody hamburgers?'
asked Mark.

The eight of them, production crew and technicians
alike, were queueing patiently for a table. There were
some tables free, for it was early as yet, and one of them
was a table for six. Mark had insisted that William go and
ask if they couldn't take that, on the grounds that it
would be easily converted into a table for eight by the
addition of an extra chair at either end. The hostess in
charge of seating arrangements had been affronted, just
as William had known she would be. She was a slender
woman of about forty in a pale-blue full-length evening
dress and she had hair the colour and texture of pink
candyfloss. Tables for six, she had told William sternly,
were reserved for parties of six. The fact that there
appeared to be no immediate call for a table for six didn't

117

mean that a party of six wouldn't come bustling in, demanding accommodation, at any moment. Parties of eight were perforce obliged to wait until a table for eight fell vacant; those were the house rules and she wasn't about to change them.

What, William enquired, if he and his group split up into a party of six and a party of two, or even into two parties of four? Why, certainly they could do that, said the hostess. The party of six could be seated immediately but the party of two, having changed its status, would have to go back to the end of the line and wait until a suitable table became available and the same would apply if they divided into two parties of four. The rules, William had to acknowledge, were quite foolproof; he said they would wait until a table for eight was free and went back to report to Mark.

Mark took the news surprisingly well, as if deep within himself he had expected nothing better, realizing that they were firmly locked into a system from which there was no escape. 'You know,' he said gloomily, 'this country isn't really all that much different from Russia. It's a question of regimentation. You're all right so long as you conform.'

They waited fifteen minutes until the hostess came by to ask if Mr Pen'leton and his party wanted to go to their table now. The previous occupants of the table, whom they passed on their way, proved to be a group of out-of-town businessmen who, on the evidence of the labels they all wore on their lapels, were in Hollywood for a convention. They were much given to Crimplene safari suits in pastel shades with shirts of violent hue open halfway to the waist. Chunky gold medallions nestled in the grey or white hair of their chests. At least half of them wore toupees in youthful colours. In America generally, and in California in particular, the second gravest sin was to be old; the gravest sin of all was to look old.

The hamburgers were delicious; all who ordered them were agreed upon that and the cameraman took particular delight in extolling their excellence to Mark who, arguing that he hadn't come all the way to America to eat bloody hamburgers, had insisted on ordering giant prawns. William had advised him against it since the prawns had probably been flown, deep-frozen, from somewhere like Alaska and would taste of nothing. Mark, who had proceeded with his original plan anyway, sampled the dish when it arrived and said that William was entirely wrong: the prawns tasted, in fact, of the spicy tomato sauce in which they were smothered and also of slightly burnt rubber, a combination so disgusting that he would have much preferred it if they had tasted of nothing. He then pushed his plate sulkily to one side and refused to take anything more except black coffee.

He was, therefore, in an extremely bad mood when they left the restaurant. Somehow in Mark's mind the disaster of his lunch was solely William's fault. This augured badly, William thought, for the afternoon which they were to spend at Mega-Star-Dynamic Studios interviewing the director of Willard Kaines's last film. He viewed the prospect with trepidation.

The table for six, William noted as they left, remained unclaimed.

Once upon a time, in the days when M.G.M. boasted more stars than there were in heaven, Mega-Star-Dynamic had boasted more stars than there were at M.G.M.

At best this had been a most extravagant claim which nobody had taken at all seriously and now it was no more than a memory, a nostalgic reminder of the days when Hollywood was exclusively a film town, before the even richer and more powerful moguls of television and the pop industry had moved in and relegated films to third

119

place in the local hierarchy.

Today M.S.D. was simply a four-waller, a collection of facilities for hire – studios, offices, cutting-rooms and the like. The permanent staff was minimal; the once-extensive back lot had been sold off for factory and housing developments; and there were no stars, no directors, no writers and no producers on the payroll. The studio stood at the end of a short street off one of the meaner boulevards in an area which had come down in the world. Around it were small factories, shabby shops and a handful of bars which catered bravely to the independent crews that used the M.S.D. facilities by stocking foreign cigarettes and copies of *Variety* and *The Hollywood Reporter*.

A messenger, a girl in pale-blue Levis and a dark-blue tee-shirt that insisted in white letters across its chest that the wearer was a free spirit, met The Great Men entourage at reception. The ghost crew, she said, had already arrived and was playing cards in an unused corner of the set.

Nobody had wanted this ghost crew. It was a necessary evil, its presence demanded by the American trade unions. Whenever a foreign unit wished to film in a studio, a duplicate American crew had to be present. It had no function but to be there and to draw its pay. But be there it must and paid it had to be.

Even Geoff Warbottle had been annoyed at William for arranging the interview with the director in the studio. It had been an appalling waste of money, he said, to spend several hundred dollars merely to enable an out-of-work American cameraman and his assistant, a soundman and a lighting man to play poker all afternoon. William had protested truthfully but uselessly that there had been no alternative: the director, a tyro when he worked with Willard Kaines but now a significant figure in the movie capital, had insisted that he could do the interview only on the set of his film and between takes.

This director was now a man whose word had become law. He was constantly in employment because he had all the qualities that commended themselves to the accountants and agents-turned-executives who dominated the film industry: he had hardly any discernible imagination but what almost amounted to a genius for completing a production on, or more often than not, under budget and schedule. The result was that he had behind him an unbroken string of box-office successes each of which had been soundly derided by the critics of every land where they had been shown – every land, that is, save one. The exception was France. The French, being a subtle race, had been quite unable to believe that any films could be as unimaginative as his and had therefore read into them all manner of sly comments and statements that had never been intended. Consequently a small cult had been built around his work by the Parisian critics and since the words 'Paris, France' still represent to Americans – especially those who cannot speak the language – the very acme of sophistication and wit, he enjoyed a reputation not only as the most bankable director in the industry but as an artist so far ahead of his time as to be recognized only by the most cultured critics in the world.

Thus he continued to turn out inferior remakes of the kind of gangster movies that Warner Brothers made so well in the 1930s and to jump on every cinematic bandwagon and to follow every trend. The mass of the public liked his pictures because of the crude violence and the explicit sex and the French critics liked them because they professed to see in them all kinds of implicit criticisms of the American way of life.

The director, therefore, had it made and knew he had it made and so when he told William that he would be interviewed by Mark between takes on his own set and only between takes on his own set, there was no arguing with him. He sounded like a higher authority granting the Pope an audience.

The messenger girl announced that her name was Charlene and she came from Georgia; she also suggested that Mark, William and Warbottle should accompany her to the publicity department while the rest waited until summoned in the reception area. As the producer, Warbottle's place was undoubtedly alongside Mark and William, doing the P.R. bit and oiling the wheels but on this occasion, he said, he would take a raincheck on the grounds that the others could cope perfectly well without him. William was a little surprised at this reaction until Warbottle pointed out that there was an interesting-looking bar across the street and decreed that, for purposes of convenience, any enquiries for him should be addressed to that establishment. Without waiting for further argument he then proceeded towards it, adding by way of afterthought that he hoped William and Mark would have a nice day.

'Something,' said Mark to William, 'will have to be done about him. He's getting worse, you know.'

'A lush, huh?' said the girl, Charlene, cheerfully. 'This is a great town for it.'

She led them through the seedy and decaying studio lot towards the publicity department, pointing out places of interest on the way.

'That's the J.J.Huxter Building,' she said, indicating a once-white edifice that was now stained with damp where water had dripped from its rotting gutters. Across its portal was the slogan: 'The J.J.Huxter Building'. J.J. Huxter, she said, was a legendary figure of the post-war era, a wunderkind, M.S.D.'s favourite son. 'He made more money for this studio when it really was a studio than any other producer they ever had.'

'Really?' said Mark. 'Good films were they?'

'Are you kidding? Good they were not. But profitable – you better believe it.'

'You seem to know quite a lot about this place,' said

William. 'You must have been here a long time.'

'Just a month, honey. But I learned all this stuff off by heart. See, I got a good memory. I'm not really a messenger, you know, I'm an actress.'

'Just filling in time, waiting for your break?'

'Right,' Charlene said, nodding.

'Tell me,' said William, 'is there anyone in this town who isn't really an actress?'

'Not that I know of. Except the guys, of course, and they're really actors.'

It was a phenomenon that William had noticed soon after he arrived. Hollywood had the most attractive waiters, waitresses and shop assistants in the world because all of them were really potential stars filling menial jobs while they waited for the big break to come their way.

One day, he thought, they would all wake up and realize that they had reached forty and had never done a day's acting since they arrived in Hollywood. They would have spent their entire lives waiting for something that never happened and that, by the law of averages, had never been much better than a million-to-one shot in the first place. They would have spent about twenty years claiming to be actors and actresses when, in reality, they had never been anything but waiters and waitresses. And what would they do then, he wondered. Come to terms with the passage of time, most likely, by insisting that they were now character actors and actresses waiting for something to turn up. In Hollywood Mr Micawber wouldn't have merited a second glance.

'Mind you,' said Charlene, 'there are times when I can hardly tell the guys from the gals in this town. Have you ever seen so many gays in your life?'

William, who had no special interest in other people's sexual tastes, grunted non-committally, but Mark, with a disdainful sniff, said he hadn't really thought about it but now she mentioned it, yes, he had noticed some rather strange men around, men who – it would not surprise him to learn – were indeed homosexuals.

'You bet,' said the girl. 'It's the fashion here. Nearly everybody's gay. And you know how you can tell a gay guy in Hollywood – the more macho he looks the gayer he is. No straight guy in the world needs to took as macho as the local faggots. That's how I knew you guys weren't gay. You don't look macho at all.'

With this doubtful compliment she led them into another damp-stained building, along a corridor of worn and cracked tiles and knocked on a door marked 'Circus of the Zombies: Publicity'. 'Good to meet you guys,' she said. 'Have a ni . . .'

'We will,' said William.

'Bye now,' she said and opened the door and ushered them in and went away down the corridor.

William and Mark found themselves in a shabbily furnished office and facing a desk behind which sat a youngish-oldish man with thin fair hair that was parted a quarter of an inch above his left ear and combed straight across his head. On the desk in front of him was a portable typewriter and a plaque that read: 'Herb Omlet, Director of Publicity.'

He got up as they entered and came out to meet them. He was a little under medium height and wore his belt below his belly. 'Hi,' he said. 'You must be the English guys. I'm Herb Omlet.' He carried, as a kind of burden, a tired, grey-flecked moustache that looked as if it had been intended for an older man and that had struggled wearily across his top lip and halfway down his chin on either side of his mouth before giving up in exhaustion or possibly despair.

The English guys admitted that they were indeed English guys and revealed their individual identities. 'Great,' said Herb Omlet, apparently much impressed by their ability to remember their own names. 'Okay, let's go across to the set and I'll introduce you to Cosmo. You know Cosmo – Cosmo Dekker?'

William said that neither of them had met Mr Dekker – for such was the director's name – but that he had spoken to him on the telephone to arrange this appointment.

'Right,' said Herb Omlet, as if he had asked the question as a sort of test and William had provided the correct answer. 'Well, he's a great guy – and talented, wow! You know how much his last picture grossed?'

'Herb Omlet,' Mark said, looking at the plaque on the desk as the publicity director led them out of the office. 'Is that, er, is that your real name?'

'Sure is. Jefferson Herbert Omlet if you want the whole bit. But I dropped the Jefferson soon as I got into publicity. I mean, like Jeff Omlet, that's a no-no name. Who's gonna remember anybody called Jeff Omlet? But Herb Omlet, now that's another matter. Nobody's ever gonna forget a name like Herb Omlet.'

'No,' said Mark. 'When you put it like that, I suppose not.'

'Darn right,' said Herb Omlet. 'You know what I called my son? Huh? You wanna guess what I called my son?

William shrugged. 'Spanish?' he said. 'Cheese? Onion? Guacamole?'

'Nope,' said Omlet smugly. 'Hamilton.'

'Hamilton,' said Mark.

'Right. Ham Omlet. 'Course he's only ten now and the kids at school give him a hard time on account of his name. But, like I keep telling him, he'll have the last laugh. When he grows up I'm gonna take him into partnership. Can you imagine it – Herb and Ham Omlet, Publicity Counsellors? Why, it's got to be the best goddamn gimmick in the business.'

'Didn't, didn't your wife object, though,' William asked. 'When you said you were going to call your son Ham, I mean?'

'Wilhelmina? Hell, no,' said Omlet. 'She didn't mind at all.'

William saw no reason to doubt the man's words. Any woman, it seemed to him, who was doomed to go through life under the name of Wilhelmina Omlet was undoubtedly too crushed to object to anything very much.

'Okay,' said Omlet, becoming brisk and businesslike now that the social chitchat was over. 'You know about this latest movie Cosmo's making – *Circus of the Zombies*? Horror picture. It's gonna cost, oh, fifteen million and it'll gross at least a hundred, no sweat. The story's about this zombie gorilla that comes back from the dead and terrorizes San Francisco. Great Story. I mean, like really great.

'So anyway, just to set the scene, this zombie gorilla who's like almost human hides out in a circus. Cute, huh? So anyway that's why we got all these animals.'

And indeed they did have animals. The trio had now reached a large enclosure just outside the studio's main sound-stage and within this heavily-wired enclosure either in cages or wandering free according to temperament were all manner of animals such as one might, or in some cases might not, reasonably expect to find in a circus. There were lions and tigers, chimpanzees, elephants, camels, seals, giraffes and even a zebra or two.

'Hell of a circus,' said Mark.

'Cosmo doesn't like to do things by halves,' said Omlet and since only the Rehearsal and not the Shooting light was flashing above the heavy double-door he led them onto the sound-stage. This turned out to be an enormous hangar, most of which was set up as a circus ring but in one corner, the corner where all the activity was currently taking place, there was a bedroom set. It was decorated opulently and vulgarly in pink and white – pink carpet, pink curtains and pink silk bedspread;

delicate white furniture with gold handles on the drawers and cupboards. It was quite clearly a woman's bedroom and had there been any doubt on this score it was immediately dispelled by the presence, reclining on the bed, of a tall, tawny blonde clad only in black-lace knickers.

'You've seen those boobs before, right?' said Omlet, lasciviously.

William had. He had last seen them, he remembered, quivering with fear in Dekker's most recent picture *The Devil from Outer Space*. Their owner was the latest in Hollywood's never-ending line of blonde sex goddesses, an actress of minimal accomplishment who had been discovered, emoting strongly, on the covers of fashion magazines.

Her name originally, he also remembered, had been something on the lines of Hackenpfeffer – not that exactly though not entirely dissimilar – but Hollywood, with rare originality, had redubbed her Harlow Monroe.

'They're just about to shoot the end of the big love scene,' Omlet said. 'See, Harlow plays the journalist who's investigating all the crazy things that are going on in San Francisco and Brett Kruger is the private eye who goes up against the zombie gorilla. This scene comes right after Brett saves her from being raped by the zombie. Except, if you mention anything about the movie, it's better you don't say anything about that part. Cosmo hasn't decided yet whether she gets raped or not. It depends on whether the picture needs it.'

At this point Brett Kruger himself emerged from the crowd of people clustered around the camera and took his place on the bed alongside Harlow Monroe. He was wearing a slouch hat and a white raincoat and, considering the girl's deshabille, appeared to be considerably over-dressed.

Suddenly there was a great uproar as about twenty people started shouting 'Quiet!' When they had finished shouting 'Quiet!' at all those who were standing quite still and saying nothing, they began shouting 'Quiet!' at each other.

'They're just gonna shoot the scene now,' whispered Omlet.

'Quiet!' shouted a man with a megaphone.

In a moment peace was restored. From the crowd around the camera William heard the clapperboy say, '159. Take twenty.' The camera moved in slowly. Just as slowly Brett Kruger moved in on Harlow Monroe, took her right breast in his left hand and kissed her on the lips. They held the kiss for the best part of half a minute then the girl broke away with a shuddering moan.

'Darling,' she murmured tremulously, as Brett Kruger continued to massage her breast, 'you'd better go. Your door is waiting at the taxi.'

'Cut!' yelled an irate voice from behind the camera. 'Jesus Christ!' it said. 'One mother-lovin' line and the stupid bitch has already screwed it up a million times. Even the goddamn gorilla coulda got it right by now.'

'That's Cosmo,' murmured Omlet, proudly. 'He's kinda temperamental.'

On the set Brett Kruger lit a cigarette, took off his hat and began to stare earnestly at himself in the dressing-table mirror while Harlow Monroe emitted a pathetic wail and burst into tears. Mascara fell in a flood down her cheeks.

'Okay, okay, take five,' yelled Cosmo Dekker. 'Jesus, somebody take this broad away and clean her up.' A small regiment of dressers and make-up artists surrounded the weeping star, put a dressing-gown around her and led her away to be cleaned and combed and decorated afresh.

During this hiatus the Great Men unit arrived, Geoff Warbottle bringing up the rear and swaying a little, his face alight with goodwill towards all. 'Oh my God,' said Mark, 'he's absolutely pissed.'

And so he was. He greeted Mark and William with the delight of one unexpectedly encountering close friends whom he had not seen in many years. He greeted Herb Omlet with an enthusiastic smack on the shoulder and laughed uproariously on hearing his name. He greeted an assistant director, who came over to ask him to keep his voice down, with many a wise and understanding nod and grimace and put an index finger to his lips and said 'Shhh' very solemnly eight times. He greeted a passing messenger girl by suddenly shooting out an arm and pinching her bottom and then he collapsed into a canvas-backed chair and said, 'Carry on, carry on, carry on, carry on.'

From a group of four men who had been playing cards in a corner behind the camera a short, stout, middle-aged man detached himself and approached Mark. 'You're the Limey crew, right,' he said.

'I suppose so,' Mark said, grudgingly, as if he felt that being addressed as a Limey was hardly preferable to being mistaken for an Australian or a Scotsman.

'Yeah, well I'm your American cameraman. Arnie Gold?' He said this in the customary American fashion with a slight note of query in his voice, as though he were not at all certain that Mark would accept Arnie Gold as being his name. 'Those are the rest of my guys over there.' He gestured towards the three remaining card players, all equally stout and middle-aged, who smiled and waved in their direction.

'You got everything you want?' he asked.

'I think so,' Mark said.

'Right. We'll stick around right over there. Otherwise we're not about to get in your way. Nice to meet you guys.' He started back towards the card school, then paused and turned to Mark again. 'Say, listen – anything you want, hesitate to ask.' He laughed immoderately at his little jest and called to his companions, 'Okay, you guys, deal me in.'

Herb Omlet who had been gazing, as one stunned, at the beaming, nodding, chuckling figure of Geoff Warbottle, took William to one side. 'Is that guy really your producer,' he asked.

'I'm afraid so,' said William. He looked with sad affection at the slumped and incapable Warbottle, who was remarking to Alice Flitton that there seemed to be a long time between drinks at this party.

'He always like that?' asked Omlet.

'More or less,' said William. 'I think he's overdone it a bit this time, though.'

'Well, look, you don't mind if we leave him here when I introduce you to Cosmo? I mean, shit, Cosmo likes a drink same as anybody but he hates drunks on the set and, you know, maybe he's got enough problems with Harlow . . .'

'No, that's quite all right,' said William and Omlet, visibly relieved, took him and Mark over to the camera to introduce them to Cosmo Dekker.

Dekker was a short, tubby man with a salt-and-pepper beard, a bald head, black-framed glasses and fierce expression.

'Cosmo, this is William Pendleton,' said Omlet, deferentially. His respect for Dekker seemed to border on fear.

'William Pendleton,' said Dekker, shaking hands.

'And this, of course, is Mark Payne.'

'Mark who?' said Dekker.

There was a slight, awkward pause as Mark bestowed a sincere frown of disapproval on the director.

'Mark Payne?' said Omlet, anxiously. Again there was the note of query. William had the impression that if Dekker gave any sign of disliking the name Mark Payne, Omlet would immediately invent something more acceptable.

'Yeah?' said Dekker. 'And what do you do, Mark? William I know about. I talked to William on the phone.

130

You I don't know. What do you do, Mark?'

Mark, deeply affronted, embarked on a potted version of his autobiography in the middle of which Dekker interrupted, 'Okay, okay, I get the picture. So, you guys wanna talk to me about Willard Kaines, right?' He shook his head wonderingly. 'What the hell for? I mean, Jesus, Willard Kaines. Who remembers Willard Kaines? I didn't even know the old bastard was still alive. God he was a mean son of a bitch. I mean, mean mean, you know what I mean? I worked two months with him on my first movie, *Mafia Boss*. Well, it was called *Mafia Boss* in those days. Now we don't mention the Mafia. I see they call it *Syndicate Boss* on TV these days. You notice that, Herb?'

'Sure, I noticed it, Cosmo,' said Omlet, eagerly. 'Gutless bastards, those T.V. . . .'

'I don't blame 'em for changing it,' said Dekker.

'Gee, no,' said Omlet. 'I don't *blame* 'em, either, Cosmos. I . . .'

'But what a tight-fisted bastard,' said Dekker. 'I never saw him pick up a tab not once in two months. Not in a bar, not in a restaurant. Why I remember . . .'

An assistant director approached, coughed apologetically and said, 'Mr Dekker? Sir? You wanna come over to the set? I think we got problems.'

'What else do we ever have round here but problems?' said Dekker with a brave wink at William. 'Well, okay, that's what they pay me for. Listen, you guys wanna set up your camera someplace around here? I'll be with you as soon as I can, though God knows what I can tell you about Willard Kaines that anybody'll wanna hear. Willard Kaines. Jesus!' He went away with the assistant director and Mark, who had been brooding silently, turned on Omlet.

'Really, Omlet,!' he said. 'You might have told him who I was. It was positively humiliating, a man in my position, having to explain himself to . . .'

William moved away. He didn't want to hear the rest. Around the camera a heated discussion was going on, in the midst of which was Cosmo Dekker, alternately listening and shouting. The man to whom he was listening and at whom he was shouting appeared to be Harlow Monroe's agent who was objecting strenuously to the fact that the director had called his client a stupid bitch.

'Well, she is a stupid bitch!' Dekker was shouting. 'One goddamn line and she can't get it right after ten million takes! Any broad who keeps her brains between her legs is a stupid . . . ' He fumbled in his pockets and produced a cigarette packet which, having peered inside, he crumpled angrily and hurled to the floor. 'Garfield, for Christ's sake get me some Camels!' he yelled.

An anxious-looking youth with a megaphone who was standing beside William said, 'Garfield? That's me! I'm Garfield. What did he say?'

William shrugged. 'He said he wanted some Camels.'

'Already?' said the anxious-looking youth. 'Well, I guess he knows best. He's the director.' He hurried away towards the heavy exit doors.

In a little while some semblance of order and calm was restored around the camera. Harlow Monroe's agent shook hands with Cosmo Dekker; Brett Kruger reappeared in slouch hat and raincoat; Harlow Monroe, still clad in her dressing-gown, was brought in reverentially by her entourage of dressers and make-up artists; a conference between the director and the stars took place on the set; Dekker made a joke; Kruger laughed sycophantically; Monroe smiled wanly; Dekker kissed her on the forehead; Monroe said, 'Cosmo, I love you really,' and threw her arms around him; Dekker said he loved her, too. And then the two stars took their places on the bed, everybody yelled 'Quiet!' at everybody else, silence descended and the

132

clapperboy said: '159. Take twenty-one.' Dekker said 'Action' and a dozen camels came onto the set.

There was a moment of appalled silence, save for the noise made by the animals as they blundered around the stage, knocking over tables and chairs.

Then Dekker said, 'Cut! Cut, cut, cut! Who the . . . what the . . . Who in the name of Louis B. Mayer brought these fuckin' camels onto this set?'

Again a moment of silence as those closest to the director moved swiftly but softly away from him.

'Sir, I did, sir,' said the youthful Garfield.

'Why?' said Dekker, clapping his hands dramatically to the sides of his bald head. 'Why do you do this to me, Garfield? Why do you hate me? What have I done to you, Garfield? In the middle of a goddamn love scene you bring me camels? Who said I wanted camels?'

The panic-stricken Garfield looked wildly around him. 'He did, Sir,' he said. 'He said you asked for camels.' And in his terror he pointed, not at William, but at Mark.

Once more silence descended; an ominous, totally unpleasant silence. Dekker took one deliberate step towards the astonished Mark and paused.

'You did, huh?' he said. His tone was quiet but unmistakably venomous. 'You did? I got all the problems in the world trying to teach this stupid bitch to say one goddamn line right and at this moment in time you decide, *you* decide that I need a herd of fuckin' camels in the bedroom! In the bedroom, already! Get off!'

'But,' said Mark. 'But . . . '

'Get off my set!' yelled Dekker. 'Get off! All of you – all you Limey assholes, get off my goddamn set! You,' he said, turning to his acolytes, 'get them off my set! Now!'

Swiftly the acolytes moved in and just as swiftly Mark and William and the Great Men camera crew backed away towards the exit doors. And at this moment Geoff

Warbottle suddenly sat up from his position on the floor at the far side of the silk-covered bed and, from a vantage point just below Harlow Monroe's naked left breast, said, 'Who do you have to fuck to get a drink round here?'

9

The journey back to the motel was not a happy one. William drove with Alice Flitton beside him; Mark sat in the back with the sleeping Warbottle.

'That fellow,' Mark said, 'did you see him – that huge fellow? He manhandled me! Me! He threw me out, literally threw me out. By God, they won't get away with this. I shall . . . I shall sue.' Warbottle, snoring heavily, slid off the back seat onto the floor of the car. Mark kicked him savagely on the leg but the producer only grunted and rolled over.

'This whole trip is a nightmare,' Mark said. 'An absolute nightmare. Everywhere we turn we're faced with unscheduled disasters. We've got nothing whatsoever, in the way of decent material. Well, I'll tell you this . . .'

'Did you,' asked Alice Flitton in a small, awed voice, 'did you see Cosmo Dekker's face when Geoff appeared beside the bed? I thought he was going to have a heart attack. He screamed – actually screamed.'

'I know,' William said. 'But it got even worse after that because Dekker was so cross he threw his script on the floor and one of the camels peed on it.' Despite himself, despite the humiliation of their exit from the studio, he began to laugh.

'You,' said Mark, 'have nothing to laugh about, William. None of you has anything to laugh about. I give you fair warning now that I intend to give a detailed account of this fiasco to Charles Kaufman as soon as we get back. All the blame will be laid at the proper doors. I seriously doubt whether any of you will ever work in television again.'

This was not, William thought, altogether an empty threat. Mark and Kaufman, Nat-Met's head of production, were old friends and though it was unlikely that any of the production unit would actually be fired on Mark's say-so, it was very likely that a bad report from him would mean that their contracts would not be renewed. His, William's, contract had only one month to run. He wondered if the B.B.C. would take him on; he wondered if he could afford to work for the B.B.C.

The powerful smell of Warbottle's breath wafted into the front of the car. 'Can we open the window?' Alice Flitton asked. 'I think I'm going to be sick.'

'If you're sick in this car,' said Mark, 'I shall rub your face in it. I positively forbid you to be sick.' William pressed the button to open Alice Flitton's window and she leaned out. Even the petrol fumes on Sunset Boulevard were preferable to Warbottle's breath.

When they pulled up in fron of the motel Mark leapt out of the car and made towards his room. 'Aren't you going to give us a hand with Geoff?' William asked.

'No, I most certainly am not. The filthy pig can lie in the gutter for all I care.'

William and Alice hauled the producer out of the car and somehow, between them, half pulled and half carried him to his room. As they laid him on his bed Warbottle opened his eyes and mumbled something.

'What did he say?' said Alice.

'What did you say?' said William, leaning closer. Warbottle mumbled again.

'Well?' said Alice.

'He said he thinks he's got the D.T.s. He said he could swear he saw a herd of camels at that party we just left.'

Dinner was a lonely affair for them all. Mark, insisting that in a decent and well-ordered world he would never again be obliged to set eyes on any of his companions, drove off by himself to Wilshire Boulevard to dine alone at the original Brown Derby restaurant. Alice Flitton betook herself to the coffee-shop, as was now her habit, to commune with Larraine Laroux. Geoff Warbottle slept.

And William, having visited Ralph's supermarket to acquire a carton of guacamole dip and a family pack of taco chips, fed on these and half a flagon of Mountain Chablis in his room and watched television.

He was not entirely sorry to be alone. The previous night had been a long one and he welcomed the prospect of an early bed. Besides, he wanted a quiet time in which to sort himself out and survey his future. He had, he realized, completely alienated Mark Payne: the fiasco at the film studio had been, strictly speaking, his fault, although he could hardly have anticipated that the eager Garfield, sent to find Camels, would have returned with a horde of animals of that name instead of a packet of cigarettes. Nor was it his fault that Garfield, in his panic, had accused Mark of sending him on this errand, on the grounds presumably that all Englishmen looked alike to him. Nevertheless, the result was that Mark now blamed William and only William for the ignominy that had been heaped upon him. Furthermore, he blamed William and only William for the fact that the interviews that had been arranged for him had yielded nothing of any real interest. And there was, William was obliged to admit, a certain amount to be said for that point of view. Of course, had they been briefed to provide an accurate portrait of Willard Kaines, instead of the eulogy which Nat-Met and the network demanded, they would by now be in possession of such material from Rex Angell and

Ida Kaines as would have scorched the eardrums of any T.V. audience. But a eulogy was what was demanded and though, with clever editing, it could be provided, there was no doubt that on the evidence so far it would be an extremely bland eulogy, even as eulogies went. William could only hope that the next week's interviews would provide something a little juicier.

And then . . . What else did Mark blame him for? Oh yes, William thought as he poured himself another glass of Mountain Chablis, there was the matter of Larraine Laroux and Alice Flitton. That, apparently, was also William's fault. It was a little hard, he reflected, upon his soul it was, that whatever action he took, or deliberately failed to take, he invariably ended up as the scapegoat. Unless he could somehow square himself with Mark his future looked decidedly bleak; in one month's time he could easily be out of work and then what – a crawl back to Fleet Street or a life of penury with the B.B.C.? Neither prospect pleased.

At this point, therefore, he switched off his mind and switched on the television set, the former, in America, being a necessary prerequisite for the latter. The programme into which he had tuned – too late to catch its title – turned out to be a species of quiz show. The contestants, eight of them in all, four of each sex, appeared to be newly married and to command a joint I.Q. of very nearly one hundred.

'Girls, girls,' the quizmaster was saying to the wives; 'how did your husband finish this sentence: "I think of my wife's figure (William assumed he meant 'figure' although what he actually said was 'figyoor') when I'm in the supermarket buying . . . " How did he finish that sentence?' He was a smooth, blond young man, presumably an Elder Brother symbol, with a wide, toothy smile and cold eyes.

The studio audience fell about with mirth while the females currently in the spotlight sought desperately to locate their brains and, having located them, racked them.

'Rib roast,' said newly-wed female No.1.

'Bananas,' said her husband, proving that this indeed had been his answer by holding up a card on which he had personally scrawled the word bananas with four 'n's.

'Bananas,' said wife No.2.

'Dogfood,' said her husband.

'Pomegranates,' said wife No.3.

'Lemons,' said her husband.

'Steak,' said wife No.4.

'Pork chops,' said her husband.

William, watching this appalled, sought refuge in another glass of Mountain Chablis.

The audience collectively held its sides and howled with glee. The huge, wide smiles of the wives narrowed: their glittering teeth vanished behind lips stretched white and thin as knicker elastic. Their husbands shifted uneasily in their chairs and tried to placate their spouses with furtive grins and playful nudges. The wives were not so easily to be placated. A young bride whose husband has admitted in public that her figure reminds him of lemons, pork chops or dogfood is a young bride into whose soul the iron has entered. And each of those young brides, realizing that their husband's answers did not correspond with their own and realizing, too, that, therefore, the chance of winning whatever ghastly prizes were on offer for the couple who scored most points was receding fast, refused to be appeased. William, observing the thin smiles and uneasy grins, didn't give any of the marriages more than another three months.

And so the frightful programme wore on and in the course of it all kinds of depressing details were revealed about the intimate couplings of these four couples.

Three out of four husbands admitted to having nibbled their wives' toes; two out of four wives had chewed the hair on their husband's chests and doubtless the others would have done so, too, had their partners been endowed with hair on the chest; one out of the four husbands had put his tongue in his wife's ear; three out of four wives had refused to perform the same office for their husbands.

All of these secrets, none of which in William's opinion should ever have been mentioned outside the privacy of the marital bedroom – and not mentioned even in there, save in muted whispers – were revealed to the studio audience and the viewing public in order to win – what? A monstrous set of living-room furniture, imitation Spanish in concept, in shades of gold, green, yellow and red. William wondered what sort of living-room furniture these unhappy people already possessed that this dreadful stuff should seem so excitingly superior.

Filled with cheap wine and also with pity for the pathetic aspirations of these contestants, queasy in the stomach at the thought of them all nibbling and nuzzling each other, William switched off the set. He had the feeling that, inadvertently, he had been shown the soft, white underbelly of America and wished somehow that he hadn't.

'Do you think,' asked Geoff Warbottle at breakfast the next morning, 'that I should do something about my drinking?' His hands were shaking but, apart from that, thanks to the fact that he had slept from about four o'clock the previous afternoon until some time after dawn, he looked reasonably well. He had even managed to shave without cutting himself more than three times.

'Have you actually drawn a completely sober breath since you arrived?' William asked.

Warbottle considered the problem. 'If you exclude this morning,' he said at last, 'and I haven't had anything at all to drink this morning, then the answer is No.'

'In that case,' said William, 'I think perhaps you ought

to do something about it.'

Warbottle nodded gloomily. 'I had an idea you'd say that,' he said. 'It shows, does it – my drinking? Well, I'm not altogether surprised.' He drank deeply of his black coffee, holding the cup in both hands. 'Yesterday,' he said. 'Bit over the top yesterday, was I?'

'Just a bit.'

'Mmmm. We were really supposed to be working, were we? I mean, it wasn't, strictly speaking, a party we were at?'

'No, not strictly speaking a party, though you did your excellent best to make it one. We were, in fact, supposed to be working.'

'What . . . er . . . what precisely happened?' War-bottle asked.

'I don't want to talk about it,' William said.

'Bad as that, eh?' Warbottle said. 'In that case perhaps it's best I don't know. You know what makes me drink, don't you?'

William shrugged. 'The fact that it's comparatively cheap and there's an awful lot of it about?'

Warbottle shook his head impatiently. 'No, no. Price and availability mean nothing to the dedicated drinker. No, it's Payne – Mark pain-in-the-arse Payne. He's the culprit. He frightens me, William.

'Frightens you? Why?'

'Because he has no humour. I can tolerate anybody, the worst person who ever trod the face of the earth, anybody -- so long as he has the saving grace of humour. Payne has none. The only thing in the world that might conceivably make the man smile is somebody else's dis-comfiture. That's terrifying, William. I can't get to grips with a man like that.'

William said, uneasily, 'Oh, come on, Geoff. Mark's all right.'

'No, he's not, William. He's not all right at all. He hates us – all of us – and he particularly hates you. He'll

141

destroy us, you know, he'll destroy every one of us, because this programme we're making is going to be quite dreadful and he'll blame us and he'll get away with it. He always gets away with it. And yet it's not our fault. It's going to be a bad programme because it was a bad idea in the first place but nobody will ever realize that – not when Mark bloody Payne has finished dripping poison into everybody's ears. I tell you, he . . . '

'Shut up,' said William. 'Here he comes.'

Mark came into the coffee-shop, nodded curtly to William and then walked to a table for two in the far corner of the room. He ordered orange juice, coffee, rye toast and when the waitress had gone looked up and said, 'William. Here a moment, please.'

William looked enquiringly at Warbottle who shrugged and muttered, 'You'd better go.'

'Why didn't you sit with us, Mark?' William asked as he joined the presenter. 'There's plenty of room at our table.'

'The less I have to do with that drunk the better,' Mark said.

They were both silent as the waitress brought Mark his breakfast and, having ascertained that nothing more was required, wished them both a nice day. Then Mark said, 'When I got back from dinner last night . . . and incidentally that's an excellent place, that Brown Derby, exactly the kind of place I should have been frequenting all the time. There were several quite well-known actors and actresses there last night, including one I'd interviewed once in London. After I'd re-introduced myself he bought me a drink at the bar . . . '

'That's nice,' William said.

'Yes. It was. Much more the kind of thing I'm used to than these blasted coffee-shops. Anyway, that's not the point. What I wanted to say was that when I got back here last night I had a good think about the way things are going. It's only fair to tell you that I'm not happy,

William. I'm not happy with you, I'm not happy with the camera crew, I'm not happy with Alice Flitton and, after yesterday, I'm most certainly not happy with Warbottle.'

William summoned the waitress again and asked for coffee. 'What are you going to do then, Mark?'

'If things don't improve I shall do what I told you I would do yesterday afternoon: I shall write a full, detailed and brutally frank account of the whole disastrous trip and send it to Charles Kaufman. I need hardly tell you what that could mean in terms of your future career situation.'

William sighed. 'No,' he said. 'That could be a bad situation. But . . . er . . . what if things do improve?'

'Then I may reconsider.' Mark gnawed fiercely at a bit of toast. 'In other words it's entirely up to you. Flitton's a mere pawn, Warbottle's beyond redemption but if you play your cards right, William, there could be a lot of hope for you even now.'

'I see,' said William.

'It's a matter of whose side you're on – theirs or mine. Simple as that.'

'Yes.'

'What I'd like right now,' Mark said, 'is a plate of bacon and eggs. But . . . ' Surreptitiously he pinched a roll of fat over his waistband and sighed. 'Better not. Well, what's on the agenda for today?'

William got his notebook from his pocket. 'Nothing for you and me this morning,' he said. 'This afternoon I'm going to see Willard Kaines.'

'The man himself.' Mark cried. 'At last.'

'Yes, well, I tried to see him just before you arrived but apparently he wasn't very well. I had a long talk with his companion, though, and got a fair bit of stuff from her. But she said if I wanted to see Kaines I'd better come back today, after lunch.'

'This companion,' Mark said, 'what's she like?'

'Brunette, late twenties, rather neurotic I'd have

143

thought. Also a bit frustrated sexually, if you ask me. I have an idea old Willard's not doing his stuff there.'

Mark nodded thoughtfully over his coffee. 'I think I might come with you this afternoon. I believe it's time I took a hand. We can't afford another cock-up, not with Kaines himself – that would be too disastrous.'

William lost his temper. 'Look,' he said, 'I haven't made any cock-ups. I've provided you with full background information on all the people you've interviewed so far. If you choose to ignore it, that's your look-out. But I'm bloody fed up with all your insinuations and . . .'

'Careful, William,' Mark said. 'Be very careful.'

William got up and turned to go.

'Are you going to pay for that coffee you had?' Mark said.

William threw coins on the table and rejoined Warbottle who said, 'Well?' in the voice of one expecting the worst. William told him briefly what Mark had said.

'So he's not happy, eh?' Warbottle murmured. 'Not happy with any of us. Well, well.' He put his head in his hands and stared for several moments into his now empty cup. 'I was thinking, William, while you were over there talking to him, and it seemed to me that there was not a hell of a lot he could do to most of us. Oh, at a pinch I suppose he could get me fired for being pissed yesterday but that's not so bad really. Twenty years I've been with that bloody company, so they'd have to give me a hell of a pay-off. And if they decided to save the money and keep me on anyway, the worst they could do would be to block my promotion and since I'm too old to be in line for much of that it doesn't really matter one way or the other. So, generally speaking, I'm okay. And the camera crew's okay, too, because Nat-Met wouldn't want to go up against the unions just because Mark's unhappy. Alice, well, he can't do a lot to Alice when you think about it, because he's not very likely to go

144

complaining that she pulled the waitress he was after, is he? So . . .'

'So that leaves me,' William said.

'Right. And you, I'm afraid, are a bit vulnerable, young William. Mark could really screw you if he wanted to. You're going to have to win him over somehow.'

William grinned – not much of a grin; very little humour in it. 'And how do you suppose I could do that?'

'Well,' Warbottle said, 'I've been thinking, like I told you, and while I was thinking I remembered what you said about being offered that good-looking whore. You know, the cut price one. Well, why don't you accept the offer and give her to Mark?'

'You really think that's a good idea?'

'Why not?' Warbottle said, urgently. 'Look, you don't want her so it's no skin off your nose. But, on the other hand, why look a gift whore in the mouth? Get her for Mark. It can only do you good.'

William nodded, considering the proposition. 'Perhaps,' he said. 'I'll think about it.' Then he said, 'How did you know Alice had pulled that waitress? It was supposed to be a secret.'

Warbottle smiled. 'There are no secrets,' he said, 'between a producer and his assistant. What about that hooker though, William? Will you do as I suggest?'

William sighed. 'I told you – I'll think about it.'

He was still thinking about it, stretched out on his bed and listening to the grass being Hoovered, when the phone rang and Rex Angell said, 'Hi, kid, how ya doin'?'

William said he was fine and asked how Rex Angell was and Rex Angell said he was fine, too, and then he said, 'Listen, kid, you wanna have dinner with me tonight?'

'I'd love to, only it's really time I took you to dinner and . . .'

'No, I mean, it's a nice thought but I meant dinner here, at my apartment. That Maria's a great cook specially if you like Mexican, and . . . ah, what the hell, kid, I don't wanna go to a restaurant but I want some company. You'd be doing me a favour.'

'Then I'll do it gladly,' William said.

'You know something? I keep going around with a kid like you people are gonna think I'm turning faggot in my old age. How does that grab ya?'

'Not much,' said William. 'But then they'd never really think that of you – not Rex Angell, the master swordsman.'

Angell gave a hollow laugh. 'Some swordsman these days, kid. I can't even raise a rubber dagger. See ya at eight.'

He hung up. Poor old boy, William thought. He must be as lonely as hell up there by himself in his apartment. Well, it was a small favour indeed to agree to be entertained by him especially as he, William, was rather partial to Mexican food.

He lay back on the bed again and resumed thinking of Warbottle and what he had said, of Mark and Stack and the cut-price whore and after a while he made up his mind what to do.

In his own room Warbottle was drinking again. Purely medicinal, he told himself, as he poured the first tumbler of post-breakfast wine. Just a little something to cure the shaking hands . . .

He had not always been a heavy drinker. It was marriage that drove him to it, that tipped him over the boundary dividing the social drinker from the boozer. More specifically it was a wife who, fifteen years into a marriage that, for no known medical reason, had remained childless, had upped and run away with the bank manager on the occasion of his transfer to the north of England.

Warbottle had been very hurt when that happened. He had liked his wife a great deal and he missed her when she had gone. He had tried for some time to entice her back and when that failed had turned for consolation to the first thing that came to hand, namely a bottle of whisky. He had imbibed quite a lot of consolation before the local vicar, learning belatedly of Mrs Warbottle's desertion, came by to offer condolences and spiritual help.

Warbottle had taken to the vicar. The man enjoyed a drink and also shared his, Warbottle's, interest in soccer generally and the fortunes of Tottenham Hotspur in particular. Before the initial meeting was over they had struck a bargain: Warbottle would take the vicar to watch the Spurs play Manchester United on the following Saturday and in return (playing, as it were, the away match) would attend Holy Communion, for the first time in many years, the next morning.

Both engagements turned out well. On the Saturday the Spurs won handsomely and the malt whisky in Warbottle's hip flask went down smoothly. On the Sunday the gentle simplicity of the early Communion service soothed the anguish he still felt over his wife's betrayal and the taste of Communion wine on his lips at 8.35 in the morning convinced him that God didn't object to a chap taking a drink or two.

After that the vicar went to soccer matches and Warbottle went to church quite regularly. Warbottle's consumption of alcohol increased steadily, too, although following one or two unsatisfactory, casual encounters he quite gave up sex. He found that in the middle of the act he kept thinking of his wife and the bank manager. It destroyed his concentration completely.

Thus matters continued for some time, with Warbottle leading a hard-drinking, celibate and vaguely religious life until, in the same week, he learned that his (now divorced and remarried) wife was pregnant and that the vicar was going to the West Country to become a rural dean. Both revelations disturbed him profoundly. The fact that another man had succeeded in impregnating his wife where he himself had failed gave him an even deeper repugnance for sex and the replacement of the vicar by a man who had no interest whatsoever in soccer quite put him off early Communion.

There followed several unhappy months during which Warbottle's alcohol consumption advanced alarmingly, partly because he no longer enjoyed the comforting presence of the man of God and partly because his work, as the producer of a series of witless and inane light entertainment programmes, was deeply unsatisfying.

And then, the morning after a breathtakingly appalling performance by the comedian of no discernible talent around whom the light entertainment programme was tailored, Warbottle received two important letters. The first, from his ex-wife and presumably sent with intent to wound, announced the birth of her son and enclosed a photograph to prove it. The second, from the rural dean, urged him not to abandon the church.

It was, therefore, in a state of some mental turmoil (not much ameliorated by a hangover) that Warbottle turned up at the Nat-Met offices to learn that a vacancy had occurred for a producer in the religious affairs department. One way and another it occurred to him that here was the hand of God. He applied for the post and, being the only applicant, was immediately given it.

At first he had hoped that he might be allowed to make something of the job but it quickly became clear that this was not to be. Nat-Met had a religious affairs department only because its franchise demanded that it have one. Consequently Warbottle found that he had little to do except arrange for a weekly five-minute sermon to be broadcast late on Sunday night. This took about half a day each week and the rest of the time was his own. He spent most of that time drinking.

Cocooned on the one hand by the Bible and on the other by John Barleycorn he had found this a not entirely unacceptable way of life. But this week he had been thrust out into the world again to make a documentary not, as was originally planned, about an heroic bishop in Burnley but about a sinful movie star in Hollywood.

Warbottle's self-confidence – a fragile commodity at the best of times – had cracked immediately. He was afraid of the work, afraid of Mark Payne, afraid for his own future . . .

Alone in his room in the motel on Sunset Boulevard he poured and drank another glass of wine. When he had finished there was a sour taste in his mouth, a taste that stemmed less from the drink than from his own self-disgust. He thought of William and Mark and the cut-price whore, he thought of his own ex-wife and the bank manager and he thought of himself and the advice that he had been offering to William. They were all of them – himself included – he thought, contemptible.

'Show me the way, Lord,' he murmured, 'show me the way.' And he poured himself a third glass of wine.

William and Mark drove alone to see Willard Kaines. Warbottle, Alice and the crew had gone off before lunch to take stock shots of Hollywood and find glamorous locations in which Mark could deliver his pieces to camera. To the uninitiated this might seem a simple thing to do in a place like Hollywood but it is not because one of the outstanding characteristics of Hollywood is the noise. Hollywood never closes, night or day, and it is particularly noisy whenever anybody wishes to film in the open air. It is only necessary to set up a camera, position somebody to speak to it and say 'Action' for seven police cars to sound their sirens, five helicopters to flutter low overhead, lawnmowers to start up in every garden in the neighbourhood and an impromptu motorcycle rally to be organized in the street outside.

In order to find one or two places where Mark might reasonably expect to make himself heard above the general uproar for as long as a minute at a time, Warbottle and the crew would be fully occupied for the entire afternoon.

William drove west along Sunset Boulevard towards the sea and turned right through the ornate, arched gate that signalled the entrance to Bel Air. Generally speaking the poor in Hollywood gaze in envy at the rich who live in Beverley Hills and the rich who live in Beverley Hills gaze in even greater envy at the very rich who live in Bel Air. In a community where the aristocrats are those who can trace their ancestry all the way back to their own fathers, wealth is the only significant mark of class distinction; a man's social status is determined by where he lives and what he drives and whether he goes to work in genuine Gucci sneakers. The ambitions of those who would dwell in the upper echelons of Hollywood society are fuelled by their dreams of building mock-Spanish castles in Bel Air.

On a Saturday afternoon, just as on any other afternoon, Bel Air was as quiet as any place in Hollywood could ever hope to be. The lawn-mowers and the sprinklers were going, of course, and the occasional patrol car roamed the streets and the security helicopter hovered overhead, watching out for any suspicious movement – such as, for example, somebody who was walking. In Bel Air no respectable person ever walks; walking is frowned upon, for anyone who is reduced to using his feet to propel himself from point A to point B must be a poor man and a poor man on a rich estate is clearly up to no good. Anyone caught walking in Bel Air by one of the patrol cars is immediately invited to lean across the bonnet of said car with his feet wide apart while he is frisked for guns, burglary equipment or drugs or, very possibly, all three. The residents of Bel Air and their security guards don't believe in taking any chances.

The narrow streets wound slowly upwards through the mock-Spanish castles and the mock-Tudor mansions nestling on their small estates among their swimming pools and tennis courts and expensively tended lawns and their gardens of lush green shrubs and vivid semi-tropical flowers. With the exception of a Mexican gardener or two, nobody was to be seen. No child played and no householder pottered on the front lawns and no human voice was heard. In a climate designed by God for outdoor living the residents of Bel Air preferred to stay indoors, possibly counting their assets. They were, in any case, far too rich to be dictated to by God.

Willard Kaines lived in the most desirable part of the estate, high up on the top of a hill, in one of the mock-Tudor mansions. His house had been built back in the early thirties before land in Hollywood became as scarce and expensive as it is now and it was surrounded by more than an acre of grounds.

'This companion,' Mark said, as they went slowly up the winding drive. 'Good-looking woman, is she?'

'Not bad,' said William. 'You'll see for yourself in a minute.'

They did not, however, see her immediately for the door was opened to them by an elderly black butler, who 'Yassuh-ed' and 'Nosuh-ed' as if he'd never heard of Civil Rights, and led them into a large sitting-room heavily furnished with great, leather-covered Victorian armchairs and settees and chaises-longues, all of which looked fairly incongruous when set against the wide french windows that led onto a patio and thence to a heart-shaped pool. William found the room, as he had on his previous visit, depressing, but Mark appeared to be enchanted by it.

'Amazing,' he said, gazing round at the Victorian

table and the Victorian desk and the Victorian prints and oil paintings on the dark Victorian walls. 'It's like the last outpost of empire. I wonder, William, I wonder if I could do my summing-up-career piece to camera in this room? Just there – in that chair, with the Landseer beside me and the swimming pool just visible in the background.'

'I was rather thinking,' William said, 'that we could put the old boy in that chair for the interview.'

'What? Good Lord, no. It's the kind of setting I need. We can find something else for him. Perfect for me, that chair in that spot – properly lit, of course, assuming our esteemed cameraman knows the slightest thing about lighting. Sitting there, casual, relaxed . . . '

'Sincere,' William murmured.

'Sincere, of course, sitting there I could do quite a long piece. Yes, quite a long piece, I think . . . ' He snapped his fingers a couple of times. 'It's all coming to me, William. Amazing, you know, the creative process of the subconscious mind. I think we'll start the programme with my summing-up of the life – the piece I did the other day – and then we'll build up to my summing-up of the career as the kind of climax, the highlight, in that chair . . . '

A voice from the door said, 'Hi,' and a tall, lean, dark-haired young woman came towards them. 'Hi . . . er, William, isn't it?'

'William it is,' said William, speaking up candidly. 'And this is Mark Payne.'

'Hi, Mark. I'm Tracy-Lou.' She shook hands with them both, her eyes bright and nervous in a thin, high-cheekboned face that somehow managed to look welcoming and vaguely dissatisfied at the same time.

Her breath smelt of wine and peppermints and her hands were never quite still, as though they led some busy, independent existence of their own. William had not been quite fair to her when he had described her as 'not bad'; she was, in fact, very pretty but she was too volatile for his taste. If asked his advice on the best way to handle her he would have said, 'Light blue touchpaper and retire swiftly.' None of his reservations, however, appeared to have communicated themselves to Mark who shook, and held onto, her hand with a frank and hungry appreciation which she, in turn, seemed to appreciate.

She offered them tea, presumably because they were English, which they, certainly because they were English, accepted and when the business of summoning the butler and placing their order had been dealt with, she bade them sit down and said, 'Gee, I feel awful bad about this but I guess I'd better give you the heavy news right out. I'm afraid you won't be able to see Mr Kaines this afternoon. He's not too well.'

'Oh dear,' Mark said. 'Nothing serious, I trust.'

'Heart,' she said, with a bright smile. 'He gets these flutters. Well, he's pretty old now.' She added, rather tonelessly, 'Bless him. Of course, the afternoon's always his worst time.'

'But you said the afternoon was his best time,' William said. 'That's why we're here now.'

'Did I say that?' Her long, slender fingers twisted nervously in her lap. 'I don't think I did. I mean, I don't remember . . . I don't think I can have said that.'

'You did,' William said insistently. 'You said . . . '

Mark, frowning darkly and sincerely, stopped him with an upraised hand. 'William, if Tracy-Lou says she didn't say that then I think we can rest assured that the error is yours. As usual,' he added, somewhat bitterly. 'And certainly I shall not allow you to distress her further by arguing with her. I'm quite sure, Mr Kaines being ill, she has enough problems already.' He directed a sympathetic gaze at Tracy-Lou and was rewarded with a tremulous smile and a quick flutter of long, curling – and probably false – eyelashes.

'You're very kind,' she said, adding softly, 'Mark.' Then, after a sigh that caused her small but by no means negligible breasts to strain briefly against her grey silk shirt – a movement that was noted and quietly approved by both men – she said. 'It's been quite a tough day, I must admit. The Old Man – Mr Kaines, that is – can be a little difficult when he's not well. And he's not well quite a lot of the time now . . . Would either of you like a drink?'

'No thank you, my dear,' Mark said. 'We have the tea coming.'

'Oh yeah. The tea,' She squeezed her hands tightly together and fell silent, staring down at the thick Victorian carpet.

'About tomorrow,' William said. 'Will he be all right? For the interview, I mean? And what would be the best time?'

'You're sure you don't want a drink?'

'Quite sure, thank you,' said Mark, smiling his thanks for her thoughtfulness. There was another brief silence.

'Tomorrow,' William said. 'Will he be all right tomorrow, do you think?'

'What? Oh yeah, he should be all right tomorrow. Ask me, the old ba . . . Yeah, he should be okay tomorrow.'

'What time then?'

'Oh, I guess . . . You'll want to talk to him first, right?' Before the interview? Right. I guess, the best thing is you two come here about 7.30 a.m. for breakfast . . . '

'Do you mean 7.30 a.m.?' Mark, said, appalled. He knew there was such an hour as 7.30 a.m.; indeed, on several occasions he had gone home to bed at it. But it was not an hour at which he would ever contemplate rising and eating breakfast.

'When else do you eat breakfast – 7.30 at night?' As if to compensate for the sharpness of her tone she gave him another quick smile and another flutter of the eyelashes. 'Then if your crew comes at, like, eight, 8.15 we can do

154

the interview right away. He'll be at his best then. Mornings are his best time.'

The butler arrived with the tea and when he had set it down and withdrawn and Tracy-Lou was playing mother, though not as if she were used to the role, Mark said, 'Have you been with Mr Kaines long?'

'About a year, eighteen months. He's a . . . ' She thought for a moment. 'He's a darling.'

'And, er, what exactly do you do for him?'

William raised his eyes to the ceiling. What, he wondered, did Mark suppose young women like this did for rich old men like that?

She paused in the act of pouring tea and gave Mark yet another smile, somewhat colder than its predecessors. 'I do a lot of things for him.'

'Of course,' Mark said. 'Secretarial work, I suppose. Er, companionship. That sort of thing.' William suddenly realized that Mark genuinely wished to believe that such were all the services Tracy-Lou performed for the ancient Thespian. He glanced sharply at his presenter and caught him gazing at the girl with sincere lust.

'It must be . . . very interesting work,' Mark said.

'Oh, it is. He's . . . such a dear. And no trouble – except when he's unwell, of course. But that's only . . . ' She paused again, the cup and saucer shaking in her hand. 'That's only most of the time. He's such a hypochon . . . he's such a martyr to all manner of complaints. Heart and chest and bowels and . . . I have to, I have to look after him like a baby and . . . He wants me with him all the time. I mean, *all* the time – like, day and night and . . . Oh but he's a darling. I love him. I'm with him here 'most every minute and he's so sweet and . . . and . . . '

'Rich,' William murmured but only to himself.

'. . . and generous and I . . . I just, I just love being with him and reading to him, and . . . and . . . doing things for him and I never go out, at least hardly ever, because he needs me so much and I never see any young people, or anybody hardly, because we never have any guests and he just likes to be with me and . . . and . . . and . . . oh, Jesus, I'm so *bored* you wouldn't believe it!' And the Crown Derby cup and the Crown Derby saucer fell into the grate and smashed and Tracy-Lou burst into tears.

Mark sprang immediately into action. With movements so fast as to deceive the eye he was beside her, kneeling, her head on his shoulder, his hand lightly stroking her hair, his lips against her ear as he murmured soft words of comfort.

'Bloody hell,' said William.

Mark looked up, frowning with sincere disapproval. 'Leave us, William,' he said.

'What do you mean – leave you? We've got to talk to her. I haven't got any background yet. For the questions. What are we going to ask the old boy tomorrow?'

'You can leave that to me. Indeed, I insist that you leave it to me. God knows, your efforts so far have been pretty disastrous. It's about time I took a hand. There, there,' he said to the sobbing Tracy-Lou who had just twined her arm round his neck and was getting lipstick marks on his collar. 'Get out, William. Go. I'll get a cab back. Just tell the others – eight o'clock, here, tomorrow. There, there, it's all right. I'm here, my dear. I'm here.' And then Tracy-Lou's delicate little earlobe disappeared between his lips.

William finished his tea and left. It wasn't particularly good tea but, as an Englishman, he felt it was his duty to finish it.

10

On the way back to the motel William stopped at the English pub where, as he had expected or anyway hoped, he found Stack, the pimp, drinking beer and eating pretzels and watching a boxing match on T.V.

William sat on the stool beside him at the bar. 'Buy you a drink, Stack?' he asked.

'What? Hey, my man! Gimme some skin.' They slapped each other's outstretched palms. It all seemed far too theatrical to William but he went through with it because he was particularly anxious to keep Stack in the good mood in which he seemed to have found him.

'Stack,' he said, as the picture on the T.V. screen faded out, to be replaced by a car commercial at the very moment when a haymaking right hook from boxer A appeared to heading directly for the chin of boxer B, 'about that offer you made me the other night.'

'Shee-it,' said Stack. 'Why the hell they put the mother-fuckin' commercial on now? They always doin' this to me, the suckers.'

'We'll find out what happened in a minute, Stack,' William said, soothingly. Deeming it politic, he stayed silent until the commercials ended and the sports pro-gramme returned. But when it did so there were two entirely different fighters in the ring and it was several minutes before the sportscaster revealed, as a sort of afterthought, that the haymaking right hand had done its work and brought a premature end to the previous bout.

'That's my man!' said Stack, whose sympathies, apparently, had been with the winner. William decided that this was the right time to return to his original theme.

'About that offer you made me the other night,' he said again.

'What offer, man?'

'You remember. you offered me one of your girls. For fifty dollars. For the night. On account of I helped you out.'

'Oh, that offer. Yeah, well,' Stack drank deeply of his beer. 'I changed my mind about that, man. I musta been high when I made you that offer, man. I can't go through with that.'

'I see. You're welshing on me, are you?'

'I'm what?'

'You're going back on the deal.'

'Right.'

William nodded. 'And they say,' he said bitterly, 'that a pimp's word is his bond.'

'They say what?'

'A pimp's word is his bond.'

Stack laughed heartily. 'Hey, man! Who been feedin' you that shit?'

'Well, that's what they say in London,' William said untruthfully. Or at least he supposed it was untruthful although, on the other hand, since he had no knowledge whatever of the moral code of pimps in London, it might even be true. It was unlikely, he was bound to concede, but it was just possible. In any event, Stack seemed impressed.

'They really say that in London, man?'

'Certainly they do. A London Pimp who went back on his word would be blackballed from his club.'

'Most of the pimps in Hollywood got black balls already,' said Stack, but it was merely an automatic response. He frowned into the pretzel bowl, his natural avarice struggling with his reluctance to appear less

158

honourable than his London counterparts. The good name of American pimps – or anyway of Hollywood pimps – hung in the balance.

'You only lent me ten bucks, man,' he said.

'I *gave* you ten bucks,' William said, pointedly. 'You never returned it. Besides, there was more at issue than a mere ten dollars. I hate to remind anyone of a favour but your attitude leaves me no alternative. I could have called the police, you know.'

Stack thought about that. 'That's true, man. You coulda blew the whistle on me and a bust is just what I don't need right now.' He ate several of the pretzels he had been frowning at. 'They really say that, huh? A pimp's word is his bond?'

'That's what they say.'

Stack shook his head. 'Those London pimps must be a buncha assholes, man. But . . . Okay, you got my marker. Which girl you want, man?'

William breathed a sigh of relief. He had been well aware that trying to hassle the powerful and vaguely menacing Stack had not necessarily been the most prudent move he had made all day but it seemed to have worked. 'Jenny. The white girl. And I want her tonight.'

'Tonight! Hey, man, you know what tonight is? Tonight Saturday. The Big One. That girl could turn a hundred tricks for me tonight.'

'Tonight,' William said, firmly. It didn't have to be tonight, of course, but now he seemed to have a slight advantage he might as well press it. 'At six o'clock.'

'Six o'clock!' Stack was almost yelping with indignation. 'That girl don't even get up till four. Man, come on, man, gimme a break! I send her to you at six and she don't even have time to turn one lousy trick for the house.'

William considered the argument. It seemed reasonable. To take the girl for the whole night from as early as six o'clock was to deprive Stack of a large slice of his legitimate income. 'Tell you what I'll do, I'll give you the fifty dollars for the night as agreed. And also I'll pay you for one trick for the house. How's that?'

Stack put his head in his hands and moaned softly. 'I don't believe this, man. I don't know why I even talkin' to you, man. Why don't I just bust you right in the mouth? Shee-it! An' I thought you was a good honky, too.'

'I am a good honky, Stack.'

'Then why you screwin' me, man? Why you rippin' me off?'

William was bold enough to pat him consolingly on the back. 'I'm not ripping you off. This is simply a deal between friends.'

Stack shook his head. 'No, it ain't, man. It's the same ol' story – a nigger works his ass off to get ahead of the game and then he gets hisself exploited by the white folks. Okay, okay. I don't wanna talk about it no more. Gimme the bread, man, and tell me where you want her.'

William counted the notes into the limp hand of the broken pimp. 'Six o'clock at my motel,' he said. 'And tell her not to dress like a hooker. I want her looking demure.'

'Lookin' what?'

'Demure. You know – like a lady.'

'Okay, I'll tell her.' He took hold of William's sleeve. 'Lissen, man, you wanna buy me a drink after all this? Or do I have to give you both my balls as a marker?'

On the plastic lawn beside the swimming pool back at the motel William bumped into Geoff Warbottle, or rather Warbottle bumped into him after bumping into several other things including two deckchairs and a palm tree.

'William! Good ol' William!' Warbottle was clutching

160

a large brown-paper bag to his chest and was very drunk indeed.

'Hello, Geoff. How's it going?'

'William, oh William, have dinner with me, William?'

'Sorry, Geoff, can't tonight. Already booked.'

'Oh, William.' Warbottle sat down heavily in the third deckchair he bumped into. 'Whassamatter with me, William? Nobody wanted to have lunch with me, nobody wants to have dinner with me. I feel like a prior, William.'

'A prior, Geoff?'

'Yes, a prior. An outcast.'

'Oh. That kind of prior.'

'Right. I asked Alice Flitton. I said, Alice, I said, have dinner with me. And you know what she said? She said, Geoff, I have a prior engagement. Not an engagement with a prior like me, but a prior engagement.' He rocked slowly back and forth in the deckchair clutching his brown-paper bag.

William said, 'I thought you were going to do something about your drinking, Geoff.'

'I am doing something about it, William. I've been doing something about it all day. Listen, listen, I said to the camera crew – all of 'em – I said to the camera crew, I said, let's all go and have dinner tonight and you know what they said? Do you know what they said, William?'

'No, Geoff. What did they say?'

Warbottle fell back in the chair, breathing heavily, his eyes closed. William waited a few moments and then, thinking the producer to be asleep, was about to tiptoe away when Warbottle sat up abruptly, his eyes gleaming. 'There's no God in this town, William. This is the most Godless town I ever saw.'

'We've been through this already, Geoff,' William said uneasily.

Warbottle nodded, several times. 'Sodom,' he said.

'Sod who, Geoff?'

'Sodom-by-the-sea. That's what this town is, William. You know what goes on here, William? In this Godless town, William? Fornication. That's what goes on. Nothing but fornication. That cameraman – old whassisname – and his assistant – the other feller – fornicators, both of 'em. Been fornicating since Day One, since the minute they arrived here. And where are they now? Do you know? I know. Fornicating, that's where they are. Couldn't come to dinner with poor old Geoff because they're fornicating.'

'Oh, I don't think so, Geoff. You misjudge them,' William said, anxiously, 'don't you think you'd better get to your room and . . .'

Warbottle waved an imperious hand, putting a stop to what he seemed to regard as William's defence of the sinful cameraman and his assistant. 'No good you speaking up for them, William. You're a nice boy, William, but it's no good you defending them. They're fornicators. And adulterers. Both married men, William. Same with the soundman and the lighting man, whatever their names are. I said to them, Soundman, I said, lighting man, I said – whatever their names are – come to dinner with me, I said. And do you know what they said, William?'

'I think I can guess,' William said, resignedly.

'You're right, William, you're absolutely right. Just as you said, William, they've gone to a brothel. They didn't admit it, but I knew. Married men, both of them. God has deserted this town, William. He's washed his hands of it. Alice Flitton's just the same.'

William was startled. 'You mean she's washed her hands of Hollywood as well?'

'No, William. No, no, no. No, no, no, William. She's fornicating, too. And with another woman. And what about Mark Payne, eh? Mark-bloody-Payne? Can you look me in the eye, William, can you look me in the eye and tell me, on your word of honour, that Mark-bloody-

Payne isn't fornicating with the rest of 'em?'

'Well,' William said. 'He wasn't when I last saw him but there's a pretty fair chance he will be later.'

'Exactly. Eggs-ackly. William, we've got to do something, William. William, you're not fornicating, are you William?'

'Not me, Geoff. I've forgotten how.' He raised Warbottle from his chair and started guiding him towards the stairs, the producer mumbling incomprehensibly to himself.

'Did I ever tell you, William,' Warbottle said, when finally they reached his room, 'that there's no God in this town? Did I ever tell you that?'

'I think you mentioned it, Geoff,' William said, unlocking the door. This was what it came to, he thought sadly; too much exposure to the religious department of Nat-Met and this was how you ended up.

'William,' Warbottle said, 'you're a good boy, William. You're no fornicator, William. Not you. Not me. The others, fornicators – all of 'em.' He staggered backwards into his room and from the paper bag clasped to his chest came a slight clinking sound as of two bottles kissing each other.

William phoned the camera crew to apprise them of the arrangements for the following morning. They were not pleased. It was unreasonable, they protested, to ask anyone to work at eight o'clock on a Sunday morning. William reminded them of the overtime they would earn. They said, Sod the overtime; this was a question of principle. William told them that Mark Payne would be reporting for duty at 7.30 and they were slightly mollified. In the end William compromised. He would tell them what, why didn't they make it 8.30? After a brief discussion, a strong case being put forward in favour of a nine o'clock start by the brothers of the camera crew, 8.30 was finally accepted.

William then called Alice Flitton. She was not pleased either. It was Larraine's night off and they were going to spend the evening at Malibu where the actress/waitress had the use of a friend's beach house, and when Alice said the evening she didn't just mean the evening. They would certainly stay over, she said, and at what ungodly hour did he, William, think that she, Alice would have to get up in order to drive herself to Bel Air by 8.30? William told her to put in an alarm call and be sure to get to the rendezvous on time. Alice informed him sulkily that he was a pig and that she jolly well wouldn't have time to pick up Geoff Warbottle, so there.

William decided not to call Geoff Warbottle. There didn't seem to be a great deal of point in it, considering the state the producer was in. Instead he phoned a taxi firm and gave them precise instructions as to the hour at which they were to collect Warbottle (early, he decided, to give the man time to arrange the various bits of himself into some semblance of a cogent whole) and the address to which he was to be delivered.

By the time he had finished that it was six o'clock and Jenny, the hooker, had arrived.

'Here I am, m'lord,' she said, dropping him a small curtsey, 'every inch the lady.' And indeed she was. She wore a classically cut navy-blue suit and a white silk shirt, high-heeled court shoes and very little make-up. 'Stack didn't say anything about the underwear but I figured that if you wanted a lady, you wanted a lady all the way down to the skin, right?'

'Right,' William said, ushering her into the room.

'On the other hand,' she said, 'if you want a lady on top and a whore underneath I got some stuff here I could change into.'

'No, no. You're splendid as you are.'

'You wanna just look at it before you really decide? It's pretty wild stuff. You might change your mind.'

'No, no. Not at all.' He scurried around the room removing papers, books and bits of clothing from the chairs and the bed.

'Okay,' she said, 'what do you want me to do?'

William glaced at his watch. 'I want you to look at television.'

She shrugged. 'Okay. Dressed or undressed? On the bed, on the floor, or where?'

'Dressed, of course,' he said, puzzled. 'And sit wherever you're most comfortable.'

'Right.' She moved an armchair in front of the T.V. set and sat down. 'And while I'm watching T.V. what are you going to be doing? Scrubbing the floor and wearing nothing but an apron, something like that?'

'Certainly not. I'll probably watch it with you for a bit. And then, if you don't mind, I'll go and shower and change.'

Another shrug. 'Well, if that's what turns you on . . . It's your big night, buster. It's your money.'

'Look, just shut up and watch the telly, will you?' He switched on the set and after a few minutes during which a succession of inevitably green people complained of the usual ailments a film came on. It was *Death on the Run*, Rex Angell's Oscar-winning movie, and fortunately it had been made in black and white so that the implacable greenness of the picture was less obtrusive than usual.

'Is this what you want me to look at?' Jenny asked.

'Yes, if you don't mind. I'd like you to watch it rather carefully, as a matter of fact.'

'Gee, I don't mind. I love old movies. I'll tell you something though – you're the weirdest john I ever had, you know that?'

'Never mind,' William said. 'Just pay attention to the picture.'

He drew up another armchair alongside hers and they watched together in companionable silence. William had never seen the film before and he was instantly impressed. It was merely another cops-and-robbers melodrama, of course, with Angell as the leading robber/gang boss/murderer but what transformed it into something far better, indeed into a genuine tragedy, was Rex's performance. In it there was an underlying note of deathly weariness that from the first reel foreshadowed his end, bullet-riddled in a gutter, and made a superb counterpoint to the snarling, tough, wise-cracking dialogue. William was not surprised that the critics and the Academy voters had mistaken this weariness, this dissolution, for true acting. He would have done so himself if Rex Angell had not told him the real cause of it.

About halfway through he showered and changed his clothes, leaving the girl so engrossed in the film that he doubted whether she even noticed his leaving or his return. And when finally, the camera drew back and then froze on a long-shot of Angell's crumpled, shattered body, she gave a deep, shuddering sigh and wiped tears from her cheeks.

'Gee, that was good,' she said. 'I mean, that was really great. I've always loved his old movies but I never saw that one before. It was fabulous, fantastic.'

'Glad you liked it, William said, 'because we're going to dinner with him right now.'

'With Rex Angell? You gotta be kidding!'

William shook his head. 'Scout's honour.'

'Wow! That's really something. He's kinda cute, isn't he? I mean, he *was* kinda cute, like back then when he made that movie. Is he still like that?'

'Give or take the hair, yes. A good bit older, of course, but pretty much the same.'

'Oh boy! I'd better go fix my face and . . .' She stopped and turned towards him. 'Oh-oh, *now* I get it. I'm not for you at all, am I?'

'No.'

'I'm for him, right?'

'Yes. Do you mind awfully? I mean, if you do, we can call the whole thing off. Really.'

'Cute.' She patted him gently on the cheek. 'Listen, why should I mind? A john's a john and I've had a helluva lot worse than him, believe me, however old he is.'

'Good. Then everyone's happy. At least, I hope everyone will be happy. Now if you want to fix your face . . .'

Ten minutes later he escorted her from the room and down to his car. Neither of them noticed the twitch of a curtain in another room on the other side of the swimming pool and neither of them noticed the out-raged, horrified, drunken face of Geoff Warbottle as he watched them go. And neither of them heard him mutter 'Fornication!' as he reached for the bourbon bottle.

William gave Jenny her briefing on the way to Rex Angell's apartment. 'The thing is,' he said, 'the most important thing is, you're not to let him know you're a hooker.'

'He doesn't like hookers, huh?'

'Well, I don't think he has anything against hookers *per se*. It's more a matter of pride with him really. He says he's never had to pay for sex in his life and he's too old to start now.'

She nodded. 'How often has he been married?'

'I've no idea. I'm not at all sure even he knows. At least four.'

'Four times married, huh? And he says he's never had to pay for sex in his life? Boy, men are such fools.'

'Well, you know what I mean. He's a romantic really. What he wants is love.'

'And he doesn't know I'm going to be there tonight?'

'No. You're a surprise for him.'

167

'I see. An unbirthday-present. Gift-wrapped.'

'Oh dear,' William said. 'I'm beginning to wonder whether this was such a good idea after all. I didn't realize it would be so . . . degrading.'

'Degrading?' she said, furiously. 'Who for, buster? For you? For him?'

'No! For you. I mean, it's a bit under the arm, isn't it, just presenting you to him, like some kind of toy.'

She relaxed. 'Forget it. It's my business. The toy business is what I'm in. I'm just a living Barbie-doll for rent. I don't mind. I make a living. So then,' she added briskly, 'let's get it all straight. I'm not a hooker, right? He'll never know I'm a hooker, I promise you. But if I'm not a hooker, what am I?'

'What do you fancy?' William said. 'A secretary? A model – no, better not be a model. A model sounds too much like a hooker. Something in public relations? An actress looking for a break? I don't think it matters what we tell him so long as we make it convincing.'

'Okay. I'll tell him I'm an actress looking for a break. What the hell, the truth never hurt.'

William glanced sharply at her. 'The truth?'

'Sure. I'm no different from anyone else in Hollywood. You think any Hollywood hooker ever arrived in Hollywood as a hooker? No way. We all arrived here as dewy-eyed hopefuls looking to bust into the movie business. Boy, I remember it well. I was gonna be this year's Jane Fonda, only it wasn't this year. It was . . . quite a long time ago now.' She fell silent, thoughtful, the bright, vivacious hooker's mask forgotten.

'It can't be that long. You're not exactly old now.'

'I'm old enough. I'm older than I look. So . . . anyway, I never did get to be any year's Jane Fonda and being a hooker was a lot better than waiting table so I became a hooker. It was easy. All hookers are actresses. Maybe all actresses are hookers, how would I know?'

They pulled up outside the apartment block and

William waited while she checked her make-up in the mirror, smoothing her hair back, adding a dab of lipstick. Then she turned to him with a sly, provocative smile. 'Do I pass?'

He nodded. 'You're fine. Just one thing though. Will you leave the hooker's underwear in the car along with the hooker's face? You know – the smile, the come-on look? I like you better without. And I think Rex will, too.'

Rex Angell, standing at the door, expansive, welcoming, natty in black slacks and white cashmere cardigan, said, 'Hey, kid, come on in . . .' He caught sight of Jenny, waiting shyly behind William and looking as dewy as any of this year's Jane Fondas. 'Hey, kid, who's this?'

William said, 'Rex, I'm terribly sorry. I should have asked you but . . . I hope you don't mind my bringing Jenny along.'

Rex surveyed Jenny with frank but wistful admiration, appreciative but regretful, remembering the days when he, too, used to arrived at somebody's house with a creature like this on his arm. 'You never told me about this one.'

'Well,' William said, 'we only met this afternoon . . .'

'This afternoon! Boy, I gotta hand it to you – you are *some* operator. Listen, come in, come in.'

He ushered them into the apartment, fussing around Jenny who, in her high heels, was at least three inches taller than he, not that Rex seemed to care or even notice. 'What is it about that kid, Jenny?' he asked. 'Why should he get so lucky? Know what I think it is? I think it's that friggin' Shirley Temple look. God knows why but the broads seem to go for it.' He went behind the bar and started mixing drinks and William said, 'Rex, if you'd just shut up a minute I want to tell you something. The reason Jenny's here is that she's a great fan of yours.'

Rex paused in the act of waving the cork of the Martini bottle over an enormous glass of gin. 'A fan of mine?' An anguished look came into his eyes and he passed his hand over his bald head. 'Jeeze, why didn't ya let me know? I woulda put the rug on!'

And then Jenny, who had been standing in the background as if genuinely shy, leading William to suppose that she was either a great loss to the acting profession or truly overcome by Rex Angell's presence, said, 'Oh, no. I'm glad you didn't put the rug on. I think rugs make men look older.'

'Yeah?' Rex said. He seemed pleased but not entirely convinced. 'On the other hand a bald head don't make you look exactly like the juvenile lead, know what I mean?'

'A bald head never did any harm to Yul Brynner or Telly Savalas.'

'You're not wrong,' Rex admitted. 'I knew both those guys when they had hair and you know what they were when they had hair? Nothing. Bald is beautiful, right?'

'Right,' she said and smiled softly, shyly, at him as he handed her a dry martini.

'Hey, kid,' Rex said to William, 'she likes me. I think she likes me!'

'No accounting for taste,' William said.

Jenny sat beside Rex Angell on the great, suede-covered, Western-style sofa. She was still smiling that soft, shy smile, the smile of a young girl; not at all the smile of a whore.

Rex spread his hands in a gesture of pretended resignation. 'Some of us got it, some of us ain't,' he said. 'Sorry, kid.'

'I wish I hadn't brought her now,' William said grumpily. He thought the evening was progressing very well indeed.

11

By eleven o'clock that night William was back, alone, in his motel room. The Mexican dinner had been superb and he had been able to give it practically undivided attention because Jenny, playing her role to perfection, had monopolized Rex Angell. William had found himself almost excluded from the conversation. On those occasions when, feeling it incumbent upon him to say something, he had tossed in the odd remark the other two had looked up blankly, as though surprised to find him there. He had stayed for coffee and brandy and then, yawning loudly, had announced that it was time to go for he had to be up early in the morning to work.

At that point Rex had begun to look anxious. It was clear that he wanted William to leave but just as clear that he was afraid Jenny would go, too. So he had said, with a curious mixture of fervour and reluctance, well, okay kid, if you must, you must . . . And William had looked at Jenny and cocked an eyebrow and said, if she was ready . . .

Jenny had delivered a quite delicious little pout of disappointment and said, gee, she was having such a good time and did they really have to leave, like *now*? Testily, William had said that he certainly must go but, of course, whether she went with him was entirely up to her. Children, Rex had said, please . . . And Jenny had said that if William was going to be so grouchy she would really rather stay, whereupon William, falling back on

171

frightfully English reserve, had said that he was certainly not about to coerce her, indeed no, and she had said that if she had to be honest she'd much rather stick around awhile and listen to some more of Rex's lovely stories . . .

Rex had taken William on one side and said, 'Look, kid, let her stay. Please? You'll be doing me a favour. I haven't had a chick like that so interested in listening to me since my peter died. I'll get her home safe, I swear it. I'll get her a cab. I'll get her an armed guard! But I'd sure appreciate it if you'd just let her stay awhile.'

And William had said, 'Oh very well, dammit,' and he had said a curt goodnight to Jenny and, with a wan smile, a warmer goodnight to Rex, who had said, 'Kid, I'm real sorry about this, honest to God,' and William had remarked that that was the way it went and had left, congratulating himself on how splendidly he had stage-managed the entire event. From now on, he thought, as he drove away, everything was in the lap of the gods or, more accurately, in the lap of Jenny and he could only hope that she lived up to the billing Stack had given her.

He put in an alarm call for seven o'clock the next morning and having ascertained that this was not one of Tina Ling's nights for reading the late news he went to bed with a book. He had read only half-a-dozen pages when sleep overcame him and he nodded off with the light still burning.

Later, thinking back on it, he was never quite sure whether it was the fact of the light being on that woke him around two o'clock in the morning or whether the noise next door would have done it anyway. In any event he became aware of a shrill cry of 'Wake up, wake up!' and he struggled towards consciousness wondering who it was that could be addressing him thus.

In a moment, though, he realized that the shrill voice was coming not, as he had supposed, from outside his door but from the next room, Mark Payne's room. Furthermore he was able to recognize it as the voice of

Tracy-Lou, Willard Kaines's companion. It thus became clear that Tracy-Lou was addressing herself not to him, William, but to Mark Payne and any doubts as to that were swiftly resolved when he heard Mark mumbling that he couldn't, he really couldn't, at least not yet, and if she would only let him have a couple of hours' sleep . . .

This was followed by much *sotto voce* murmuring and then Mark said, reluctantly, 'Oh, very well,' and then there was silence, after which Mark said, 'Oh, my God!' and then there was a fair amount of noise, some of it provided by the human voice and some by bedsprings under strain and in the midst of it all William heard Mark cry, 'Not on the face! I have to go before the cameras tomorrow!' And then there was more thumping and bumping and humping and a few shrill cries, at which William switched off the light and pulled the pillow over his head and settled down to sleep again. He slept deeply and well because the last thought that entered his mind before he dozed off was that, intentionally or not, he had made two people – Rex Angell and Mark Payne – happy that evening. At one point during the night he dreamed of himself as Santa Claus.

Just after 7 a.m., showered, shaved and dressed, William rapped on the wall between his room and Mark's and shouted: 'Coffee up! Come and get it.'

A few minutes later Mark came in, wearing dark glasses. It was difficult to understand why he was wearing dark glasses because whatever scars the previous night's exertions had left beneath his eyes they could hardly have been more startling than the scars they had left on his nose, which was red and swollen and bore quite clearly the indentations of toothmarks.

'Good God,' William said. 'Whatever happened to you?'

'What do you mean?' Mark said.

'Well, who bit you?'

'Ah, shows, does it?' Mark said gloomily. He thought for a moment. 'It was a dog. I was bitten by a dog.'

'Oh? A dog or a bitch?'

'I didn't inquire as to its gender,' Mark said haughtily. 'I was merely bending down to stroke it when it leapt up and bit me.'

'I bet it was a bitch,' William said.

'What do you mean by that?' As far as it was possible to tell, the glance that Mark was aiming at him from behind the dark glasses was a suspicious glance.

'The female of the species is more deadly than the male,' William said innocently. 'Tell you what, though, you're going to look very odd on camera today.'

'Yes, well I thought we might do without the reverses. Just let old Kaines talk, you know. My voice will be there, asking the sharp, pertinent questions. I don't necessarily have to be seen.'

'What? In the main interview? Just Kaines rabitting on, no sign of you? Come, come, Mark. We can get round it somehow. You could hold your hand over your nose or . . .'

'Be your bloody age, William,' Mark said, furiously. 'I can't do noddies like this. I'll look like bloody Karl Malden with my nose all swollen up. I'll look *worse* than Karl Malden. At least he doesn't have tooth marks on *his* nose.'

William moved in closer to examine the nasal wound. 'What sort of dog was it? I mean, it had a smashing set of choppers. Those marks are absolutely perfect. I bet it must have worn a brace when it was a puppy . . .'

'For God's sake, William, leave it alone!' Mark cried. 'I don't want to talk about it any more!'

So they drank their coffee in silence and maintained this silence till they were in William's car and on their way to Bel Air, at which point Mark said, 'Did you . . . er . . . did you hear any strange noises last night?'

'Odd you should mention that,' William said. 'I did, as a matter of fact. I heard some very weird noises. As far as I could make out there was a man and a woman and she was trying to persuade him to do something or other to her.' He laughed heartily. 'He seemed very reluctant. I'm not sure but I think she accused him of being some species of fruit or faggot.'

'She did not,' Mark said sharply. 'I mean . . . well, what I mean is I think I heard those voices, too. I didn't hear anything about fruits or faggot but the rest of what you said sounds familiar.'

'Where do you suppose the voices were coming from?'

'Oh, the floor above ours,' Mark said firmly. 'No doubt about that. They were virtually over my head.'

'Really. Isn't that strange? I thought they were a *lot* closer.'

William had his eyes carefully on the road ahead but he still had the strong feeling that the look Mark directed towards him above the swollen nose and behind the dark glasses was a look that was intended to kill.

'Hi,' said Tracy-Lou. 'You're right on time.' She gave William a perfunctory nod, stared sharply at Mark and began to giggle. 'What happened to your nose?'

'It's not worth talking about,' Mark said coldly.

'No?' She gave him a sly look. 'Well, I'm surprised. I'd have thought it was *well* worth talking about.' She giggled again. 'Tiger,' she murmured softly.

'Tiger!' William said.

Mark looked at William and the rest of his face had turned the same angry red as his nose. 'You'll forget you heard that.'

'Heard what, Tig . . . er, Mark?'

Tracy-Lou led them into the kitchen-cum-breakfast room. It was still pretty Victorian, though less Victorian than the sitting-room they had been in the previous day.

Bright sunlight shone through the non-Victorian venetian blinds and there was coffee and toast and orange juice on the table. On Sundays, Tracy-Lou explained, the staff didn't report for duty till nine o'clock so she was going to cook the breakfast. They could have bacon and eggs, she added proudly, as though the cooking of bacon and eggs required such a degree of culinary expertise as to merit a round of applause.

William and Mark made noises which, though appreciative, fell short of ecstasy. On the wall a bell rang. Tracy-Lou said, 'That's the old boy. I'll go get him.'

From the hallway came the sound of an elevator clanking down from the floors above and in a moment Tracy-Lou reappeared pushing Willard Kaines before her in a wheelchair. As far as it was possible to judge the height of a man who was slumped in a wheelchair and covered from the waist down by a Navajo blanket, he appeared to be exceptionally tall and certainly he was exceptionally thin. Delicate blue veins stood out at his temples and on the backs of his long, gnarled hands. He had a full head of long white hair and a long white moustache to match and his skin was deathly pale. When he greeted the visitors his voice was frail and thin. Whether or not the man was a hypochondriac, William thought, he was definitely rather ill.

The introductions over, Kaines murmured something to Mark who said, 'Pardon?' and leaned forward with his ear to the old man's mouth to catch the repetition. 'Oh yes,' he said, straightening up, 'ha, ha.' He wore the ghastly, forced grin of one who has failed to comprehend or even to hear one syllable of what has been said to him.

Willard Kaines murmured something else. 'Sorry?' Mark said and leaned forward again. When he straightened up once more, saying, 'Quite so. Quite so indeed, sir,' his grin was strained to the point of idiocy.

'Now you just sit over here, darlin',' said Tracy-Lou, wheeling Kaines to a position by the window. He seemed quite contented, sitting there, nodding at the garden. Mark grabbed hold of William's sleeve.

'William,' he whispered urgently, 'what are we going to do? I can't understand a bloody word he says. I can't even hear what he says. Dear Lord, what kind of an interview are we going to get?'

'Perhaps he'll be better on camera,' William said. 'The old warhorse coming to life when the trumpet sounds.'

'Do you really believe that?'

'I dunno.'

'Oh, God,' Mark said. 'This is a nightmare. This whole trip is a nightmare. Why on earth did I ever let myself get talked into it? This is going to be the worst documentary ever made.'

'Perhaps we can ask him to shout?'

'Shout? What do you mean, shout? He's hardly got the strength to whisper. Oh God, I think he wants to talk to me again. Shall I ignore him?'

'Better not,' William said. 'At least it'll give you practice in trying to understand him.'

'What's the bloody good of that,' Mark said, 'if I'm the only person in the world who can?'

Reluctantly he joined Kaines by the window and knelt beside him, his ear virtually pressed to the old man's lips, his grin converting itself into a kind of rictus. Tracy-Lou, frying bacon at the kitchen range, beckoned to William. 'Aren't we lucky?' she said. 'The old boy's in such good form today.'

'This is good form, is it?'

'Oh yeah. Some days he can hardly speak at all. But this morning he's so clear, so vigorous, so . . . so articulate. I bet you're going to get one hell of an interview.'

From his kneeling position by the wheelchair Mark Payne, who had taken off his glasses the better presumably to hear what Kaines was saying, looked up at them, wild-eyed, scarlet-nosed. From his lips came a peal of hysterical, uncomprehending laughter.

'Isn't that cute?' said Tracy-Lou. 'They're getting along so well. I know this morning's going to be just beautiful. Okay, you guys,' bestowing a maternal smile on the nodding Kaines and the madly grinning Payne, 'come and eat. You wanna wheel Willard over here, Mark honey?'

Mark honey got up and pushed the wheelchair viciously towards the table.

12

Geoff Warbottle awoke that morning to find a fat man in a toupee performing miracles on T.V. How long he had been performing miracles Warbottle had no idea but he seemed to have been at it for some time because he was well into his stride. He appeared to be performing about two miracles every three minutes.

Warbottle was fascinated. He was also extremely uncomfortable for he had spent the night lying on the carpet in his suit with an empty bourbon bottle for a pillow. He looked awful; his eyelids and eyeballs were the identical shade of angry red, his skin was blotchy and his cheeks, chin and upper lip were lightly covered with dirty grey stubble. His suit was crumpled and smelled of bourbon; his shirt was grubby and his tie had worked its way round his neck till it was practically under one ear. He sat up, moaning, to concentrate on the T.V., and the events of the previous night flashed before his eyes. Actually, they passed even more quickly than that because his booze-ruined recollection of them was not even enough to occupy an entire flash. Indeed, the only vivid memories he had were of William leaving his room early in the evening with a girl and Mark Payne going into his own room later in the evening with a different girl. A spasm of anger shook Warbottle's frame and the word 'Fornicators!' sprang unbidden to his lips.

He sat up, dizzy, light-headed, and his hand brushed against another bourbon bottle – a full, unopened

179

bourbon bottle – lying under the bed. He unscrewed the cap, took a deep gulp and turned his attention back to the T.V. screen. He felt weak but strangely exhilarated with no trace of hangover, probably because he was still extremely drunk.

He had been drunk since lunch-time the previous day and he had eaten nothing since lunch-time the day before that. He sucked at the bourbon bottle and watched the fat man in the toupee performing miracles on T.V. On closer inspection he discerned that, along with the toupee, the fat man wore a pale-blue Crimplene suit, a sunburst tie, a benign expression and eyebrows like a pair of socks. He stood on the stage of a large auditorium with a choir, now silent, behind him, a choir of young people all dressed in white and of such gleaming beauty and cleanliness as to make the Osmonds look decadent. And towards him down the aisle of the auditorium limped a procession of very old and crippled people leaning heavily on sticks and crutches.

'Come on, praising the Lord,' the preacher cried. 'Thank God, come on. Here they come, here they come, praising the Lord. This is a parade, this is a parade of people being healed and praising the Lord. Thank God, come on . . .' He had a dramatic, declamatory style and a Midwest twang and the benign expression never moved from his face.

The first cripple reached him and paused, panting. The preacher turned away, his face and arms uplifted in prayer. 'Oh Lord,' he said, 'oh Lord, forgive these people of their sins. Cast out their sins, dear Lord, cast out their drinking, cast out their smoking, cast out their fornicating . . .'

'Fornicating!' Warbottle murmured, his eyes gleaming.

'. . . Cast out all these things, dear Lord.' The preacher beamed upwards towards heaven. It was as though God was some kind of superior Tooth Fairy and if all these people would only lay their sins beneath their pillows at night He would take them away and leave something preferable in their place.

'Fornicating!' Warbottle said, nodding.

'Okay, sir,' the preacher was saying to the First Cripple. 'Okay, sir, take a miracle. Here it comes now. Take a miracle. In the name of Jesus, in the name of Jesus, in the name of Jee-zers, cast aside your crutches and walk! Come on, sir, come on. Leave your crutches and start walking. Come one, praising God, come on. That's it, stand up. Come on, throw away the crutches . . .' The First Cripple took a tentative step and stumbled. The crutches fell from under his arms; he lurched forward another pace unaided and the preacher caught him. 'Come on, sir, praising the Lord, Come on.' With the preacher's arm around his shoulders, the cripple shuffled another three paces forward. You see? You see? cried the preacher. 'This man threw away his crutches and walked. It's a miracle!'

'It's a miracle!' cried the congregation in the dimness of the auditorium.

'It's a miracle!' cried Warbottle, waving his bourbon bottle. He was extremely impressed. He took another drink and by the time he returned his gaze to the screen the First Cripple had gone, he knew not where or how, and the preacher had turned his attention to another bent and twisted old man leaning on a stick and complaining of some ailment whose nature Warbottle did not catch.

'It's in your kidneys,' the preacher was saying, his eyes closed, his hands upraised. 'I have it in the vision. I have it, I see it, I see a mass of black in the vision. It's in the kidneys all right, sir. Okay, take a miracle, sir. Lay your hands on mine. Oh Lord, dear Lord, God Almighty, heal! Heal! Heal! Hee-yall! I have it in the vision. Heee-all, hee-yall, heeeee-all!'

He opened his eyes and beamed at the bewildered old man with the stick. 'Okay, sir, start moving, do anything you want to do.' The old man swayed precariously on his stick. 'Something's happening to you, isn't it? Something's happening to you, sir!' The audience applauded wildly.

'Okay now, praising the Lord, pick 'em up, put 'em down. That's it, sir. You can walk, sir, you can walk! Isn't God beautiful? Isn't he beautiful?' The old man swayed from side to side. 'That's right, sir, try 'em out.' The preacher turned to the congregation. 'This man, this man, this man got right out of his wheelchair and walked right up here, praising the Lord.' More frantic applause. 'Okay, sir, put out your hand, decide this is it, decide this is the end of being rolled in a wheelchair, this is the end of the stick and the crutches.' He put his palm against the wavering, outstretched palm of the swaying old man. 'Now take that power from your hand and put it to your body, any where you want to, anywhere you want to. This is it – any where you want to. Yeh-yah! In the name of Jeezerz!'

Warbottle experienced a marvellous feeling of exultation. He had been wrong, he had been wrong, he thought in the repetitive style of the preacher. God was alive and well and living in Hollywood, after all. God was alive and this fat man with the toupee and the Crimplene suit and the eyebrows like a pair of socks, this unlikely-looking man, was His messenger. The discovery was so overwhelming that he felt the need of another swig of bourbon to calm himself.

On the T.V. screen the preacher, having apparently cured every cripple in sight, had now turned his attention to lesser complaints. A succession of people, the poor and the old of every colour, came before him to be purged of their addictions. To each of them the approach was the same.

'Okay, sir, are you saved? And you drink, right? And you smoke, of course. Okay, get 'em out.' Packets of cigarettes were sheepishly handed over and tossed to one side. 'No more smoking, sir. This is the end of smoking, right? Right.' And then the preacher sprang suddenly at his supplicants and smote them each a terrible blow on the forehead with the heel of his hand, while crying, 'Out, foul spirits called alcohol and tobacco!' And the supplicants reeled backwards, half-stunned by the unexpected assault, and when the preacher said, 'You're never going to smoke again, are you?' they mumbled something that was presumably an affirmative and the preacher cried, 'It's a miracle!' and the congregation cried, 'It's a miracle!' and Geoff Warbottle cried, 'It's a miracle!' and because, during the many seconds they were up on the stage, none of the supplicants even so much as reached for a hip flask or a cigarette, Warbottle truly believed it was a miracle.

He was more excited, more uplifted than he had ever been in his life. Through the window a bright light from the east suffused his room. Scoffers and unbelievers would have said it came from the sun, which had just moved round to the right position to shine onto the motel but Warbottle knew it came directly from God. He knew, he positively knew, that he had been Chosen.

And now the preacher, whose gifts, whose capacity for miracles knew no bounds, was curing people of deafness. His method was very similar to the one he used for curing people of smoking and drinking and it was equally effective. He would stick his finger violently into the ear of the sufferer and then pull it out just as violently and with a loud popping sound, while crying, 'Out, out, foul spirit called deafness!' And Warbottle cried with him, 'Out foul spirit called deafness!'

In fifteen minutes twelve deaf people were cured and Warbottle knew they had been cured because as soon as the foul spirit called deafness had been evicted the preacher would gaze closely into the sufferer's eyes and shout, 'You hear me now, don't you, sir? You hear me now!' And the sufferer, instantly cured, would nod and rub his ear and the preacher and the congregation and Warbottle all cried, 'It's a miracle!'

Once, when a formerly deaf person had been sent back with stinging ears to his seat, the preacher raised his hands and said in a loud voice, 'Come in, Jee-zers!' as if Jesus was himself slightly hard of hearing and was waiting outside the door to be cured in his turn.

'Come in, Jesus!' echoed Warbottle fervently. And the door opened and Jesus came into the room.

Warbottle recognized him at once. He was a young man of slender build and medium height and he had long, dark hair and a long, dark beard and moustache and burning eyes. Warbottle knew beyond doubt that this was Jesus. Of course, if such a suggestion had been put to him directly the newcomer himself would have denied it. He would have insisted staunchly that he was a taxi driver, the one ordered the previous night on Warbottle's behalf by William, and if questioned about the burning eyes he would have said they were due to the fact that he had been on duty since midnight already and, boy, was he bushed.

But Warbottle saw no need to question him because the light, the light from the east shining through the window, fell full on the pale, olive face and the hair and the beard and the burning eyes and Warbottle knew who he was.

'Jesus!' Warbottle breathed.

'What? Oh. Hey, I'm sorry to startle you, man, but . . .' the newcomer looked pointedly at his watch. 'It's time.'

'Time?'

'Yeah. Time to go, man. You ready?'

'Ready?' Warbottle gazed at him in awe. 'Oh, yes. Yes, I'm ready. Lead and I will follow.'

Oh my God, thought the taxi driver. Why does it always have to happen to me? Why do I always have to get the drunks, even before eight o'clock in the morning, for Chrissakes? 'Okay then, let's go.' He turned and walked away, along the passage and down the stairs to the parking lot at the side of the motel and Warbottle lurched after him, clutching the half-empty bourbon bottle. On the television set, unheeded, one of the preacher's young, beautiful, shiningly clean acolytes was saying '. . . . send in your tithes and offerings. The Reverend needs your help. He cannot do this great work alone. Everything you send in is used entirely to save souls and you will share in the reward for all the souls that the Reverend saves. Send in your tithes and offerings . . .'

'Wait,' Warbottle said. 'Wait. What . . . shall I call you?'

'What? Call me?' The taxi driver shrugged. 'Hell, I don't know. I don't even care what you call me, man. We're not gonna be together that long.'

Not long, Warbottle thought. Not long. So this . . . he hardly knew what word to use . . . this Experience, this Visitation, was only to be brief. He must listen carefully to what was said to him. 'Please, I'd like to know. What shall I call you?'

The taxi driver sighed. He needed his bacon and eggs, he needed his bed; he didn't need this drunk. 'Okay, if you insist. Call me Claud, why not?' Well, why not, he thought; it was his name after all.

'Lord,' Warbottle whispered to himself. Of course. What else should He be called but 'Lord'?

'Yes, Lord,' he said. 'Lead on.' The taxi driver led him to a battered Ford Sedan with a 'Taxi' sign on top. Warbottle was rather surprised. He had half expected an ass, or perhaps two asses, one for each of them. But after all, he reminded himself, this was Hollywood in the penultimate decade of the twentieth century; it was un-reasonable to expect Christ to visit this modern Sodom on an ass. And after all, a battered Ford taxi was probably the latterday equivalent.

185

'Get in,' said the taxi driver and Warbottle, stooping, half fell onto the back seat. The car started up with an unhealthy grating sound and lurched out onto Sunset Strip and up the hill past the Hamburger Hamlet to where Sunset Boulevard widened into two carriageways with a grassy intersection between them and trees and well-kept lawns on either side. The shining light from the east came in through the back window and lit up both Warbottle and the driver.

'Where are you taking me, Lord?' Warbottle asked.

'Don't you know?'

'No.'

'You're going to work,' the taxi driver said. He knew that because it had been on the instructions he was given. Something to do with T.V. What the hell, wasn't everything in this town? Movies or T.V. or the record business.

'What work?' Warbottle asked.

The taxi driver laughed and shook his head. Boy, he'd carried some drunks in his time but these Limeys were the worst kind. Once they got a sniff of the sauce they never seemed to stop. This one had obviously been working at it all night. 'You'll know when you get there,' he said.

Warbottle was mystified. He took a gulp of bourbon to clear his mind and spilt a little from the bottle as the cab suddenly turned right through some arches – heavenly arches they seemed to Warbottle. 'Are you quite sure I'll know, Lord? he asked.

'Yeah, yeah, you'll know.' The taxi driver thought maybe he wouldn't have bacon and eggs after all. Maybe he'd have a stack of pancakes with butter and syrup and about a gallon of coffee.

In the back seat Warbottle sat shaking and anxious. He had been Chosen; there was no doubt about that – he had truly been Chosen. But for what? He wished, and hoped the wish was not blasphemous, that the Lord could be just a little more explicit. Of course, he knew that traditionally Christ spoke in parables but did He have to speak in riddles? Warbottle wondered desperately what it was that he must do.

The car drew up in a quiet, expensive-looking street. There were other cars parked in the driveways of the houses but there was no living thing in sight. 'This is it, man,' the taxi driver said. 'That'll be . . .' he glanced in the mirror at the crumpled, bleary figure on the back seat and wondered how much he could take him for. 'That'll be twenty bucks.'

'Twenty bucks?' Warbottle said. He had never before heard of Jesus taking twenty bucks off anybody.

'Yeah,' the taxi driver said. He watched as Warbottle fumbled obediently for his wallet and extracted a twenty-dollar bill. Dammit, the taxi driver thought, I coulda asked for more. 'And how's about five for the tip?'

'Five . . . Oh yes, Lord. Of course.' Warbottle produced a five and handed both bills across to the driver. It must be just another sign of twentieth-century wickedness, he thought, if even Christ couldn't pursue his Ministry in a capitalist society like America without a plentiful supply of dollars.

He got out of the cab and stood swaying on the narrow sidewalk. Before him stood a pair of wrought-iron gates and beyond them a long driveway and at the end of that a large, opulent house. The front door of the house was open.

'Is this the place?' he asked.

'Yep, this is the place, man.'

'But . . . but what do I do now?'

'You'll know once you get inside,' said the taxi driver, though privately, and considering the state of the man, he doubted it. 'Bye, now. Have a nice day.' And tucking his ill-gotten twenty-five dollars into his shirt pocket he drove off rapidly.

Warbottle pushed open the wrought-iron gates and

187

started off up the drive. He was still exultant but equally puzzled. Where was he? Why was he here? He had never seen this place before in his life. What was it the Lord wanted of him? He was still pondering such questions and had nearly reached the house when, from within, he heard a woman's laugh and in a flash he remembered the miracle-worker's prayer and he knew what he had to do.

'Fornicators!' he cried and plunged into the house.

13

At the moment when Geoff Warbottle, led unerringly to his destination by the evil, Siren sound of the fornicating woman's laughter, burst into the kitchen, the occupants of the room consisted of William, Willard Kaines and Tracy-Lou. A few moments earlier Mark Payne had escaped thankfully to the lavatory.

For him breakfast had been more of a penance than a meal. To begin with, the food itself had been appalling. Though he had asked for only one egg and that over-easy, Tracy-Lou had insisted on giving him three, sunny-side up, and the upsides had been half raw. She had watched with a lover's tenderness as he forced down every disgusting forkful. And on top of that she had placed him alongside Willard Kaines, who had whispered incomprehensibly at him throughout the entire meal. His cheeks ached from smiling, his neck from nodding, his stomach from the barely cooked eggs. Nor was that the end of his tribulations for his jacket was stained with yet more egg that had dribbled from the lips of his aged neighbour. That Kaines had dribbled onto Mark's jacket and not his own was due to the fact that Tracy-Lou had been feeding the old man with a tea-spoon and her timing was not in sync. with his. Each time she thrust more egg at him Kaines turned towards Mark to impart another piece of indecipherable information, with the result that the egg fell from his open mouth onto the imitation Yves St Laurent safari suit.

'Ha, ha, yes indeed, sir,' Mark said, dismally, as a fourth blob of yolk landed on his lapel.

'You're getting on awfully well with Mr Kaines, Mark,' William said, encouragingly. He was quite enjoying his breakfast, plain though it was. Having seen what Tracy-Lou dished up for Mark he had wisely cancelled his order for more of the same and settled instead for toast, marmalade and coffee. And since, given the electric aids of a toaster and a percolator, there was little that even Tracy-Lou could do to spoil toast and coffee, neither was at all bad.

'Yes,' Tracy-Lou said. 'Gee, I'm getting so excited about the interview, aren't you, honey?' She put her arms round Willard Kaines's neck and hugged him gently. Mark glared at both of them and then at William. 'William,' he said, 'a word with you.' He stalked to the far corner of the wide room and William followed him.

'This is impossible,' Mark said, in a low, urgent voice. 'I mean, it's just impossible. I can't interview this old fool. It'll be pointless.'

'You still can't understand him?'

'Understand him? I don't even know what language he's speaking! Dear God, what are we going to do?'

William shook his head. 'I really don't know. The crew will be here in about fifteen minutes. We'll have to go through with it. We can't just cancel everything now. The old boy would be so hurt . . . '

'Hurt!' Mark cried. 'Hurt? What does he know about hurt? I'm the one who's going to suffer. I . . . '

'More coffee, boys?' Tracy-Lou called from beside the percolator.

'No,' Mark said. 'No, thank you. I don't . . . ' To William he muttered, 'I'm going to the loo. I've got to get away and think.' He left the room, frowning in a desperate sort of way, and William sat down again at the breakfast table. Tracy-Lou was singing softly as she made more coffee and Willard Kaines was staring out of the window and nodding to himself. William studied him closely. It was impossible to believe that this skinny, weak old man whose body and limbs appeared to have been constructed entirely out of pipe-cleaners could be a murderer, a wife-killer. And yet Ida Kaines had been so certain about it, had made the accusation so calmly, so matter-of-factly, had signed her statement so unhesitatingly . . .

'Mark looks upset,' Tracy-Lou said, bearing coffee to William.

'Yes, well, I think he feels a bit off-colour,' William said, guilelessly. 'It appears he was bitten by a dog last night,'

'Bitten by a do . . . ! Is that what he told you? He was bitten by a dog?' It was at this point that Tracy-Lou uttered the joyous fornicating woman's laugh that had revealed to Geoff Warbottle what it was he must do.

'Bitten by a dog!' she said. 'Oh my dear, that is the funniest thing . . . ' And then she had uttered a second laugh, the one that led Warbottle from the front door to the kitchen and now caused him to reel ferociously into the room, waving his bourbon bottle and roaring, 'Fornicators!' in a loud and terrible voice.

At the sight of this grubby, drunken apparition Tracy-Lou emitted a loud scream and William jumped up from his chair, saying, 'Oh, my God! Geoff! Oh, my God!'

The scene upon which he had stumbled, or more properly lurched, was even worse than Warbottle had expected – the woman screaming, William leaping up, both obviously ridden with guilt, and by the window a foul old man, no doubt the master of whatever evil, fornicating ceremonies had just been performed. The other fornicator, Payne, was not present but he was certainly somewhere about in this house of sin, recovering perhaps from a night of excessive copulation.

'Pen'leton,' Warbottle cried, staggering uncontrollably about the room, brandishing his bottle. 'I know you, Pen'leton. Fornicator! And you . . . ' he added, turning his wrath on Tracy-Lou, 'Scarlet Woman, I know you too – you're Mark Payne's whore!' The last word was uttered on one long, venomous breath and Tracy-Lou screamed again and said, 'Oh, my God! He's a psycho! We got a psycho in the house!'

'Geoff!' William said. 'For heaven's sake, Geoff . . . ' He moved quickly forward to restrain the wild figure but his foot caught against the leg of the chair and he tripped and fell to his knees. And now Warbottle advanced on the panic-stricken Tracy-Lou, waving his bottle around his head like a club and crying, 'Scarlet Woman! Fornicator!' and then, tying both thoughts together in one neat package, 'Fornicating Scarlet Woman!'

Quite what he planned to do once he reached the cowering, panic-stricken girl nobody knew, least of all Warbottle. All he did know was that he had been Chosen to come to this place and denounce the fornicators. Well, denounce them he had; nobody could deny that, but what next? Drive them into the street perhaps, loudly declaring their infamy for all the world to hear? It was with some such thought in mind that he lurched towards Tracy-Lou but to William, still half-crouching on the floor, it seemed that Warbottle was about to offer her physical violence, possibly even to go so far as to beat her about the head with a quart of Jack Daniels, and so he launched himself in a desperate, flying tackle and caught the Chosen Messenger of God around the waist, bringing them both painfully to the floor.

The bottle flew from Warbottle's hand and smashed -against the wall, only a foot or so from the head of Willard Kaines. The old man, who had watched the scene fearfully and helplessly from his wheelchair, raised his hands to protect himself from the shower of bourbon that descended upon him and if he didn't exactly let out a piercing cry he certainly uttered the loudest sound he had made all morning.

Meanwhile, Mark Payne, who had listened with astonishment to the beginning of this uproar from a point of disadvantage – sitting on a pink, nylon-covered lavatory seat with his trousers around his ankles – had swiftly adjusted his dress and now came running to the rescue, though too late to be of any effective help. For as he entered the room Warbottle, escaping from William's clutches, was about to leave it by another door.

'Warbottle!' Mark cried.

'Fornicator!' Warbottle riposted and made his exit. Mark plunged after him but unfortunately collided with the slightly groggy William who had just risen to his feet, and by the time each had recovered his balance the front door had slammed shut and Warbottle had gone from the house.

'What . . . ' Mark said. 'What on earth . . . ?'

'He's drunk,' William said.

'Drunk? He can't be just drunk. He must be insane. You're both insane.'

'Me?' William said indignantly. 'What are you talking about?'

'I heard you. You were shouting at him. You were both shouting. You were quarrelling.'

Before William could reply to this accusation Tracy-Lou had launched herself, sobbing, into Mark's arms. 'Mark,' she said, 'oh, Mark, you saved me. That terrible man . . . he . . . Oh, Mark.' He soothed her, murmuring to her and holding her rather awkwardly away from him so that her tears wouldn't add further stains to his egg-splattered suit. 'There, there,' he said, glowering at William above her head.

'Brandy,' said Tracy-Lou. 'Oh God, I need a brandy.'

'Get her a brandy,' Mark said.

And it was while William was looking around for the brandy bottle that he discovered that Willard Kaines was dead.

The old man had, in fact, died in the act of uttering his

equivalent of a piercing cry. The events of the morning had simply been too much for his already weakened heart. The fact of visitors for breakfast and the prospect of a television interview had been excitement enough but when an unexpected lunatic had erupted into his house, accusing him of fornication and pelting him with bourbon bottles, he really couldn't stand the pace. His heart gave a final leap and promptly threw in the towel.

'He's what?' said Tracy-Lou.

'He's dead,' William said. There was no doubt about it. The old man's eyes were open and staring and his face was already the colour of death.

'Dear Lord,' Mark said. 'What are we going to do?' He and William stood side by side staring down at the corpse. Tracy-Lou went to a cupboard on the wall, brought out a brandy bottle and poured herself a stiff one. 'I know what I'm going to do,' she said. 'I'm going to call the doctor.'

William turned to her in astonishment. 'A doctor's no good. It's too late for doctors. It's even too late for a bloody heart transplant! The old boy's a goner.'

'I know that.' She collected the breakfast things from the table and put them into the dishwasher. Then from another cupboard she took a dustpan and brush and carefully swept up the remains of the broken bottle. After that she found a cloth and dabbed the bourbon from the wall. Mark and William watched her in silence. There was no sign now of the tears and near-hysteria of a few minutes ago; she looked pale, admittedly, but also composed and determined.

'What are you doing ?' Mark said.

She turned to him, exasperated. 'God, men are so useless. Look, what do you want me to do? You want me to call the cops, tell 'em what went on here? You want that kind of scandal? Can you handle that?' She put the dustpan, brush and cloth tidily back in their places and looked critically at the stain on the wall. 'Not too bad.

194

Unless you look close you can't even see it's fresh. God, this place stinks of bourbon.' She threw open the windows and then sprayed the room liberally with an aerosol can of air-freshener.

'Listen,' she said, speaking slowly as to a pair of backward children. 'I'm gonna call the doctor and I'm gonna tell him we'd just finished breakfast, Willard and me, and Willard had a sudden heart attack and I think he's dead. I may even cry a little.'

'Strewth,' William said.

'Yeah, I know. I'm a hard lady. But, look, it's not like he was cut off in his prime exactly. With his heart he could have died any time in the last ten years. Okay, so maybe throwing bottles at him didn't help a lot but do we want people to know about that? Do we?'

'No,' Mark said. 'No, we certainly don't.' He glared at William.

'I didn't throw bottles at him,' William protested.

'Hey,' said Tracy-Lou, 'fight about it someplace else, will you? Right now I want you out of here. I'll tell the doctor you called, I'll tell him I sent you away because the old guy wasn't feeling well and then I'll tell him he died. Okay? Okay. So now go.' And she ushered them to the door.

'I don't know what to say,' William said. 'I mean, you're sure you're all right?'

'I'm all right. Don't worry.' She watched from the door as they went down the steps to William's car and as they were about to get in she called, 'Mark.'

'Yes?'

'I'll be in touch, Mark.'

'Oh,' he said. 'Yes. Of course.' The prospect didn't seem to please him a great deal.

Two carloads of technicians were just approaching the wrought-iron gates when Mark and William came down

195

the drive. They all stopped and got out. 'What's going on?' said the cameraman. 'I thought we were doing an interview.'

'Not much point, is there? Mark said. 'The old fart's dead.'

'What? Dead? What do you mean, dead?'

'Just dead,' Mark said. 'I can't think how else to put it.'

'But, I mean, how is he dead? What happened?'

'He killed him,' Mark said, jerking his head bitterly towards William. 'Him and Warbottle. They gave the poor old bugger a heart attack.'

'I didn't!' William said. 'It's not true. I had nothing to do with it. I . . . '

'It's unbelievable.' Mark plunged his hands into his trouser pockets and looked blankly at the sidewalk, shaking his head and sniffing sincerely. 'I mean, you simply wouldn't credit it. They were fighting. Him and Warbottle. Fighting! I saw them. Rolling around on the carpet, they were, and throwing bottles about. God knows what they thought they were doing . . . '

'You're mad,' William said. 'You're out of your . . . '

'They had a quarrel first,' Mark continued as if he hadn't heard the interruption. 'I don't know what it was about; I was out of the room at the time. When I came back in, there was this wrestling match going on and Willard Kaines dead in his wheelchair. God, what a mess. I can hardly believe it myself.'

'Is this straight up?' asked the cameraman of William.

'Of course it's not. What happened was Geoff Warbottle came in and . . . '

'Where is old Geoff then?' said the soundman. 'I thought he'd be with you.

'God knows where he is,' Mark said. 'With any luck he's dead, too. I sincerely hope so anyway.

'I don't understand all this,' said the cameraman. 'I suppose, I mean if old Kaines is dead, I suppose it means the job's over, does it?'

Mark gave him one of his most sincere glares. 'I'm surrounded by idiots. Idiots and incompetents. And drunks. What on earth have I done to deserve this?'

Another car, a small rented Pinto, turned into the street and drew up behind the others. Alice Flitton got out. 'What's going on then?' she said.

'Don't ask,' said the cameraman. 'You won't believe it if we tell you.'

'I wonder where old Geoff's got to,' said the soundman.

'Oh,' said Alice Flitton. 'Yes, well, I was going to tell you about that. He's stretched out in the back of my car as a matter of fact.'

'Is he dead?' asked Mark, hopefully.

'I wouldn't say dead exactly but, if pushed, I might say drunk. I found him in the next street lying in the road. What on earth's going on?'

'You might as well know,' Mark said. 'Everyone else does. Warbottle has just murdered Willard Kaines.'

'What?'

Mark nodded. 'Warbottle and him.' He jerked his head in William's direction.

'Why?'

'They had a drunken brawl.'

Alice Flitton said carefully, 'They got into a drunken brawl with Willard Kaines? What kind of dreadful old man was he?'

'Never mind the details. Just take it from me.'

'Which of them bit your nose then?' she asked.

'Yes, I was wondering about that,' said the cameraman.

'It's gone a very funny colour,' said the soundman, critically. 'Wouldn't be surprised if gangrene set in.'

'Look, never mind my nose,' said Mark. He turned to William, his hand stretched out imperiously. 'Keys,' he said.

'What?'

'Give me the car keys.'

'Why? It's my car. I rented it.'

197

'Give me the keys!' The fiercely red and swollen nose shone with anger.

'Oh, all right,' William said and handed them over. Mark snatched them from him, got into the car and drove away, with neither a look nor a word for any of the group around him.

They watched him silently till the car disappeared round the corner.

'Lovely bloke,' said the soundman. 'Not so much as a goodbye, kiss my arse, or anything.'

'Will somebody please tell me what's going on? said Alice Flitton but nobody took any notice.

'Old Kaines really is dead, is he?' asked the cameraman.

William nodded. 'Stiff as a board by now, I should imagine.'

'What did happen then?'

'I don't want to talk about it,' William said. 'I really don't. I've had a very bad morning.'

'Not as bad as old Kaines has had,' said the lighting man, unsympathetically.

The cameraman thought for a moment. Then he said, 'Well, if old Kaines is dead and the job's off and it's all been a right cock-up anyway, you know where Mark's gone, don't you?' He looked around the assembled company as they stared back at him inquiringly. 'Well, it's obvious, isn't it? He's gone to phone Nat-Met and start spreading the blame around, that's where he's gone. And judging by what he said before he left, young William, I reckon that when the sticky and smelly hits the fan most of it's going to fall on you.'

'Oh, Lor',' said William. None of this had occurred to him before. 'What shall I do?'

'Well, if I were you, mate, I'd get back to the motel and start letting London know my side of the story pretty damn fast. Come on, hop in the car. We'll take you back.'

14

It was no use, of course. William realized that as soon as he got through to the National Metropolitan switchboard in London and asked for Charles Kaufman, the head of production, and the girl said reprovingly, 'On a Sunday? He's never in on a Sunday.' William had forgotten it was Sunday. He asked the girl if she could give him Kaufman's home number and she said, not reprovingly this time but with genuine pleasure, as if this were the kind of moment that made the whole day worthwhile, that she could not under any circumstances divulge the home telephone number of anybody in the entire organization. William pleaded with her but the pleasure in her voice deepened as her refusal to part with the information grew ever more adamant. Finally, and as a concession, she unbent so far as to say that if he, William, wanted to leave his own number she would contact the head of production and see whether he wished to call William but that was as far as she was prepared to go.

William said not to bother and hung up.

It was too late anyway and he had become aware of that in the last few seconds of his argument with the switchboard girl for during that time he had heard, through the partition wall, Mark's strong, confident voice speaking on the telephone. It was the phrase, ' . . . extremely grave news, Charles,' that brought the realization that he, William, had never been in with a fighting chance in the first place. Mark wouldn't need to go badgering switchboard girls for people's home numbers; he would already be privy to such things.

William pressed his ear against the partition wall and listened. He couldn't hear everything that was said but he heard enough. Snatches of Mark's end of the conversation came through to him, the occasional word, the occasional phrase, the occasional sentence . . . 'abortive mission, I fear . . . ' and ' . . . Pendleton's fault entirely . . . ' and 'quite unreliable' and ' . . . outrageous behaviour' and ' . . . let camels loose on film sets. Yes, camels . . .' and ' . . . Warbottle equally at fault . . . ' and ' . . . drunk all the time . . . ' and 'today was the last straw' . . . and then disconnected words like fighting, bottles, quarrelling and dead. And finally, and this time very clearly and with a note of deep satisfaction, 'Right, Charles. Yes. I'll tell him. Sorry about this, Charles. No, certainly not my fault. Right. Goodbye, Charles.' He heard Mark put the phone down and moved to an armchair and waited.

A minute later there was a knock on the door and Mark, without waiting for a response, entered the room. He had a glass of wine in one hand and he snapped the fingers of the other to demonstrate all the pent-up creative energy within him while he bestowed upon William a frown of sincere disapproval.

'Do you know when your contract expires?' he asked.

'Yes,' William said. 'In a month's time.'

'Well, that's precisely how long you have to find yourself another job. I have it on the highest authority. And if you don't believe me, I suggest you phone Charles Kaufman tomorrow. Of course, if you wished to confirm this news immediately I suppose I could let you have his home number but I don't really think he'd want to be disturbed on a Sunday. Not by you.'

'I'll take your word for it, Mark,' William said. 'All of it.'

'Oh,' Mark said. He looked disappointed as if he'd expected something else, something more spirited, or more emotional. Cries of horror and despair perhaps or pleas for forgiveness and help. 'I've given Charles a detailed report of what has happened on this nightmare trip and I shall post him an even fuller, more detailed report tomorrow. I hold you entirely responsible for the whole disastrous business and what I want to tell you now is . . .'

William got up. 'Don't tell me, Mark,' he said. 'Just piss off.'

'Wha . . . ? Well, really!' And Mark went out, slamming the door shut. From outside in the corridor he called, 'You know what this means, don't you? You're finished in television. Absolutely finished. When the word gets round, and I'll make damn sure it does get round, nobody – not even the bloody B.B.C – will give you a job!' And then he went into his own room and slammed that door, too.

William thought it over. He was quite sure Mark was right. Mark had access to the right ears; his version of recent events was the one that would be believed, while he, William, would probably go down in television folk-lore as the lunatic who introduced camels into a bed-room scene on a film set and gave fatal heart attacks to interviewees. So now he had a month, or more precisely a month and a couple of days, to work out a new future for himself. But what kind of future? A shamefaced shuffle back to Fleet Street? Unlikely. In Fleet Street they were trying to get rid of people, not take on more. An advertising job then? Something in publicity? Neither prospect held any appeal at all but there seemed to be nothing else. He wasn't qualified for anything else.

He sighed and got up and went out and found a cab and set off early for brunch with Rex Angell.

*

201

Stack, the pimp, opened the door and for a moment William thought he must have come to the wrong address. 'Stack?' he said.

'Hey, my man, come on in.' Stack was dressed, *en fête*, in a purple Hawaiian shirt with a sort of hibiscus pattern, pink slacks and white loafers. He had a large glass of Scotch in his hand.

'What are you doing here?' William said but before the question could be answered Rex Angell came hurtling like a small, bald missile from the Western-style living-room to kiss him warmly on both cheeks. Behind him, in the doorway, Jenny, the hooker, smiled demurely.

'Congratulate me, kid,' Angell cried. 'My peter's come back from the dead.'

'What?'

'My peter. It's alive and well and living in my pants. And I got you to thank, kid. You and my future bride.'

'Your what?'

'My bride, my future bride. Jesus, wassa matter with you, kid, you hungover or something? You understand English, don't you? You know what a friggin' bride is?'

'Yes, but . . . '

'Well, give her a kiss then, goddammit.' He beckoned and Jenny came forward, smiling shyly and William dutifully kissed her on the forehead. 'I don't know what to say,' he said.

'Congratulate me, you asshole,' said Rex Angell. 'And, lissen, we're gettin' married just as soon as I can fix the licence and you're gonna be my friggin' witness, right? Right. I don't want no arguments.'

'You're going to marry Jenny?'

'Damn right I am.'

'But she . . . but she's a . . . '

'A hooker. Sure I know. And I don't care. And what's more you're living in the past, kid. She useda be a hooker. She ain't no more. I bought her contract.'

'You did what?' William tagged along, bewildered, as they all moved back into the living room. There was champagne, half-a-dozen bottles of champagne, in buckets and Rex Angell poured him a glass and thrust it into his hand.

'I bought her contract from my friend Stack – my new friend Stack. She's a free agent now and I love her and she's gonna marry me. Okay? You unnerstand or you want diagrams?'

'A little explanation might help,' William said. 'I won't bother with the diagrams.'

'Okay,' Rex Angell said. He sat on the sofa with his arm round Jenny's waist. 'Siddown and I'll tell ya what happened . . . Jesus, it's friggin' unbelievable, kid, but it really happened . . . '

What exactly had happened, it transpired, was this: after William had left the dinner party, Jenny had gone about her work with a skill and subtlety that had swept the delighted, though amazed, Angell off his feet and into his bed at which point he was about to tell her that, gratified though he was by her attentions and efforts, the fixture would have to be cancelled due to the unfortunate demise of his peter. But then, to his inexpressible joy, a miracle – greater than any that had been performed on T.V. that morning – took place. In response to Jenny's delicate ministrations the late, great peter began to make its comeback.

'I swear to you, kid, it stood up and took a bow. Took a bow – what am I saying? It gave itself a friggin' standing ovation. I couldn't believe it . . . '

Later, when the deed was done, Rex Angell and Jenny lay and talked and she confessed all. So he learned who she was and what she was and how she came to be in his bed that night and he didn't care. The revivification of the peter (henceforth, according to Angell, to be known to its friends and well-wishers as Lazarus) had driven all anti-hooker prejudice from his mind. He was

203

deeply touched by William's thoughtful gesture and also madly in love with Jenny, to whom he swiftly proposed marriage. She said she would like to sleep on it and so they slept for four hours after which, pausing only to reassure themselves that Lazarus had not flattered merely to deceive, she accepted Rex's proposal and as early as seemed reasonable – bearing in mind that a hard-working pimp needed his rest – they had phoned Stack and summoned him to the apartment to work out the financial details.

'Then I tried to call you, kid,' Rex Angell said. 'But first you were out and then the line was busy. What the hell you been doin'?'

William said, 'Ah, yes, well . . . I'll tell you later but first, if it's okay with you, I'd like a private word with the future bride.'

'Be my guest, kid,' Angell said and ruffled William's curls. 'Do you think I oughta get a curly-blond rug, kid? Do you think she'd love me even more if I looked like friggin' Shirley Temple, too?'

William took Jenny into the master bedroom and they sat, side by side, on the bed. He said, awkwardly, 'I don't really know how to put this but what exactly are you up to?'

'Are my intentions honourable, do you mean?' she asked.

'No. Or rather . . . well, yes. Look, what I want to say is this: he's a very nice and very lonely old man. Okay, I know he talks dirty but it really doesn't mean anything. I like him a great deal and I don't want to see him hurt and I don't want to see him ripped off. And, if you'll excuse my saying so, what's happened in the last few hours looks like a perfect, instant get-rich-quick set-up.'

'Well,' she said, thoughtfully, 'in a way I guess that's what it is. Listen, I'll level with you – I don't love him. He's old enough to be my grandaddy, for God's sake.

But I do like him a lot. He's sweet and gentle and he doesn't talk dirty to me. So when he asked me to marry him I thought, What the hell, why not? I can make him happy. Hell, I've already made him happier than he's been for ten years. I know about making men happy – it's what I'm good at. So I figure it's a kind of deal – I'll stay with him and keep him happy until he dies.'

'And when he does you'll be very rich,' William said.

'Yes, I will. So? He's gotta leave it all to somebody, he can't take it with him, so why not leave it to me? It's going to be a good deal, William, good for both of us. What's wrong with that?'

William studied her carefully and she looked back at him with the candid gaze of one who had nothing to hide.

'All right,' he said at last. 'So long as you keep your side of the bargain.'

'I will,' she said. 'I'm an honest hooker, William.'

They went back into the other room and Rex Angell refilled the champagne glasses and said, 'Okay, kid, now it's your turn. Where the hell you been all morning?'

So William told his tale and when he was halfway through Tina Ling arrived and greeted him with a firm kiss on the mouth and ran her hand through his hair and seated herself beside him on the settee with her arm linked through his and he had to begin the story all over again.

When at last he had finished, Rex Angell said, 'Jesus, I can't believe it. You really mean Ida Kaines signed that statement?'

'Yes.' William had it folded in his pocket and he brought it out and showed it to them. When they had all read it and Rex had said, 'Jesus!' and Jenny had said, 'Goodness!' and Stack had said, 'Shee-it, man!' Tina Ling said, 'What are you going to do now, William? The way she said it, it sounded like Willy-yam.

'Well, I don't know. Get myself another job, I suppose.'

'No, no, no,' she said impatiently. 'What are you going to do about the story, William, the Willard Kaines story? You call yourself a reporter and you haven't even thought about that? Oh, William, William.'

'You mean . . . sell it?'

'What else? What contacts do you have?'

'With newspapers, do you mean? Gosh, yes. Well, there's my old paper in Fleet Street, the *Daily Journal*. They'd . . . why didn't I think of this? . . . they'd jump at it. Of course! There's nothing to stop me selling the story right away.'

'So go call them, William. Now. Oh, William, who's your agent?'

'Agent? I don't have an agent.'

Tina Ling shook her head exasperatedly, affectionately. 'Oh, William, how have you survived so long in this wicked world? You don't even have an agent? Well, okay, leave it to me. You go call the paper, William, and tell them what you have to deliver, but don't make any deals, okay? Tell them your agent will be calling – within the hour, pro'lly – and he's the only one can talk numbers. You got that, William? Can I trust you to do it right?'

'Yes, Tina,' he said meekly. 'Thank you very much indeed.' And he went away to call London on one of Rex Angell's phones while, on the other, Tina Ling called her own agent and recruited him on William's behalf.

By noon it was all arranged. William had contacted the *Daily Journal* in London and informed its night editor, Henry Tyson, of the tale he had to tell and Tyson had accepted it with alacrity. A little later Tina Ling's agent, now William's agent, had also contacted the *Daily Journal* and had laid out the financial terms, which Tyson had accepted with considerably less alacrity. Indeed, Tyson felt that he and the paper were being screwed so hard that he called William back to try to persuade him to drop the price but Tina Ling, who had anticipated just such an event, insisted on talking to him first so that by the time William himself was permitted to say a word or two, the distant Tyson was both weary and defeated. 'Blimey, William,' he said. 'Who's that Chinese bird? She sounds like the daughter of Fu-Manchu.'

'She is the daughter of Fu-Manchu,' William said. 'When do you want the copy?'

'Five minutes ago,' said Tyson and hung up. It was his sole small triumph of the day.

'Listen,' William said, as Tina Ling led him by the hand to Rex Angell's office where a typewriter and a supply of paper lay ready, 'how much am I getting for all this?'

'Don't worry your pretty head about that now, darling,' she said. 'I'll explain it all later. Right now you just sit down there and write the news story. Just the facts, okay? Nothing more. The rest of it you give them tomorrow.'

Later, when William had dictated his story – a fairly bald revelation of the fact that (according to his widow) the late, lamented Willard Kaines had murdered his first wife, the allegation being backed up by a quote or two from the statement of Ida Kaines – to the *Daily Journal* and he and Tina and Stack and the betrothed couple had sat down to a belated brunch, Tina Ling filled in the details. For the exclusive story of the murder William was to be paid what, in his modest expectations, seemed a large sum of money plus a percentage of the syndication rights. For a more detailed, and possibly three-part examination of the life and times and crimes of said Willard Kaines (which the *Daily Journal* would print later in the week after advertising the forthcoming event on commercial television to gain the maximum publicity and circulation) he would be paid a far larger sum. Even after he'd sent half the proceeds to Ida Kaine's Brazilians he still stood to make quite a lot of money.

'It's fantastic,' he said. 'But . . . Well, look, it's not going to work out. Once the story breaks in Fleet Street the other London papers and all the local Californian papers will get their stringers and staff men onto it at once and they'll go round to Ida Kaines and she'll give them the story too.'

'No, she won't, William,' said Tina Ling, 'because she's not here any more. While you were slaving over a hot typewriter I was checking her out and she's gone already. She's gone to Brazil and the only forwarding address she's left is her bank in Rio de Janeiro. So you've got the whole story to yourself, my pretty one.'

Then Rex Angell raised his glass and said, 'To Willard Kaines, the son-of-a-bitch,' and they all solemnly drank this toast and later they went to the new, fashionable restaurant, the one on Rodeo Drive, for spare ribs and onion rings. And when the meal was over Stack said it had been a great day, a memorable day, but he was, he would like to remind them, a working man and it was time he went off on his rounds to make sure his remaining hookers weren't taking advantage of his absence and skimming. He said, too, that it had been great doing business with Rex Angell, who was the first honky he had ever met, not excluding William, who'd offered a fair shake and hadn't tried to screw a poor nigger and that if Rex had other friends who might wish to buy a bride they could always call on him. They all shook his hand or kissed his cheek depending on sex and it was a quietly emotional scene as only befitted an engagement party.

Rex said, 'See ya at the wedding, Stack?' and Stack said the whole mother-fuckin' L.A. police department armed with nightsticks and tear gas couldn't keep him away.

And then it was Tina Ling's turn to leave. They stood on Rodeo Drive on this warm, spring night, the air lightly scented with a mixture of high-octane petrol fumes from the Rolls-Royces and the Porsches and the exciting smell of money that emanated from the most ludicrously expensive shops in the world, and Tina Ling said she really must go because she had a production meeting early in the morning. She and William looked at each other for a long time and William said the least he could do, as the closest equivalent to an English gentleman in the immediate vicinity, was to see her safely home, but she smiled and shook her head and said, 'Not tonight, I think, William. Call me tomorrow,' and then she got into her little, gold, open Mercedes and drove away.

So that left Rex Angell and his bride-to-be and William. Rex said, 'What kind of a friggin' celebration is this that breaks up at ten o'clock at night? Come back for a nightcap, kid.' William was only too pleased to accept since he had no desire to return to the motel and another unpleasant encounter with Mark Payne.

An hour later, when Jenny had gone to bed and William and the old man were perched on bar stools in the Western-style sittingroom, Rex Angell said, 'I owe ya, kid.'

'*De nada*' William said.

'Yes, I do. Lissen, kid, if I'd died a week ago I'd have died a rich, lonely old man. If I died tonight I'd die happy. I don't know what the hell happened or how it happened but . . . I was just living out the rest of my life, that was all, and then you come along, Shirley Temple with a friggin' baritone, and suddenly I'm having a better time that I've had in a decade, so I owe ya, kid. I really owe you.'

'You don't, Rex. Honestly. Whatever I did I was glad to do. Forget it. It was my pleasure.'

'Why did you do it, kid?' Why did you send Jenny to me?'

'Oh, I dunno,' William said and wondered why he had done it. Out of pity, he supposed, but he could hardly tell the old man that. Affection had played a part in it too, of course, but he had never thought deeply about his motives until now. It had been very much a sudden whim – in a sense Jenny had been a sort of impulse buy – but at the back of it all pity had been the overriding motive. 'It just seemed a good idea at the time. Now I think about it, it wasn't really. I mean, you know, buying a girl for a friend . . . it's not exactly a commendable thing to do, is it? All right, it seems to have turned out fine but it could have been awful, it could have been disastrous for all three of us.'

Rex Angell patted him gently on the cheek. 'Yeah, I know. But it has turned out fine and you better believe it. You've made an old man feel very happy.'

'Yes,' William said, and grinned wryly. 'And by all accounts last night Jenny made a happy man feel very old.'

'Enough with the crappy jokes, kid. Lissen, what are you gonna do now? You got no job, right.'

'Well, I've got a job for another month. But after that, you're right. I'm on the streets.'

'So what are you gonna do? Do you wanna go home, back to England?'

William shrugged. 'Not particularly. At least, not right away. Besides, I can't for a few days. I've got to stay here and write that Willard Kaines stuff. What I think I'll do is, I'll send a letter of resignation to the T.V. company, give them a month's notice. At least that way they can't say they fired me. And then, well, I think I'll stick around, have a holiday . . . '

'See a lot of Tina Ling.'

'. . . see a lot of Tina Ling and try to work something out.'

Rex got up and from a cupboard behind the bar produced a letter. He handed it to William. 'Remember this?'

It was the letter from the New York publishers offering

Rex a fortune for his unexpurgated memoirs. 'Yes?' William said.

'I've decided to go ahead with it. What the hell, it'll be one fantastic, friggin' book. It'll make me really big again in this town – hated, but big. And maybe not so hated at that, on account of most of the people I could dish the dirt on are long dead.'

'Are you really sure you want to do it?'

'Yeah. I been leading a quiet life too long. I don't even get asked to go on the friggin' talk shows on T.V. any more, you know that? Any asshole with one movie to his name gets on the Carson show and the Griffin show and the Today show, but me they never invite. Well, believe me, kid, when my book comes out they'll be standing in line, begging me to go on. It's gonna be exciting and I need some excitement and . . . well, it'll be fun for Jenny, too.'

William read the letter again. 'Okay, why not? Apart from anything else, it's an awful lot of money, Rex.'

'What, that? That pisswater offer? That's a friggin' insult, that's what that is. That ain't half of what they're gonna pay me. Besides . . . Ah, it ain't the money, kid. I want the notoriety, I want the attention. I want people to read my memoirs and say, "Jesus, do you know what that old bastard did?" It's gonna be great, kid.'

William handed the letter back. 'Well, that's marvellous, Rex. I'll expect an autographed copy.'

'Don't you wanna know who's gonna write it for me?'

'The publishers will decide that, surely. They said they'd send someone to . . . '

'Uh-uh. No way. No Harvard snotnose is gonna write my memoirs. You're gonna write 'em for me, kid.'

'Me?' William was astonished. 'But I . . . '

'You're a journalist, aren't you? You're a writer? So, okay then, it's settled. Call your agent tomorrow, then he can call my agent and we'll make a deal. It'll be a nice deal, kid, I promise you. We're gonna be rich, only of course I'm gonna be a lot richer than you.'

'Rex,' William said, 'you can't do this! I've never written a book. I don't even know if I can.

'Sure you can. You could write a million books. No problem, believe me. This is what I want and I always get what I want. Okay? You agree?'

William thought it over. Despite his doubts it was a hugely tempting offer and even the doubts weren't too grave. He knew he couldn't really ruin the book, despite his inexperience, because the publishers wouldn't let him. If it started going wrong they'd tell him so, very swiftly indeed. So that wasn't the problem. The real difficulty lay in deciphering Rex's motive. Was this simply an exchange deal, a *quid pro quo*, a lucrative commission in exchange for a bride? Because if it was, William could have no part of it. He'd done quite enough bartering in human flesh already and though no harm – and indeed a great deal of good – seemed to have come out of it he had no desire to base his immediate future career on what would amount to poncing.

He glanced up and found Rex staring at him anxiously. 'Come on, kid, please,' he said.

'Yes, but . . . why, Rex? You don't owe me, really you don't.'

Rex said, 'Okay, you're right. I been thinking about it and I don't owe you a friggin' thing. You introduced me to Jenny, I introduced you to Tina – we're quits. So this book is something different. I like you, kid. I trust you and I like having you around. So this way I get what I want and you get the chance to make yourself some dough and give yourself some time to plan out what you wanna do with your life. What's so bad? Come on, for Chrissake, give me your friggin' hand and tell me we got a deal.'

'All right.' Impulsively, William gave him his friggin' hand and said they'd got a deal. He also promised he would phone his agent in the morning, just as soon as he could get in touch with Tina Ling and discover from her who his agent was, to arrange the details.

And by then it was midnight and time to go. Rex took him to the door. 'It's been a great day, kid,' he said, 'it's been the greatest day of my whole friggin' life. And, you know something, there are even better days to come.'

'I do believe you're right, Rex.' William opened the door and stepped out into the corridor.

Rex said, 'Hey, don't worry, huh? About me and Jenny, know what I mean? I may be goddam old, kid, but I'm no fool. I know she doesn't love me but it don't matter. Hell, how could a young girl like her love an old fart like me? But it don't matter because I love her and I know she at least likes me a lot. It's gonna be okay, kid, you'll see. It's gonna be fantastic.' He closed the door and from inside William heard him say, 'G'night, kid. See ya tomorrow.'

15

The light was still on in Alice Flitton's room when William returned to the motel. He phoned her first to make sure she was alone and then went up to see her.

He had, it appeared, missed a fairly eventful day. Geoff Warbottle had been attended by a doctor and was now asleep under sedation; Mark Payne had called a conference of the crew and what remained of the production staff (in a word, Alice) and informed them that their mission was aborted due to Willard Kaines's total lack of basic human decency in dying at such an inopportune time.

'You wouldn't credit it, would you?' Mark had said, bitterly. 'Two old buggers dying on me in barely a week. Why did they have to pick on me? First, that sodding bishop, then Kaines . . . What have I done to deserve this?'

The cameraman had suggested that perhaps the two old buggers might have wondered, in their last moments, what they themselves had done to deserve it, but Mark had treated this frivolous comment with understandable contempt. The point was, he had said, that there was no reason for them to remain in California any longer and they must return to London as soon as possible. The whole enterprise, he added, had been a major disaster from its ill-conceived start, but fortunately Nat-Met knew where the guilt lay and he could tell them with some assurance that (a) William Pendleton would be on the dole in five weeks' time and (b) Geoff Warbottle – even if he were fortunate enough to escape the sack himself – would spend the rest of his working life in the T.V. company's religious department picking out apt Biblical quotations for the Sunday prayer.

At this point, Alice Fritton said, the conference had come to an abrupt end with the arrival of Tracy-Lou demanding that Mark take her to lunch. He didn't appear to want to take her to lunch, Alice Flitton went on, but there seemed to be an underlying note of menace in the way Tracy-Lou couched her demand. If you asked her, Alice Flitton said, that girl seemed to have some kind of hold on Mark and it wouldn't surprise her at all if it had a lot to do with those toothmarks on his nose.

'Probably,' William said, and didn't add that it also had much more than she knew to do with the curious circumstances surrounding the death of Willard Kaines. The less said about that, he felt, the better.

So anyway, Alice Flitton said, the party was over, although she personally was going to take her annual leave – and she didn't care whether Nat-Met approved or not – and go off somewhere with Larraine. 'And what about you, William?' she asked.

'Oh, I don't know,' William said, vaguely. 'I'll just stick around Hollywood for a bit. Don't worry about me, Alice. I think I'm going to be all right.'

And he *was* going to be all right, too, he thought, as he got into bed and turned off the light. He was going to be better than all right.

William awoke early the next day. It was a bright, sunny morning on Sunset Boulevard although the smog was already beginning to form over downtown Los Angeles. On T.V. the news was as familiar and reassuring as ever, the only development of any importance being that nasal

215

catarrh appeared to have ousted acid indigestion from the headlines.

He made some coffee and took it out onto the open corridor so that he could drink it while leaning on the rail in the sunshine. On the plastic grass around the swimming pool below him a couple of dedicated sunbathers were already stretched out in deckchairs and bikinis. On the Boulevard the commuting traffic was getting thicker by the minute and the coffee-shop was rapidly filling with office workers grabbing their eggs and bacon and hash browns preparatory to a hard day at the desk.

Mark Payne's door was closed but the picture window was open a little at the top and so William was in a perfect position to hear all when the telephone rang and Mark answered it with a sincere sniff and a crisp, 'Mark Payne . . . Oh hello, Charles. To what do I owe . . . Well, no, I haven't seen the *Daily Journal*, Charles. They don't sell it here. It's an English paper, you . . . Oh my God . . . Oh my God . . . Pendleton wrote that? But he had no right! He . . . Well, yes, Charles, I did interview Ida Kaines but not exactly on that particular subject, the murder of the first wife, I mean . . . Really, I don't think there's any need for that sort of tone . . . What? Well, I'll tell you why the hell not. She was asking 5,000 dollars and . . . Well, yes, now the old bugger's dead, of course, it's peanuts but how was I to know he was going to pop off like that? . . . Now listen to me, Charles . . . No, no, I'm sorry. By no means did I intend to shout at you . . . Look, please can I explain? I knew we couldn't possibly use the interview while Kaines was alive and it didn't seem to me to be worthwhile tying up 5,000 dollars in a piece of film we might not be able to use for ten years or more . . . Well, yes, I was aware that Kaines was very old but these people live a long time out here in Hollywood. Monkey glands or something . . . Yes, but Charles, Nat-Met could have lost its franchise by the time he shuffled off the mortal . . .

I'm not making excuses, Charles, I'm merely trying to explain . . . No I'm sure it's not too late. I'll get the crew together and go round to her house right away. You're still prepared to pay the five thou . . . ? Oh. Really? Up to 25,000? Are you sure? . . . No, no, of course I'm not questioning your judgement, Charles . . . Yes, yes, you're quite right. No point in wasting time arguing. I'm on my way, Charles . . . Oh, but Charles, there's one thing I would like to point out. It's almost entirely Pendleton's fault that this happened. He really under-played the story most disgracefully when he was telling it to me. I suspect that he intended all the time to sell it to the newspapers and . . . Charles? Hello? Are you there, Charles?' He put the receiver down. 'Oh my God,' he said. 'Oh my God, my God.'

William stayed where he was, sipping his coffee and smiling down upon the sunbathers. In a moment he heard Mark pick up the receiver again and then the phone rang in his own room. He ignored it.

A couple of minutes later Mark came out into the corridor frowning with sincere anxiety. He stopped when he saw William and briefly a look of relief crossed his face. 'Oh there you are. Look, I really don't know why I should have done this but I've just been on the phone to Charles Kaufman and I've persuaded him to reconsider. He's prepared to give you another chance, and so am I.'

'Gosh,' William said.

'Yes, well, there's no need to thank me. I was perhaps a little hasty yesterday. Now then, what I want you to do is to go and see Ida Kaines; keep all other newspaper-men and television people away from her until I can get there with the crew. Charles is very anxious that we should have an exclusive interview with her and every moment is precious, so don't hang about.'

A sharp note of comand had entered his voice whether he intended it or not, and William reacted by snapping smartly to attention.

'Yes, Mark,' he said. 'Right, Mark. What time's the next plane to Brazil, Mark?'

'Brazil? What are you talking about? What's bloody Brazil got to do with it?'

'Bloody Brazil is where Ida Kaines is, Mark. In the middle of some bloody jungle in bloody Brazil to be precise.'

'You're lying!' Mark said.

'No, I'm not. She's gone. I checked yesterday. She left the day after you interviewed her.'

'Oh my God!' Mark said. 'Oh my God!' His fingers clicked frantically and this time, William was sure, he had no idea he was doing it. 'This is your fault, Pendleton. You're a disgrace, you know that? Selling that scurrilous story to the papers. It wasn't even your story to sell. It belonged to Nat-Met. Every penny you're being paid for it is rightfully theirs.'

'Right,' William said. 'Well, I'll wait for their lawyers to sue me, shall I?'

'You think you're so clever, don't you Pendleton? You . . . ' Mark's eyes narrowed suspiciously. 'You're lying, aren't you? She hasn't gone at all. You're just trying to put me off, to stop me going down there to see her. This is another of your filthy, underhand little plots, isn't it?' A look of wild, desperate hope crossed his face. 'Well, it's not going to work, my friend. I'm going to get the others and go and see Ida Kaines now.'

'Suit yourself,' William said. 'It's a nice day for a drive.'

Mark dashed along the corridor towards the stairs leading up to the floor above where Alice Flitton and the still presumably comatose Warbottle had their rooms. 'Warbottle!' he shouted, staring upwards. 'Flitton! Get up!' At the stairs he paused and looked back at William.

'I'm going to fix you,' he said. 'I am really going to fix you.'

William shrugged and turned back to the sunbathers.

It was going to be a busy day, he thought. He had to phone Tina Ling and the agent and then he had to write the first instalment of his series for the *Daily Journal* and then he'd better start looking for an apartment to live in for the next few months while he worked on Rex Angell's memoirs. Oh yes, and he also had to write his letter of resignation to Nat-Met.

There was a hammering on the door above his head and then Alice Flitton murmured something and Mark said, 'Well, never mind about that. Ring the crew, tell them to be ready in ten minutes. I'll go and get the car started.'

Next came the sound of running footsteps, a clattering on the stairs and Mark, flushed and anxious, reappeared briefly on the landing. He stopped and glared with deep hatred at William. 'I mean that, you know,' he said. I'm going to fix you so that you never work again.'

William finished the last of his coffee. 'Yes, well, right-ho,' he said. 'Have a nice day, Mark.'

A SERIES OF DEFEATS

Barry Norman

Henry Tyson is floundering in the widening gap between expectation and achievement as he approaches middle age. His wife leads such a busy, successful life as a writer that he has to cook his own dinner on returning hom frome a dreary day's reporting for the *Daily Journal*. He's been passed over for promotion and the executive editor is out to get him. Dismayed, he takes a mistress and his wife consequently leaves him. He's already been beaten up by another woman and Henry's misogyny is becoming as rampant as his sense of failure.

But Henry's defeats – from being locked in the lavatory to being coolly appraised by his wife and mistress as though he were not in the room – and his wanderings through the jungles of television and journalism, London and the permissive society, are recorded in a chronicle of brilliant hilarity and acute observation, and *A Series of Defeats* will delight Barry Norman's present fans, and make him many more.

85p

THE UNLUCKIEST MAN IN THE WORLD
and similar disasters

Mike Harding

Born in the picturesque spa of Lower Crumpsall, he spent his early years in the brooding shadow of a cream cracker factory. At the age of seventeen he bought a set of Mongolian bagpipes and joined a rock and roll band. Much of his manhood has been spent waiting for a girl wearing red feathers and a hulu skirt to come into his life. He is the incorrigible, irrepressible and slightly mad Mike Harding.

The Unluckiest Man in the World takes us into the world of Mike Harding with an inimitable collection of happy, sad, ridiculous, profound and simply hilarious songs, poems and stories.

£1.25

LOOSELY ENGAGED

Christopher Matthew

'The hilarious follow-up to *Diary of a Somebody*' *Punch*

Newly promoted and loosely engaged to the boss's daughter, Simon Crisp finally seems all set for success. But whether he is dancing pink-haired in New York's Studio 54 with a model called (he is sure) Ernest Hemingway, or wrecking the central heating system in a Moscow hotel, or attempting to join the Freemasons and winding up with a lifetime membership of the National Trust, Simon is never quite the man he would like to believe he is. Surely even Simon should know by now that nothing succeeds like failure – and that, though he never knows at whose expense it is, there is always a joke going on.

'Addictive' *Evening News*

£1.25

THE BOOK OF DAYS

Bob Monkhouse

Take a day-by-day look at some of the more outrageous and unusual events of history through the eyes of one of TV's zaniest personalities, Bob Monkhouse.

Remember these red letter days:

2nd November

This is the birthday of the world's first test tube baby rabbit! The bunny-under-glass was presented to the New York Academy of Medicine today . . . in 1939. I wouldn't have thought rabbits needed any artificial help with that sort of thing.

19th September

False teeth were first advertised for sale today in America in 1768 by a goldsmith named Paul Revere, born – are you ready for this? – in Massachusetts!

24th June

The Battle of Bannockburn took place in 1314. Sir Harry Lauder said, 'The British dispersed the Scottish army with an underhand trick. They passed the hat around.'

11th July

Two totally blind soccer teams played to a 2–2 tie in Lima, Peru, today in 1973 . . . using a sonic ball and a handful of dried peas.

£1.75

THE DIETER'S GUIDE TO WEIGHT LOSS DURING SEX

Richard Smith

Tired? Listless? Overweight? Open this book at any page and discover everything you wanted to know about sex, food and dieting but never dreamt of asking.

Activity	Calories burned
REMOVING CLOTHES	
With partner's consent	12
Without partner's consent	187
Unhooking bra	
Using two calm hands	7
Using one trembling hand	96

EMBARRASSMENT	
Large juice stain on shorts	10

ORGASM	
Real	27
Faked	160

(Continued on page 81)

95p